Praise for Louie The Lynx and Ryan the Lion

2024 IndieDiscovery Award Winner: Romance

"A delightful exploration of love, serendipity, and the unexpected twists that make romance stories truly enchanting." —Readers' Favorite

"Sparkling real dialogue and true 'characters,' will grab readers and lovers of chick-lit and romance right from the start." —Indie Discovery Review

"Loved it!! Love, love, love Ryan the Lion and Louie the Lynx. A well-paced rom-com drama. So sweet!!! So good!!! —BookSprout

"Oh man, I did not want to stop reading this book! I loved Louie and her sweet dog. What a gem of a book!" —LibraryThing

"Easily, one of the most favorite books I've read. I fell in love with the characters."— BookSirens

"A journey filled with laughter, sighs, and the sweet unpredictability of love." —Reader's Favorite

"This is a great romance, I loved both characters, and I loved Louie's dog. Great book." —BookSirens

"A gorgeous and joyful novel." —Readers' Favorite

"A balance of chemistry and chaos. With all the necessary elements of a romance . . . the tender realism lends itself to the literary genre." —BookLife

I0593158

PRAISE FOR SARAH LAHEY ROMANCE BOOKS

"A must-read, second-chance romance with the perfect level of romantic sizzle."—Reedsy

"...all the romantic scenes you could hope for from the genre, from sweet to steamy." —The Independent Book Review

"Oh man, I did not want to stop reading this book!" —LibraryThing

"Easily, one of my favorite books I've read. I fell in love with the characters." —BookSirens

"Beautifully written, compelling, and truly delightful." —Readers' Favorite

"This was more than satisfying and fun. It warmed my heart."—BookSprout

"You want to read her books when it is raining, if that makes sense."— LibraryThing

"Lahey writes with warmth and wit. I couldn't put it down. It had me rooting for their future."—Readers' Favourite

"An absolute gem. Buckle up—you're in for one unforgettable trip!" —Bookish Mom

"This book felt like sitting down with a fluffy blanket and a cup of tea." —NetGallley

ALSO BY SARAH LAHEY

Cross Over Press acknowledges the Traditional Owners of the land on which they work, the Gadigal people of the Eora Nation, and the Djiringanj Clan of the Yuin Nation, and they pay their respects to the Elders past and present.

Published by Cross Over Press
168 Pacific Parade, Dee Why, NSW, Australia
www.sarahlahey.com/cross-over-press

EBook ISBN: 978-0-6458358-3-0

Print ISBN: 978-0-6458358-0-9

Hardcover ISBN: 978-1-7640954-0-2

LOUIE THE LYNX AND RYAN THE LION

SARAH LAHEY

Cross Over
Press

AUTHOR'S NOTE

Dear Reader,

While my Southern Skies Series of books are romantic comedies, some themes in these stories may be triggering for readers. If you feel trigger warnings are spoilers, and you don't need them, please skip the following paragraph and jump right into this book.

This book depicts scenes containing real life issues, such as anxiety and depression.

For Andrew Aitken

"So don't study and swot too much, for that makes one sterile. Enjoy yourself too much rather than too little, and don't take art or love too seriously—there is very little one can do about it."

~ Vincent van Gogh

1

A TREASURE HUNT

Late Friday afternoon, Louie Leon entered Max Cabot's office at City University. The office was empty, but she wasn't there to see Max. She was searching for a book—an art book—and the shelves in his office held hundreds of titles. As a regular borrower, Louie knew the books were sorted by art movements, then chronologically, and finally alphabetically. Finding a title was always easy, and the one she wanted was on Van Gogh—specifically, the letters he had written to his brother Theo when he lived in Arles, in the south of France.

The section on Van Gogh was located at the end of Impressionism, and there were three versions of the book she wanted—each with a different self-portrait on the cover. Multiple editions confirmed the letters held important ideas about life and art. She wiggled a copy out of the shelf and studied the image on the cover. A green-eyed man smoking a pipe. Rust-coloured hair and an angular face. A sombre expression. A bandage covering one ear. That ill-fated ear. *Imagine that,* she thought, *cutting off your own ear after a heated argument.* And not just a small part of the ear, but the whole thing, and then he offered it to a woman as a heartfelt gesture. Was this a story of love and sacrifice, or insanity and art?

He must have endured many dark hours before he took a knife to his ear.

In the self-portrait, Van Gogh wore a fluffy hat and a heavy jacket that was clasped at the neck by a large button. He looked warm and he seemed content, apart from his ear, which must have hurt. The portrait was finished in 1889, a week after he left the hospital, and Louie knew what lay ahead—golden fields of wheat, starry nights, and sunflowers.

Louie shivered; it was chilly inside the office. Outside, it was raining, and storms were forecast for the afternoon. The two-piece plaid suit—a short skirt and a cropped jacket—that she wore once belonged to her grandmother. (A well-made outfit can last for decades if properly cared for.) Her bare legs were covered in goosebumps. That morning, she had worn tights to work but she snagged them on a twig. The ladder ran from her ankle to her thigh, so she slipped them off and threw them away. Under her jacket, her thin linen shirt wasn't keeping her warm. But she wore thick socks and heavy boots, so her feet were comfortable. Her dark hair was pulled back into a high ponytail. Her blunt fringe finished low over her eyes—it needed a trim.

The door opened. Max entered and Louie turned.

"Hello," Max said. "Did you find what you were looking for?"

Max, a compact man in his mid-fifties, was head of the Arts Department at City University. He wore black-framed glasses, crisp jeans, and a soft jacket. This was his signature academic attire.

"I did." She held up the book.

He glanced at the front cover and smiled. "You might also try *Dear Theo*."

Louie turned back to the bookshelves. She found the volume and pulled it down. Another self-portrait on the cover, this one with both ears.

"I'm glad I caught you," Max said.

"What?" Louie dragged her eyes away from the book.

"I need a favour." He collected a piece of paper from his desk and waved it in her direction.

She froze, clutching the books to her chest. She didn't have time for favours on Friday afternoon, and Max knew she didn't have time. "Are you about to take advantage of me because you're in love with my uncle Filip?" she asked.

"No, absolutely not. This is a work favour. It's a fundraiser for the arts, and we have a sponsor!" He looked like he'd just uncovered a dark family secret, which everyone thought was dead and buried long ago. "I need someone to do a test run on this year's treasure hunt for the undergrad students." He handed her the sheet of paper. The page had *Treasure Hunt* written across the top.

She stowed the books into her shoulder bag, took the paper from him, and read through the instructions. "One hundred dollars for each completed list doesn't seem like much," she said.

"It's accumulative. Save the cents and count the dollars."

"The cents aren't worth as much as they used to be," she grumbled.

"That's why we need more of them. You teach first year, so you'll know if it's the right level of difficulty—we need to keep the students engaged. Besides, it might be fun." He grinned.

Roaming around the university on a wet Friday afternoon didn't sound like fun.

He checked the time on his watch. "How about I buy you a glass of bubbles at the student bar before it closes?" He collected a large book from his desk and handed it to her. "Here, you'll need this. It's your last task."

Never one to turn down a large book, or a glass of bubbles, Louie accepted both offers and accompanied Max to the student bar.

The appeal of a treasure hunt was twofold. First, there was the promise of a reward at the end of the quest. It might not be gold or silver, but it could still be something of value. Tickets to see a show at the university theatre. A free lunch in the cafeteria. A box of chocolates. A bottle of wine. A cinema coupon. Some sort of remuneration for your efforts. That's the reason it was called a *treasure* hunt—because if you found what you were looking for, in all likelihood there would be a reward.

Then, there was the *hunt* part of the task. This implied a search or a journey, where the participants might find a link from one secret clue to the next, or they untangle a tricky riddle right before their lightbulb moment of discovery.

Perhaps Max was right—a treasure hunt might be fun, and there were worse things she could be doing on a cold and wet Friday afternoon. Besides, the arts certainly needed the funding.

Louie left the student bar with the large book that Max had given her wedged under her arm. In her other hand, she held her list. She headed outside into the drizzling rain to complete her first challenge.

Two hours later, she had completed every task on her treasure hunt, except for the last. She had found nothing remotely resembling treasure and had undertaken no hunting whatsoever. Max couldn't call this a treasure hunt if there was no treasure and no hunt. At best, it was a scavenger hunt. At worst, it was a waste of her time. But she had never abandoned anything in her life, so she would forge ahead and complete the final task.

As she entered the tutorial room at the end of the corridor, Louie slipped her hand into the pocket of her jacket. Her fingers reached for the stone she kept there. Holding the stone was her coping technique. It distracted her and calmed her nerves.

Her eyes were fixed on the man leaning against the front desk—Ryan McDermott. He was reading something on his phone. Louie had never met Ryan, but she had carried out a brief internet search on him, and she wondered if this was the modern equivalent of hunting. Probing the internet for information felt like a pursuit. Perhaps there was some hunting involved after all, but still no treasure.

The outcome of her search revealed that Ryan was an architect. An intense, but good-looking man. Dark hair. Serious eyes. A moderate smile. The editor of the book she held under her arm.

The message on Ryan McDermott's phone must have been captivating. With the skill of a Navy SEAL moving through an obstacle course, Louie had successfully navigated her way around dozens of skewed chairs and tables— covered in sheets of A2 drawing paper and precariously placed pencil containers—without Ryan noticing her.

When he finally looked up, he was surprised to see her standing a few metres away. His gaze flicked over her—head to toe and back again. He placed his phone on the desk and folded his arms over his chest. "Can I help you?"

"Yes, you can." Leaving the maze of tables and chairs behind, she stepped into the moat of empty space that lay between them. "This is room twenty-two and you're Ryan McDermott?"

He nodded.

"Okay, great. The thing is, I need something from you—it's a small thing, and it won't take long." Stepping closer, she showed him her list.

He dipped his head toward her.

Did he just smell my hair?

"Have you been drinking?" he asked.

"Perhaps, I have," she confessed.

"I see." He paused. "Do you have a drinking problem?"

"What? No, I do not have a drinking problem." She glared at him. "What I do have is this." She tapped the sheet of paper in her hand. "I'm on a *treasure hunt*. And you're the last item on my list."

"Really?"

"Yes."

He stared at her. His eyes were green.

She held his gaze for a moment, then she looked away. "I don't think you're giving my list the full attention it deserves."

He glanced down, scanning the items. "Comprehensive. Did you find someone in the Quadrangle with a guitar, a Frisbee, or a dog?"

"No." She shook her head. "But I have a Frisbee, so I gave

it to some random—I mean student—I gave it to a student for the photo."

"You carry a Frisbee?"

"I do. I also have a dog . . . but I don't have a guitar." She pointed to the other challenges. "I've had my photo taken in the library, the lost-and-found department, at student services—they hate me—and in the science building wearing safety goggles. Now, you're the last item." Looking up at him, she smiled. He had attractive ears with plump earlobes. She had never considered ears to be a sensual part of the body, until now.

He held her gaze.

A tingling sensation. She turned away and told herself to focus—complete the list, get out of there, and head home.

"I need you to focus—I mean sign. Sign this book on sustainable design, which you edited—well done you." She pulled the book out from under her arm. "Then it will be auctioned at the trivia night. To raise money." She placed the book on the desk beside him and took a small step back.

"What's the money for?"

She had no idea.

"Supplies . . . maybe? The department also receives one hundred dollars if, and only if, I complete every task."

"Incredible."

"Yes, I thought so."

"Who's the generous benefactor?"

She had no idea.

"Probably a bank? They like to donate small amounts in high profile ways to the arts."

He smiled. "Are you an undergrad?"

"God, no. I'm finishing my PhD. I teach art history—

Modernism, the Romantics, the Industrial Revolution, that sort of thing. I got roped into this by Max Cabot. He gave me the list, along with two glasses of prosecco. When he told me my final task"—Louie ran her finger between Ryan and the book—"he topped up my glass. He said you might be intimidating." She paused. "But you're not. You're quite attractive."

Ryan rubbed his forehead.

"He was wearing a blue velvet jacket," Louie continued. "Seriously, who owns a velvet jacket these days? You know him?"

"Who?"

"The man wearing the velvet jacket. Come on, keep up. I'm the one who's had two glasses of bubbles and nothing to eat since . . . I can't remember." She paused and lowered her voice. "Secretly, I've always loved the feel of velvet—it's the queen of the textile family."

He stared at her, bemused. "What's your PhD topic?"

"Ahh, that's a good question. It's light and air. Essentially, how the aesthetic nature of atmosphere is represented in art. I'm nine years in. Follow your dreams, they said. But what am I going to do with a PhD in light and air? What kind of job will this qualify me for?" She made a mock sad face, with a down turned mouth.

"Something outdoors?"

"Perhaps." She glanced around the tutorial room, noting the paper and pencils scattered across the desks. "You teach drawing?"

"Architecture—I make them draw. So far, they hate it."

"Well, you know what Van Gogh said?" She picked up a Lego block eraser from one of the desks and examined it. "Cute." She placed it back on the table.

A long pause.

"Are you going to tell me what Van Gogh said?" Ryan asked.

"Yes, I am. He said, 'Drawing is the root of everything!' And he used an exclamation mark at the end of everything. Perhaps drawing was his truth. For me it's light. Light is everything." She waved her hand toward the papers and pencils covering the desks. "Do you need help cleaning this up?"

"No."

Leaning back against the edge of a table, she looked him over. He wore navy trousers, a jazzy blue shirt, and expensive-looking tan shoes. The colour of his socks matched his trousers, so details mattered. He had an alluring presence, and he was certainly cute and amiable, but she'd had enough bantering. It was getting late, and she wanted to complete the list, tick off the last task—get the book signed —and go home. Eva, her dog, would be waiting for her. They had an evening run scheduled. It was a long-standing arrangement that couldn't be broken. It kept them both sane.

She collected a pen from the table, handed it to him, and nodded toward the book.

He crossed his arms over his chest. "I'm not going to sign it."

"Why not?"

"Because I don't want to."

"But you have to."

"No, I don't."

She put the pen down.

This was an inconvenient response. He seemed determined. Perhaps the task was more difficult than she anticipated. Suddenly, she felt tired. It was getting late, the effects of the prosecco were wearing off, and she was losing her momentum.

"What's your name?" he asked.

"Oh, it's Louie. Short for Elouise." Holding out her hand, she stepped toward him.

At the same time, he moved toward her. Like two disoriented ships, they collided in the moat of empty space. Neither knew what the other was doing or in which direction they were going.

"I think that was my fault," she said.

"It was no one's fault."

He took her hand.

She gasped. A warm, tingling sensation settled in her chest, right on the edge of her heart. She glanced up at him.

He stared down at her, a curious look on his face. He dipped his head toward her.

He was going to kiss her.

"Is this okay?" he whispered.

Her heart raced, and her stomach flipped. She hadn't kissed a man in quite some time, and kissing Ryan McDermott on a rainy afternoon at the back of the tutorial room, at the end of a treasure hunt seemed like the most natural thing in the world.

"Yes," she whispered.

He placed his lips on hers. His hands cupped her face. She wrapped her arms around his neck and ran her fingers through his hair.

They continued to kiss—like castaways searching for hope. An adventurous duo, they had taken a risk, and they were in this together. But neither knew where they were headed or how it would end.

Eventually, they pulled away.

"That was . . . unexpected," Louie said.

"It was," he agreed. "Spontaneity is not normally my forte."

"But it's an admirable quality. We don't do it enough. Can I kiss you again?" she asked.

"Absolutely."

She fell into him, pressing her mouth to his.

He grabbed her waist and lifted her onto the desk. His mouth skated down her throat. Again, she wrapped her arms around him, but this time, she grabbed his earlobes and rubbed them with her thumbs. A heat source surged through her. She slipped off her jacket, and it fell to the floor. Wanting more of him, she tugged at his shirt. "Am I allowed to do this?" she mumbled into his chest.

"Yes." He chuckled into the side of her neck.

They paused and stared at each other.

He planted an affectionate kiss on her mouth, then turned his attention back to the side of her neck while she continued her inspection of his shirt. After pulling it up, she ran her hands across his stomach, loving the feel of his warm skin. "Oh my," she mumbled.

Following her lead, he also pulled at her shirt. After slipping his hands underneath the thin fabric, he trailed his fingers over her stomach. His thumb grazed the edge of her breast.

"How about this?" he whispered. "Can I do this?"

"God, yes."

It was the most wonderful spontaneous moment she had experienced in some time. His lips on her neck felt divine. His hands on her bare skin were bliss. He must be the sexiest, most attractive, warm-hearted man on the planet. How lucky was she to have him on her list? She could now confirm it was indeed a treasure hunt, and she had hit the jackpot.

Soon, propriety outwitted her lust for him—they were, after all, in the tutorial room of a prestigious university, and they had just met. Out of respect for them both, she pulled away.

He smiled down at her. "Are you okay?"

She nodded.

"I didn't intend for that to happen." He looked her in the eye. "I'm sorry if I overstepped—"

"It was mutual." She patted his chest, a reassuring gesture. "I did start the lifting of the shirt thing."

"You did." He flattened down her collar, which had risen around her neck, and then he attempted to fasten the buttons on her shirt, which had fallen open. But he was all thumbs and couldn't get the buttons inside the little holes, so she took over and fastened them herself. After tucking a few strands of hair behind her ear, his gaze wandered over her face and clothes, checking that nothing else was astray.

She felt a mix of desire and regard for him, and she thought he felt the same for her. She had closed her eyes when he kissed her—they both had—and in that moment, they had fallen off the edge of a high cliff, and neither knew where they had landed.

She slipped off the desk and began adjusting her clothes. Her skirt was up around her thighs, and she pulled it down. She tucked in her shirt.

He gazed at the floor. "That was—"

"Spontaneous."

He smiled. "You are absolutely gorgeous."

She blushed and cast her eyes to the side. Opening her mouth, she wanted to tell him that he was also quite handsome, but nerves overcame her, and the words didn't come. She closed her mouth and turned away. She hadn't expected their exchange to be so passionate, so intimate—his tongue in her mouth and his fingers grazing the edge of her breast. During their first kiss, he had captured a small piece of her heart—she hadn't found treasure; she had relinquished it.

"I've had the worst day," he said. "Now, it's vastly improved. I'm about done here. You want to get a drink? Something to eat?"

She shook her head.

"A walk. Maybe a coffee?"

"I need to go."

He paused and looked her over. "Are you okay?"

No, I'm completely overwhelmed.

"I'm fine. Absolutely fine," she said and tucked an invisible hair behind her ear. "If you'd please just sign the book."

"I told you I'm not going to sign it." He started to pack items into a laptop case—a computer lead, USBs, a sketchbook, and pencils.

"I don't understand."

"What happened between us was separate." He paused his packing and looked at her. "That was about you. Come on, you can't be mad at me. I told you I wasn't going to sign it."

"Oh, my god. You're a cad." She glared at him.

He frowned. "A cad?"

"Yes. A cad!"

She turned and walked across the moat of empty space and back through the maze of tables and chairs and out the door. In the corridor, she wanted to break into a full sprint and flee the building. Instead, she settled on a fast, dignified walk down a very long passageway and then two flights of stairs.

Once outside, Louie made her way through the campus, a mix of mid-nineteenth-century buildings constructed in the Gothic Revival style. They were adorned with multiple spires and towers, decorated with gargoyles, statuettes, and finials. The arched windows were filled with elaborate stained-glass leadlight.

She was headed for the Quadrangle—a small, enclosed park with an immaculate lawn, bordered on four sides by sandstone buildings. This was the oldest part of the university and her favourite place. At the Quadrangle, she paused and leaned against the stone wall, which, after decades of rain and wind, had weathered to a deep honey colour.

Her heart thundered, and her hands were cold and clammy. She peered up into the dark, cloud-filled sky, and her eye caught the figure of a monster-like gargoyle hanging over the edge of the roof, water dripping from its open mouth. *Some guardian*, she thought. It wasn't doing any protecting today. She had never felt more defenceless.

What had just happened?

The last item on a treasure hunt was supposed to be challenging. There were supposed to be obstacles. But it was not supposed to be this disheartening. Her list was incomplete—the arts were not going to get their much-needed funding. She had lost the book and along the way relinquished her dignity. This was no treasure hunt, and she was no adventurer. But he was a cad.

2

LIGHT IS EVERYTHING

RYAN LEANED against the edge of his desk and stared out the door of the tutorial room.

"Ahh, she meant *cad*, not CAD."

Of course, that made more sense. She thought he'd behaved badly and not considered her feelings, and he could understand how she might feel that way. On one level, he admired her restraint; she could have called him something far worse. But who used the word *cad* these days? CAD meant computer-aided design. Everyone at his architectural practice, himself included, used CAD. It referred to a software system, not a jerk.

"Fuck." He sighed and ran his hand through his hair.

In a heartbeat, the situation had turned from delight to disaster. She had completely misunderstood his motives. If she knew his reasons for not wanting to sign the book, she would understand. If he explained his position, she would change her mind about him. He was sure of it. She was finishing her PhD, obviously, she was smart, and she seemed reasonable.

Spying her jacket on the floor, he picked it up and studied the large *C* motif on the buttons. Was she really wearing a Chanel suit? There was no label on the collar, but it was fully lined, and it looked well made. He lifted the garment to his nose—a floral scent. Roses?

He felt a hard lump in the pocket of her jacket. Slipping his hand inside, he pulled out a smooth stone. Rolling it between his fingers, he studied it for a long moment. There was something he liked about this woman. The way her fringe fell over her forehead. Her serious frown, which was endearing but also amusing. She had the most beautiful dark brown eyes.

He dropped the stone back into the pocket.

He wanted to see her again. Ask her more about her PhD on light. She'd dismissed the topic too easily, but he knew the significance of light. He spent an inordinate amount of time talking to his clients about the subject. It was the most important element in an architect's toolbox. Studying it for nine years made sense to him—the sun was a phenomenon. It was an excellent topic. He needed to see her again, so he could tell her she was right—light was everything. That was not the truth though. He needed to see her again because her presence had left a warm, tingling sensation in his chest, which was only now beginning to fade.

He didn't have her number.

But he had her jacket. He had to return it.

Less than five minutes had passed since her untimely exit—he might still catch her. Then, he could explain about the book, and she would forgive the misunderstanding. She might even slip her arms around his neck and kiss him again. It was not out of the question—it would be like a reward for returning her jacket.

He could fix this. He threw her jacket over his arm and headed out the door.

By the time he reached the university Quadrangle, it was almost empty. The second week of the term, a cold and rainy Friday afternoon, and the old sandstone campus had already lost some of its charm.

He spied Louie leaning against the wall on the far side of the lawn. "Hey, Louie," he called.

She turned, surprised to see him.

He held up her jacket.

She offered a curt nod—acknowledging she had left it behind.

He approached slowly. Extending his arm, he passed her the jacket. "Please, let me explain."

"I'm not interested." She reached for her jacket.

He pulled it away. "I just need five minutes."

"I don't have time." She held out her hand, demanding the garment.

Again, he offered it to her. "Three minutes—I'll talk fast."

"I've already told you I don't have time." Again, she reached for her jacket.

Again, he withdrew it, and she was left empty-handed.

"Oh, my god," she muttered.

"It was just a misunderstanding, and if you let me explain—"

"I don't care," she snapped. "In fact, I think I hate you—and that doesn't happen to me very often."

He swallowed. "Fair enough."

"Give it to me."

Sheepishly, he handed over her jacket.

"Please, leave me alone."

After slipping on her jacket, she placed her hand in her pocket and walked away.

As dean of the Arts Department, Max Cabot was entitled to a private office—a privilege that most faculty members didn't have. During recent renovations, administrators had decided private offices for staff were elitist. Faculty didn't require personal spaces because they could share the public spaces with the students. After all, the university belonged to students and faculty. Max had argued he needed an office so he could discuss delicate topics, like student grades, and this was true, but he also needed a place to store his collection of art books, which was over fifty years old. His partner, Filip, published academic textbooks, and he also had an extensive library. The home office in their new house belonged to Filip. With no place for Max to store his books, he packed them up and took them to work.

Max also kept a two-meter-tall potted saguaro cactus in his office, which he had inherited from his grandmother. She'd smuggled the plant into Australia after a trip to California in the early 1950s. The plant was seventy years old. In good health, it would live to one hundred and seventy and grow twenty metres tall. Again, Filip saw no need to keep the prickly plant at home, so Max took it to work.

Ryan rapped on the open door of Max's office.

Max looked up and smiled. "Come in, I'll be one minute," he said, shuffling some papers.

Ryan entered. He placed the book he'd edited on sustainable design on Max's desk, then he strolled across the room and peered out the arched leadlight window, which overlooked the Quadrangle.

"What happened with you and Miss Universe? I saw you talking outside—she didn't look happy," Max said.

"Miss Universe—you mean Louie?"

"Yes. Student services call her Miss Universe—behind her back of course." Max chuckled.

"Because she's so attractive?"

"No. It's not a term of endearment—they think she's aloof."

Aloof didn't reconcile with Ryan's intimate meeting with Louie. "Is she aloof?" he asked.

"Sometimes." Max shrugged. "Apparently, she explained to a member of the student services team that the word *service* means *to serve*."

Ryan smiled. "Brave woman. They're a formidable bunch."

"They are—and they wield more power than the United Nations."

Outside, it had started raining again, and Ryan watched a handful of students flee the Quadrangle and seek shelter inside the building. He turned and pointed to the saguaro cactus. "Does this ever flower?"

"Early summer—white flowers, red fruit."

Ryan raised an eyebrow, impressed. He turned his attention back to the view outside the window. "Is she really nine years into her PhD?"

"She told you that?"

"Yes. Why?"

"She doesn't like to talk about it—we refer to it as the thing she does that takes up all her time."

"She only gets ten years, right?"

"Yes, she needs to finish this year. It looked like the two of you were arguing," Max said.

Ryan suppressed a smile. "We were. I kissed her."

"You did what?" Max stood up. He scurried across the room and closed the door. "Why in the world did you kiss her?"

"It was impulsive. I've never done anything like that before, but I really wanted to kiss her."

"Jesus Christ, Ryan. Is this going to be a consent issue? Are we going to need HR, the lawyers? Didn't you watch the videos I sent you?" Requiring the support of a solid object, Max clutched the corner of his desk.

"I know what consent is, and for the record, I watched the videos." Ryan ran his hand through his hair. "I asked her. She said yes, and then . . . we sort of made out."

"Good god. This is your second week on campus, and you *made out* in the tutorial room?"

Ryan nodded. "Then . . . I didn't sign the book." He pointed to the book sitting on Max's desk. "And she wasn't happy."

"Why didn't you sign it?"

"I had an argument with the publisher. We had a profit share agreement. Fifty percent was going to the foundation for low-income housing. We need another print run, and they wanted a larger percentage—for themselves. Substantially larger."

Max picked up the book and eyeballed the publisher's logo on the spine. "Greedy pricks."

"Exactly. I was pissed off. I didn't want to sign it."

Max put the book down. He rubbed his temples. "Tell me again—why did you kiss her?"

"I had dinner with Kat last night and—"

"I didn't know Kat was in town?" Max said. "Filip was at

some book thing. He's always at some book thing. I was free."

"It was a . . . a family thing."

"Of course, of course. How is she?"

"She's fine. Still living in Melbourne. Renovating her house."

"Is she . . . seeing anyone?" Max asked.

"No. Anyway, last night she said we were both stuck. She said something was missing from our lives. Neither of us did anything spontaneous. We're problem solvers and rule followers, which is great for architecture and sympathetic renovations, but not so good for life . . . and love." Ryan rubbed the back of his neck. "She said if I wasn't careful, all the fun girls would be taken, and I'd end up single and lonely, or worse—with a partner as boring as fuck."

"No one wants that," Max agreed. "Go on."

"Honestly, we drank a lot of wine. It's been a long day, and when Miss Universe walked into the room, all I wanted to do was put my arms around her and kiss her. Actually, that's not entirely true. I wanted to do a few other immoral things to her as well." Ryan paused. "I can't believe how quickly it fell apart. She hates me. She called me a cad."

Max snorted, and then he chuckled. "Apologise."

"I tried—she's not interested."

A long silence.

Ryan rubbed his hands together. "What do we know about Miss Universe?"

"She's Filip's niece and—"

"Filip's *niece*?" Ryan folded his arms in front of his chest. Max nodded.

"You gave her alcohol and sent her into my room?"

"Yes, I did."

"Why would you do that?"

Max blinked. "It was a treasure hunt. We do it every year for the undergraduates; it gives them a feel for the place." He shuffled some papers on his desk. Moved a document from one tray to another and then back again.

Ryan stared at Max.

"Okay, there may have been an agenda," Max confessed. "There aren't many faculty members under thirty-five who are single. It's week two of a very long year—we thought it might be fun to mix things up a bit. You're single. She's single. You both have a pulse."

"You set her up?"

"It wasn't my idea—some of the others . . . Meredith, the sustainable design lecturer, she was especially keen on the idea."

Ryan grabbed the book from Max's desk. "By the way, I'm thirty-eight."

"Then, you're not as accomplished as I first thought."

3

RAIN WORDS

LATER THAT AFTERNOON, a monsoon-like weather event hit the city. Soon, the streets and pavements were slick with water, and the gutters ran like fast-flowing tributaries. The drains overflowed and flooded low-lying intersections. The traffic stalled. After decades of drought, the country faced a fluctuating weather system. A La Niña sat off the northern region of the Australian continent, and rain was predicted to fall over the eastern coastline for the next six months.

Ryan headed toward the university car park to collect his car. He drove a red two-door 110 Land Rover Defender, which was built in 1989. The vehicle had a soft-top roof and a cavernous interior with enough space to move furniture, mountain bikes, surfboards, and camping gear.

He'd purchased the car two years ago, and since then, he had replaced the lights, wipers, shock absorbers, suspension gear, tires, and bull bar. He'd fitted the vehicle with heated leather seats and a high-end audio system. Like a Lego model with interchangeable parts, the vehicle had now cost him more than the price of a new car. But he loved the low-tech engine and the tough reliability—the thing was bullet-proof—it would go anywhere. The classic, boxy shape harked back to a 1940s design, which was the epitome of urban sophistication. He washed it every Sunday afternoon and had it detailed once a month.

After leaving the university grounds, Ryan headed to his architectural practice, SLD Projects, in The Rocks. Situated on the western side of the Harbour Bridge, the area was originally called Tallawoladah by the Cadigal people. When the First Fleet arrived, they moored their boats against the rocky foreshore and it earned the nickname, The Rocks. The name stuck.

The suburb was now a commercial hub that drew tourists to its historic attractions: cobblestone streets, narrow laneways, heritage-listed shops, charming bars, and modern restaurants. Georgian and Victorian architecture.

Stopping by the office meant Ryan didn't have to tackle the Harbour Bridge traffic in peak hour—ten lanes merging into four on a wet evening—it would take him twice as long to get home. The rain was so heavy, he could hardly see out the windscreen.

He parked the defender on Cumberland Street. It was a short walk through the Argyle Cut, a passageway carved through the sandstone hill by convict labour, to the SLD Project offices.

Friday night drinks were a regular occurrence at SLD, and Freddie, the receptionist and business manager, mixed a different cocktail every week. With no plans for the evening, the appalling weather set to continue, and an early meeting at the art museum scheduled for tomorrow morning, Ryan opted for a quiet night. After a cocktail, he would head home.

Freddie had a sweet tooth, and the cocktail on offer that evening was a rum and passionfruit concoction called a hurricane. The name suited the weather, and the golden colour of the drink lifted Ryan's spirits.

Cocktail in hand, Ryan listened to Sophie, the new graduate, talk about the value of wombats as pets, but all he could think about was Louie—how her too-long fringe covered her beautiful dark eyes. Half an hour later, he nodded sympathetically as Amos, one of the directors, discussed the plight of his Dutch girlfriend's visa application—permanent visa, bridging visa, partner visa—Ryan couldn't follow the conversation or the application process. Louie continued to fill his thoughts. He recalled her soft lips and the floral scent on her skin. When Freddie introduced a conversation about cantilevered concrete slabs—one of Ryan's favourite topics—all Ryan could think about was the stone he found in the pocket of her jacket.

"Are you okay?" Freddie asked. "You've hardly said a word. What's on your mind?"

Ryan paused. "A Chanel suit."

"Is that a cocktail?"

"I don't think so. I'm not even sure it's Chanel."

After her encounter with Ryan in the Quadrangle, Louie made her way through the torrential rain to her car, a fifteen-year-old Hyundai Elantra, which was parked a brisk twenty-minute walk away. Parking on the university grounds was expensive, and the surrounding suburbs only offered two-hour metered spaces, which were monitored by vigilante-style ticket inspectors. When it came to parking fines, Louie was risk averse. She would happily walk for twenty minutes.

Her heavy boots fared well in the downpour, and she carried a large, industrial-style umbrella purchased from a well-known hardware chain. It was the most popular item they sold.

The Elantra was an unremarkable vehicle—light brown exterior with greige (a colour somewhere between brown and grey) upholstery. The backseat held an assortment of tennis and soccer balls, Frisbees, takeaway coffee cups, and piles of dog hair. The vehicle had been cleaned three months ago when Louie drove her mother, Tara, to a corporate lunch. Tara was a working artist—she painted—and she was also on the Board of the Arts Council. It was a provision of her membership that she attend social functions and business lunches, mingling and delivering speeches when required. Tara didn't want to arrive at lunch smelling like a wet dog with her clothes covered in dog hair, so Louie acquainted herself with the vacuum.

After reaching her car, Louie climbed inside and threw her wet umbrella onto the back seat. She wiggled the radio controls until she found a station she liked and started the engine. After easing the vehicle through a series of congested side streets, she entered the throng of peak-hour traffic on the motorway. It was a long, hazardous journey home. The vehicle's seats were hard, and she had to lean forward and hover over the wheel to get comfortable. The interior fogged up, forcing her to continually flick the air-conditioning on and off, as she tried to find a balance between clear vision and Arctic temperatures.

An hour later, she arrived home and parked her car on the street directly outside her house. This never happened. Finding an unoccupied parking space within three hundred metres of her home was rare. She lived across the road from Sydney Park—a popular recreation area south of the city—and torrential rain had kept the park-goers away. The surrounding streets were littered with storm debris—leaves, tree branches, and rubbish—but they were free from cars.

Louie rented a caretaker's cottage in a heritage-listed housing commission property. The estate had once been a grand, stately home, built by wealthy sheep farmers when the nation thrived on the profits from the wool industry. In the mid-1800s, the country rode to wealth on the back of sheep revenue. One hundred and fifty years later, the main house was a warren of dilapidated flats earmarked for renovation.

The caretaker's cottage was in a similar state of disrepair —the foundations had subsided, and the gutters leaked on all sides. But it was a stand-alone building with a separate entrance and a small garden.

Opening her side gate, Louie found Eva, a black and tan kelpie, waiting for her on the front veranda. Eva came from a long line of intelligent sheepherding canines, so it was appropriate that she now lived in a property built by sheep farmers. When the dog rooted around the foundations of the building, Louie wondered if she was sniffing the scent of old sheep, left there by the original owners.

The kelpie was a lithe and active breed of working dog; Eva could run tirelessly all day if Louie let her. Three years ago, when Louie hovered over the litter of eight pups, she had no idea which one to choose. Then, Eva scurried toward Louie, climbed onto her shoes and sat down. The dog looked up at her with moist, amber-coloured eyes, and it was love at first gaze. They were naturally drawn to each other.

At the sight of Louie, the dog's eyes lit up. Wagging her tail and pricking her ears, Eva leapt off the veranda toward her favourite human. Together, they sat on the doorstep, cuddling and patting and pawing each other for several minutes. Home alone all afternoon, the dog needed a run.

"I've missed you, too. Yes, I have. Sorry, I'm late—the weather, the traffic, and an annoying man at the university made me feel very bad. But you're such a good girl. Yes, you are. Have you had a fun afternoon?"

Marvellous afternoon, I made friends with a lizard, but it's good that you're home.

The caretaker's cottage was a Federation building—red brick with a wide, covered veranda that had turned timber posts and lace fretwork. The front door opened to a central foyer, which led to the living area, and beyond that, the bathroom. The main bedroom was to the left of the foyer, and to the right was the kitchen, which had a small sitting room at the far end. A wood firebox was the only heating.

The windows of the cottage were small, but the ceilings were high. The walls were covered in original artworks— mostly landscapes—that belonged to Tara; the house was Tara's overflow gallery space, and some of the pieces were over one hundred years old. The furniture was a mix of secondhand items—a kitchen table, a few wicker chairs, and a bookcase—and a few pieces that Louie inherited when her grandmother died last year. These included an Edra sofa covered in a floral print and an old Thonet cantilever armchair. This was Louie's favourite item in the house.

Chairs mattered to Louie. They were essential household

items, and comfort was paramount, but when Louie looked at a chair, she didn't just see a functional item of furniture. A single chair could encapsulate a design movement, and therefore, a moment in time. Chairs said something about a home and its occupants. (A well-made chair could also last for decades if it was properly cared for.)

After opening her front door, Louie ducked through the entrance and nervously scanned the walls in her foyer. For the past two weeks, a large huntsman spider had been roaming around the interior of her house. She had named the spider Harry.

Harry was an intimidating, but humble, breed that hunted more troublesome bugs, like smaller spiders, insects, and ants. He was twice the size of her hand. He had eight eyes aligned in two rows across the front of his head. A flat brown body and long hairy legs. Louie was happiest when Harry was at least three metres away from her.

Louie had unhappily shared her home with many smaller huntsman spiders. These she had managed to catch and release herself—an unpleasant task that she never enjoyed—but someone had to do it. With Harry, however, she had lost her nerve for trap and release—he was just so . . . big . . . and furry . . . and scary. When she saw him, she quivered.

Harry hovered on the wall between the kitchen and the foyer, which was a good position for him because it was the wall opposite her bedroom. If Harry decided to go hunting in her bedroom, she might never sleep again.

After dropping her bag and keys on the kitchen table, Louie pulled out her phone and checked her messages and emails. She had a second job as a tour guide at the National Art Museum, and she had a booking the following morning.

An email from the museum confirmed her tour was almost full.

She messaged her mother. They had plans for the following morning. Tara had a painting entered in the National Portrait Prize. She would be at the art museum tomorrow to deliver her artwork, which meant Louie could jog with Eva to the museum, and then leave the dog with her mother, while she conducted her art tours.

Louie opened the refrigerator and selected a punnet of raspberries. After placing the punnet on the kitchen counter, she sorted through the berries, discarding the limp ones and popping the plumper fruit into her mouth. She had ceased the preparation of food some time ago—why cook when she could forage in the fridge or the pantry? The kitchen was small—the five food groups were within arm's reach. Tara also cooked for two, delivering Tupperware containers filled with hearty meals every week. Her mother was an excellent cook.

As Louie sorted through the berries, she also shifted through the events of her day. Two art history classes in a row, as well as tutorials, was unfortunate scheduling. She made a mental note to change her timetable for next term. Also, sixty-five new students were too many—both classes were over-enrolled. Faculty should have created a third class, but that meant allocating another lecturer—more money, more resources—and highly unlikely. But Carl had re-enrolled, which was good. She could get him through if he stayed focused and came to class.

The treasure hunt was a complete waste of her time. She should never have agreed to do it and she was annoyed at Max for pressing the task upon her.

Ryan McDermott entered her head. What a pretentious,

selfish, ill-mannered prick of a man. Who did he think he was, not signing the stupid book? What an idiot! He made her feel awful. So much for spontaneity. And the stupid game with the jacket, pulling it out of her reach. That was so annoying. Why did men do that? Tease and pester. They all did it, even her best friend Henri did it. It was pointless, inane behaviour.

She should never have agreed to kiss Ryan—a total stranger. That was a mistake. That was her downfall. Live and learn. She'd never do that again. Never.

It was, however, a spectacular kiss; she couldn't deny it. In the most unlikely of places—the tutorial room—with the most obnoxious man—Ryan McDermott. Life was perplexing. She had no idea how the universe worked.

Suddenly, her heart rate quickened. A warm tingling sensation spread through her body. A distracting and inconvenient sensation to be having while standing at the kitchen sink eating plump raspberries. She paused her foraging for a moment, hoping the hot tingling sensation would pass. But her thoughts stayed with Ryan. How could he kiss her the way he had, and then not sign the book? How could he look into her eyes, then not do the one thing she'd asked? And she wasn't asking much. Put pen to paper and write his name. How could he say it was separate? What did that even mean? Separate. Wasn't it all about the book? That was her reason for being there in the first place.

It was such a confusing encounter. Delightful and terrible. Passionate and crushing. But she knew the truth about him—he didn't care about her. That was fine; he didn't have to care.

She tossed the remaining imperfect berries into the trash.

Eva dropped a toy octopus at Louie's feet. Louie collected the toy with her foot, then kicked it into the air, and the dog caught it.

In the bedroom, Louie threw herself onto her bed. Rolling over, she stared up at the ceiling. She couldn't get Ryan out of her head. If he didn't care, then why had he fixed her shirt? And straightened her hair? Tell her she was gorgeous? Smile and look into her eyes and be so concerned for her? She rubbed her chest. The hot stone was still there.

"Fuck him."

She wanted to hate Ryan McDermott. She wanted to write him off as an idiot. That would be easier—but she couldn't do it.

Eva skipped into the room, carrying her toy octopus. She sat on the edge of the bed. Louie rolled over and looked the dog in the eye. Eva's amber eyes were bright, alert, and glowing—she was ready to work, play, run, swim, chase, and catch. The dog needed to get the nervous energy out of her system, and Louie needed to get Ryan out of her head.

"Rain be dammed, we both need a run," Louie said.

Eva dropped her toy and retreated to her mat in the sitting room. *You might want to check the forecast.*

Louie changed into her running gear. After grabbing Eva's lead, she coaxed the dog to the front door. "It'll be fine once we get out there," she said.

Eva hung her head—she didn't think it would be fine.

Outside, the downpour continued with no respite in sight. The rain looked like it might hurt.

"Oh, dear," Louie said.

I tried to tell you. Eva sighed.

The outing quickly lost its appeal. Getting drenched halfway through a run was inconvenient. Willingly heading out into a downpour like this took dedication and motivation. At seven on a Friday evening, Louie lacked both. They would have to wait until tomorrow.

Eva gave Louie her best *Let's have an early dinner* stare.

After Louie fed the dog, she grabbed a blanket from the daybed on the veranda, wrapped it around herself, and sat beside Eva on the doorstep. Together, they watched the rain fall. The heavy pitter-patter sound on the tin roof was hypnotic. Words floated inside her head—how to describe the rain? After nine years of studying atmospheric art, descriptive words were effortless—aqueous, deluge, barrage, torrent, volley, spate, bombardment, buckets.

"Mizzle," she whispered in Eva's ear. "Mizzle is a good rain word."

Sensing Louie's serenity, Eva lay down on the step. *So, this is what we're doing now?*

"Yes, it's one of those days—again. Sorry about that." She patted the dog, and Eva pressed her ears back.

"I like this flat ear look on you. It's regal. Very dignified."

You should start calling me princess. Eva had always wanted to be called princess.

Soon the air became dark and clammy, and Louie's mind began to shut down. Slowly, the garden dissolved into the rain. Through the downpour, she saw the world as a symphony of green and grey mist.

An hour passed.

Louie roused herself. She took a long, slow breath, then she glanced to her left and then to her right. After realising where she was, she recalled her day, the incident with Ryan, and how he made her feel.

She turned to Eva. "Somewhere inside this house is a vibrator."

Louie searched the bathroom cabinets but found no sign of the device. She checked the bedside drawers and then the kitchen drawers, but it was not there. It was small and egg-shaped, so easy to misplace, but it was also bright orange, an obvious colour. She had no idea where she'd left it.

4

THE ART HUT

At eight, Louie and Eva set off on their morning run to the art museum. Louie's tour didn't start until ten, but she would need food and a shower before work, and Eva liked to chase her Frisbee at the end of the run. They would also swing by the duck pond at the bottom of the park. For two years, Louie had watched a pair of brown and white wood ducks. The birds were monogamous and returned to the same place to breed. It was autumn, and soon the baby ducklings would take flight.

Eva ran off the lead, close to Louie's side, never wavering, always mirroring Louie's pace and direction. Despite obstacles they encountered—park benches, ill-placed posts, trees, rubbish bins, small wayward children, other dogs on extendable leads—Eva always anticipated the direction Louie would take, and she was never wrong.

At the bottom of the park, they turned into a scrappy wooded area—a low-lying watercourse and marshland where birdlife gathered. As Louie and Eva approached the small brown pond, which lay in a dip at the bottom of a hill,

Louie spied the wood duck couple resting under a gum tree at the edge of the water.

"These lovers, same place, same time, every day," Louie said, creeping through the long grass toward the ducks. She saw no sign of any ducklings.

Eva turned and grinned at Louie. *Can I chase them? Please, please can I chase them? They want to be chased. They really do.*

"Don't we all?" Louie said, patting the dog's head. "But you can't. You're a city dog. City dogs chase balls and Frisbees, not ducks."

Twenty minutes later, they arrived at the museum, and Louie pulled a flexible, rubber Frisbee from her backpack. Eva's ears pricked at the sight of the toy. Executing a statue-like stance, with her front leg raised, the dog was ready to sprint and pounce. Louie flicked the Frisbee, and Eva took off after it. She caught it mid-air and headed back to Louie.

Ryan lived in Kirribilli. A picturesque waterfront suburb on the lower north shore, close to the city. It got its name from an Aboriginal word meaning good fishing spot—the area was an outcrop of hilly land that overlooked the harbour. A small but adequate shopping strip marked the centre of town, and a second-hand, bric-a-brac market was held on the last Saturday of every month. The suburb was also home to Kirribilli House, the official Sydney residence of the Prime Minister.

Ryan's home was a one-hundred-year-old two-storey terrace house located on a narrow, tree-lined street. He bought the place a year ago and immediately gutted the interior. The new renovations included a luxury kitchen and

36

two sleek, travertine bathrooms. The rear deck was extended and covered for indoor-outdoor living. At the front, the dark iron railings and ironwork matched the colour of the glossy front door. The house had a covered driveway with ample parking and a garage.

After an early CrossFit class, followed by breakfast at his favourite café, Ryan returned home to change. At nine, he jumped into his Defender and headed toward the National Art Museum. He had a meeting with Evin French, the museum's director. Evin wanted to discuss an extension to an existing wing. SLD Projects rarely took on commercial work —they designed houses—so a gallery renovation would make a good addition to their existing portfolio.

The museum was surrounded by the city's Royal Botanic Gardens. A verdant oasis in the heart of the city, which included acres of lush parkland. Built in a neo-classical style, the historical building rested on a raised podium and the façade resembled an ancient Greek temple—two rows of Ionic columns framing a deep portico, where patrons could gather before entering the main gallery.

Ryan pulled his Defender into the car park at the rear of the museum. After gathering his belongings, he glanced through the windscreen—on the opposite side of the road he spied Louie walking under a row of Moreton Bay fig trees. She wore running shorts and a sweatshirt. Her hair was tied in a ponytail, and she carried a backpack over one arm. She travelled at a formidable pace—she was headed somewhere specific. The only place around was the art museum.

Ryan smiled. He raised his gaze skyward. "Thank you," he said.

Yesterday afternoon, Max hadn't just set Louie up. He had set them both up. This was not an uncommon experience for Ryan. His friends, his mother, and even his favourite clients, the Haigs, had set him up with a friend of their youngest daughter's. A casual BBQ, a picnic, an extra ticket to an event or the movies. It took him somewhere between five and forty minutes to realise the event was planned around a matchmake. It was usually awkward, but he complied and went along with the plan, asking the girl out on a date. He'd had some fun, and occasionally, a few more dates followed. Nothing ever came of them.

He felt for Louie. She'd been duped, and he pictured her wandering around the campus ticking all the boxes on her list. He wouldn't have called it a treasure hunt; the organisers had gotten that wrong. Her final task was never going to happen. It was a waste of her time—until of course he kissed her. That wasn't a waste of anyone's time.

However, a chance meeting like this—he didn't care if it was fate or coincidence or just wonderful luck—he would take full advantage of the situation.

After jumping out of his Defender, he made his way toward the building.

As Louie approached the museum, she paused. She loved this building. She found the grand scale of neoclassical architecture inspiring. She thought the geometric form, with its formal columns and deep triangular pediment, was beautiful. It was built from the local sandstone, with travertine floors and marble staircases; she loved the serenity of the stone materials.

She scaled the front steps two at a time and headed to the cafeteria for a muffin and coffee. Then, she quickly showered and changed.

The meeting point for her tour was outside the main entrance, next to a large brass statue of Captain Cook riding a horse. Instructions were printed on the tickets. *A large statue of a man on a horse.* They were also included in the email the recipients received, and verbally delivered to the patrons who purchased their tickets at the museum.

Only half the ticketholders ever managed to make it to the large statue of a man on a horse. Louie usually found the wayward tourists inside the foyer or waiting on the front steps. She understood colonialism and the representation of historical figures like Captain Cook was under scrutiny—and rightly so—but the meeting point was very clearly articulated. She couldn't fathom why it was so difficult to get twenty-five people to gather in one place at the same time, but it never happened. She thought perhaps the intellectual rigour of the environment distracted the patrons, causing them to lose all common sense and walk in circles.

Louie stepped outside onto the covered portico of the building to check on any early arrivals. The area was empty, but leaning against a fluted column was Ryan McDermott.

Louie froze.

Ryan held a sketchbook and a pencil—he was drawing something. He looked up, saw her, and promptly closed his sketchbook.

"Hello." He smiled.

She took a step back. "What are you doing here?"

"Looking at art." He slipped his sketchbook and pencil into his shoulder bag.

"Really? On a Saturday morning at ten a.m. Looking at art—by yourself?" She wondered if his presence was a coincidence, fate, or just terrible luck.

She pulled a sticker out of her pocket, peeled the backing

off, and slapped it onto the breast pocket of her shirt. The sticker said *Tour Guide.*

Ryan ambled toward her. "What are *you* doing here?"

"I work here." She pointed to her sticker.

"The university—"

"I'm casual. I also work here. I give tours of . . . of stuff," she said, flustered by his presence.

"Stuff." He grinned.

She frowned, unamused. He was such an annoying man, and the hot stone in her chest was beginning to fire up again.

"What do you want?" she asked.

He dug his hands into his pockets. "I wanted to explain about yesterday—the whole miscommunication about the book. If you have a few minutes—"

"No." She shook her head.

"Just hear me out—"

"I can't. My tour starts soon, and honestly, I don't care."

He stared at her for a long moment. "What's the tour on?"

"The building."

"*This* building?" He pointed to the looming presence of the museum behind her.

She nodded.

His lip curled. "You like neoclassical architecture?"

"Yes, of course—it's a beautiful building. Don't you like it?"

He stepped back. Standing on the edge of the marble steps, he looked up and considered the museum. "No. I think it's hypocritical for an art gallery to be so monumental."

Louie joined him at the edge of the steps. "You're wrong.

It's beautiful. It aspires to classical perfection. How can you not like it?" She glared at him.

"Because it's pretentious. Architecture—and art—should be less intimidating and more accessible. Less like a temple and more like . . . a hut."

"A what?"

"A hut, an art hut."

Good god. How could anyone in their right mind not like this building?

"Is this some sort of test? Has someone put you up to this?" she asked.

"No." He smiled. "I'm interested in your opinion."

"Why?"

"Because you're the tour guide."

"Okay." She turned back to the museum. "I love this building. Sometimes, if I'm having a bad day, I come here and stare at paintings of landscapes. Art helps reframe our worldview. Don't you think?"

He nodded.

Unconvinced, she pointed to the entrance. "Inside, there are paintings that take my breath away. That's what life is about, finding those moments." She turned to him. "Please don't ruin this for me."

"I'm not trying to ruin anything." He turned back to the building. "What about the names carved on the front." He pointed to the bold lettering across the façade. "Rembrandt, Michael Angelo, Leonardo da Vinci? A bunch of outdated European artists with no relevance to our own country. We have a culture of indigenous art that's far more interesting."

"Yes, you have a point. But at the time, these were the luminaries of the arts; they were meant to be aspirational."

She paused. "Are you sure this is not a test? Because it feels like a test."

He smiled. "It's not a test."

She rubbed her neck. "I agree with you about indigenous art, but there are many things to be unhappy about, and this building isn't one of them."

"Agreed. Can I join your tour?"

"God, no!"

He raised an eyebrow. "Is it sold out?"

"No, there are two places left."

He pointed to the entrance. "I could just go inside and buy a ticket?"

"Please don't."

"What if I—"

"No."

"I could—"

"No. Whatever it is, no."

A cold breeze blew up the marble steps and across the podium. She shivered and rubbed her arms.

"Are you cold?" He stepped toward her.

"No. I have a very good umbrella."

He frowned. "With you?"

"Actually, it's at home." Louie gave him a curt nod. "Goodbye. I need to find my people, and I think they might be lost."

An hour later, after Louie's tour of the building had finished, she entered the admin wing of the museum. After peeling off her *Tour Guide* sticker, she dropped it into the trash. From across the room, Evin French, the museum director waved an envelope in her direction.

Louie had never met a person with more qualifications than Evin. He had a Doctor of Philosophy, a master's in theology and science, and another in arts and humanities. She had also never met anyone as tall as Evin. If she had to guess, she would have said he was three metres tall, but math was not her strength. Evin was two metres tall—six foot six. He had hands like bear paws. His ears flared, and his large blue eyes took up a third of his face.

Evin made his way toward her, an oversized raincoat draped over one arm. It looked like a tarpaulin.

"Someone left this for you." Evan's bear-paw hand passed her the envelope.

"For me?"

"Yes, for you." Evin slipped on his raincoat. He looked like he was slipping on a two-man tent. Louie wondered where he shopped for his clothes.

"Are you going to open it?" he asked, raising both eyebrows—like two twitching moustaches taped to his forehead.

Louie suspected he already knew what was inside the envelope. It wasn't sealed, and she wondered if he'd peeked. Evin loved water cooler gossip. If she wanted to know what was going on in the office, he was the first person she asked.

From inside the envelope, Louie pulled out a sheet of white cartridge paper. She flipped it over and revealed a sketch of the museum. The front façade—eight Ionic columns, a large triangular pediment, and a wide portico. Effortlessly, the picture defined the looming presence of the building. At the bottom, the words *the art hut* were written.

Evin peered over Louie's shoulder. "I like the way *art hut* is written—all in lowercase. It's quite good, don't you think?"

Louie nodded.

The proportion was perfect, and it confirmed everything she thought about its classical legacy—it was a work of art.

"Tell your mother hello," Evin said. "I missed her this morning, but I'll see her at the gala dinner in a few weeks. She's giving the introductory speech for the arts medal recipient. And wish her luck in the portrait prize—her entry is marvellous."

Louie smiled. "It's a painting of my uncle Filip."

5

STILL LIFE

Two weeks earlier, at the beginning of the term, Max Cabot had reminded Louie that she was due to present a lecture on her thesis topic to the arts faculty. Over one thousand people—students and staff—would attend. At the time, she had thanked Max for the opportunity, then she'd walked out of his office and thought, *What the hell have I done? Why did I agree to do that?* A thousand people were not fine. It was nowhere near fine.

Perched at her desk, in the corner of her sitting room, Louie put the final touches to the slides and notes for her lecture. On the bookshelf beside her was a bowl filled with smooth stones. She picked out a polished amber rock and held it in her hand.

"Scary things build resilience," she said, taking in a long breath and releasing it slowly. "I can do this." She placed the stone back into the bowl.

Keeping a stone in her pocket was her counsellor's idea. He said it might help her control her nerves, and he was right—the world was a calmer place when she was holding onto it. Somehow, a small piece of rock grounded her thoughts, and it fixed her feet firmly to the planet. Just knowing it was there helped to settle her anxiety.

She had spent more than a third of her life studying her thesis topic: three years on her arts degree, one year completing her master's, and nine years on her PhD. She knew how to study, so compiling the information for the lecture was not a problem. Some nights, she dreamed about light and air. She had memorised hundreds of quotes and could talk about her topic for hours.

Except she didn't like to talk about it all. It had become a task she had to finish. Something to tick off her to-do list. She was on track to finish on time, in six months, and she would be free. By the end of winter, the weight would be lifted. All she had to do was focus, put her head down, and follow her study plan.

Before shutting her computer down, Louie ran an internet search on useless PhD topics. The results always amused her, and her search revealed that students had completed PhDs on *Do mosquitoes like cheese?* and *Do woodpeckers get headaches?*

Compared to woodpeckers and cheese, Louie's topic seemed reasonable. Even justifiable. Light was everything, and art was important. Surely, other people besides herself would be interested to know how the effects of light and air in landscape painting affected the viewer.

Her phone rang. The call was from Tara. Louie picked up.

"Can you please move your car?" her mother asked.

"Why?"

"Because I have things—art and clothes—for you."

Aware that she had the prime parking spot right outside her house and her car had been parked there for less than two days, Louie was reluctant to move the Elantra.

"I can help carry," Louie volunteered.

"No, no, it's too much. I have fifteen pieces."

"Fifteen pieces! Why do you have fifteen pieces?" Louie grabbed her car keys and walked out the door.

"I'm swapping. We talked about this."

"I didn't realise you were taking fifteen." Louie headed out the side gate.

"I'm not taking—I'm replacing."

Tara ended the call.

Louie had lived with the artwork on her walls for the last two years, and she was very happy with all the pieces. But they belonged to Tara—who had inherited a collection from her own mother.

Every so often, Tara decided she needed to move a few of the pieces around. But fifteen pieces was everything Louie had. This was not an art swap; it was a cull—a complete overhaul. Louie suspected Tara's behaviour was triggered by her entry into the National Portrait Prize. The painting of Filip was the best piece Tara had produced in years. The finalists would be announced in two weeks. Unsettled while she waited for the results, Tara threw her nervous energy into distracting herself, and an art swap was something she could control.

Louie moved her car, eventually finding a space three blocks away. Sunday afternoon was premium recreation time at the park, possibly the worst time of the week to move her car. When she returned home, she found her friend Lila helping Tara haul the fifteen canvases and a box of clothes onto Louie's front veranda.

Louie held the gate open for them.

Lila had Shirley Temple's blonde curly hair, a pale complexion, and rosebud lips. But today, her cheeks were flushed, and her forehead glistened with sweat. Her hair was pulled off her face and secured with a headband.

Lila wore running shorts and a T-shirt. She was not a jogger. In the twelve years that Louie had known her, Lila had never once jogged—anywhere. (They met in university in a first-year, common core, design studio class that was supposed to teach ideation, and to this day neither could tell say what the subject was about.)

"Since when do you run?" Louie asked.

"Since I got the lead in that play, the Greek tragedy thing. It starts next month. I want to look good."

Acting was Lila's true profession, but fringe theatre productions didn't pay the bills. She also worked at the opera house in ticket sales, and sometimes in hospitality at a four-star steak restaurant, which paid her well and the tips were good, but she was a vegetarian. Her advice to customers about the menu was limited to sides and desserts.

Louie looked Lila over. "You look great. Did you get the job for the diet pet food commercial?"

"Second, again. Always the bridesmaid."

"Do you get something for that?"

"I get paid for attending the call back."

"Is that like getting money for doing nothing?"

"No, it's nothing like that."

As they entered the foyer, Tara and Lila scanned the walls, searching for Harry.

"He's in the kitchen, behind the cupboard," Louie said.

The women let out a collective sigh of relief.

Tara handed Louie a bag of Tupperware containers. "A

vegetable curry, a caponata sauce—which is okay, but honestly, it's not great. Leftover pumpkin risotto, which is always better the second day—maybe have that tonight. And double chocolate lamingtons—gluten-free—which are to die for."

"Thank you." Louie dropped the food containers onto the kitchen table, and Lila packed them into the fridge.

Tara began plucking paintings from the walls in the foyer. Then she moved to the living room, the bedroom, and the sitting room. It took her less than three minutes to stack fifteen canvases against the foyer wall. These she would be taking home.

Louie scratched her thumbnail over her palm. Her mother was taking her friends.

Tara ignored her daughter's concerns.

"Lila, there are clothes in that box. Help yourself." Tara pointed to a cardboard carton on the floor. "I bought the grey suit for Louie and a handful of other things, but the cocktail dresses I'll keep at my place."

Lila picked out a paisley shirt from the box and held it up. "These are your nan's old clothes?"

"Yes." Louie pulled out a grey pinstriped suit. "At first, we didn't want to wear them because they were a dead person's clothes. Then we decided she was dead and it was fine to wear them."

Louie slipped on a grey jacket, pulling at the cuffs, as she tried it on for size.

Lila sniffed the collar of the paisley shirt.

"We had everything dry cleaned," Louie confirmed.

"What's the suit for?"

Louie explained she would wear the suit when she presented her lecture this week. She didn't want to compete with the colourful art on her presentation slides, so the suit was the perfect choice. "I'll fade into the background—no one will even notice me," she said.

Tara pointed to the canvases stacked against the wall. "I'm feeling closed in. I need to look at something epic. I'm taking all the landscapes and giving you flowers . . . and fruit. It was so cold here last winter; flowers will warm the place up, don't you think?"

Louie frowned at the new paintings that Tara was hanging on her walls.

"I'm not a fan of . . . still life." She screwed up her nose. "I love landscapes. You know that. Landscapes make me happy. Flowers are for . . . old people. Life should never be still."

Collectively, the women took a step back and considered the floral canvases that were now fixed to the walls of Louie's house: paintings of gum blossoms and banksias, native wildflowers, and proteas. Canvases filled with azaleas, ranunculus, and cornflowers. Apples and pears were also prolific. The painting included kitchen artefacts: household jugs, vases, and pitchers (because the bouquets needed to be contained in vessels of some description), teapots and teacups, and platters holding lavishly decorated cakes.

"You'll get used to them," Tara dismissed. "Now, I need to choof off. I've a board meeting this week and a ton of emails to get through."

Lila pointed to a painting of lemons and limes on a white tablecloth. "If I stole this and sold it, would I be rich?"

"Define rich?"

"Could I buy a house?"

"Not in this country. But you might get a nice car."

"I do need a nice car—actually, I just need a car." She turned to Louie. "I think I'll stay for tea and cake." She headed into the kitchen and filled the kettle.

"I've also organised a delivery of wood for your fire," Tara said.

"Mother, you didn't need to do that," Louie scolded.

"It cost nothing—literally. I paid for this man's entry into the portrait prize. He has a farm, down south . . . somewhere." She waved her hand in a southward direction. "He'll deliver the wood once a month. Think about where you want him to stack it."

Louie stepped out the front door and onto the veranda. Tara followed.

"Maybe by the lilly pilly trees, on the left. It would be out of the way, and I'd keep it covered."

"No," Tara dismissed. "Let's put it on the veranda, on the right, so it's near the side door—closer to the fireplace. We could move the table and chairs to the other side, and shuffle the daybed this way, so it catches the afternoon sun."

Tara walked over to the outdoor setting and picked up a chair.

Louie took the chair out of her mother's hands. "Leave it. I'll do it later."

With the landscape paintings safely packed in Tara's car, they said their goodbyes, and Louie went inside to help with the tea.

Lila sliced two double chocolate lamingtons in half and placed them on a plate. She poured the tea, handed Louie a serviette, and they sat down at the table. A moment later, the sound of chairs scraping across the veranda drifted into the kitchen.

Lila paused, a slice of lamington halfway to her mouth. "Is your mother moving the furniture?"

Louie nodded. "She can't help it. It's in her DNA. I'll move it back later."

Henri arrived at Louie's house later that afternoon. He carried a bag of coffee beans, another bag holding two almond croissants, and a small pair of sharp scissors. Louie had an appointment to have her hair cut—a fringe trim and two centimetres off the length. Henri wasn't a hairdresser. After his arts degree, he trained as a lighting designer, specialising in theatre productions. After a few years, he realised there was a lot of downtime in the industry and he needed a job on the side to make ends meet. He opened a café, and soon it became a full-time job. He called it a pivot. He said everyone was allowed a few pivots in life. This was his first, and he was going to make a go of it.

Steady-handed and keen-eyed, he was also handy with a pair of scissors. If the café folded, he was one step ahead; he knew what his next pivot would be.

Henri had come straight from his café. He wore a checked shirt, jeans, and trainers. His dark hair flicked across his forehead, revealing his receding hairline. He smelled like coffee.

Spying the double chocolate lamingtons, Henri dropped his croissants in the trash. "Yesterday's," he said.

"You bring me yesterday's croissants?" Louie complained.

"Yesterday they were croissants. Today they're almond croissants, but they won't keep until tomorrow. Besides, you're poor, and poor people can't be choosy." Henri placed the bag of coffee on the kitchen bench. "Do not store this in the fridge. Ever."

"Oh, my god, you tell me that at least once a month," Louie muttered.

Henri helped himself to a lamington, then scanned the new art on the walls. "Good god, we're surrounded by flowers on all sides." He frowned. "It's delightful, I guess."

"But not soulful."

"Don't take it too seriously. It's just art." He moved to the sink and dusted the coconut from the lamington off his hands. Noticing the sketch of the art museum pinned to the fridge, he asked, "What's this?"

"An annoying man drew it for me."

"You have an annoying man in your life, besides me?" Henri studied the image. "Isn't this your favourite building?"

"It is. I'm not sure how I feel about the sketch. I'm leaving it there for a few days to gauge its effect. Perhaps the austerity will cancel out the flowers." She rubbed her nose.

Henri directed her to a chair. He placed a towel over her shoulders.

Louie wiggled.

"Stop fidgeting. Now tell me more about this annoying man." He combed and trimmed the length of her hair.

Louie sat back and made a full confession to her hair-dresser. The treasure hunt, the kiss, the unsigned book, the incident with the jacket, and then the art museum encounter. "It's a confusing gesture, don't you think? He didn't like the building, but he drew a picture of it," she said.

"Not confusing at all. He likes you. Stay still." He ran the scissors along her fringe. "Obviously, he has a reason for not signing the book. Probably justified—why else would he try so hard to explain himself? And teasing you with the jacket, that was hilarious. I can imagine the look on your face. Do we have a picture?"

"Of my face?" She pointed to her face. "It's right here."

Henri handed her his phone.

Louie searched for Ryan, then showed Henri an image of the intense, serious man with green eyes and formidable ears.

"Attractive, for an older man."

"Yes, but his dislike of neoclassical architecture might be unforgivable."

Louie felt something tickle her neck.

"It's Harry," Henri shrieked. "He's on your neck."

"What the fuck?" Louie jumped up, knocking the chair over. She stood rigid with fear. "Get him off. Get him off."

"Kidding," Henri said, deadpan. "Okay, we're about done here."

Later that evening, after Henri had left, Louie once again went in search of her vibrator. Undertaking a more thorough search in case she'd missed it the first time, she looked in the same places she had previously searched. Her efforts were fruitless. Other less obvious locations around the house—the side table drawers, her wardrobe, the kitchen cupboards—also proved futile.

"If I could just remember where I left it," she mumbled.

Eva sauntered over and sat beside her. *It's in the bathroom. The top shelf of the shower caddy.*

Louie sat on the floor next to the dog and stared deeply into Eva's eyes. The dog returned her gaze.

"You know everything, don't you?" Louie said. "I wish

you could talk. Say something. Go on. Anything. Tell me you love me, unconditionally."

Talking is overrated, Eva thought. She placed her head on Louie's leg.

Louie wrapped her arms around the dog. Sometimes you didn't need words.

When Louie Leon's name turned up as a subject line in Ryan's inbox, he thought the universe had it in for him—he couldn't seem to escape her. Not that he wanted to avoid her, but her presence was a persistent diversion, which he found equally delightful and torturous. When he thought about her, time evaporated, and hours passed. He couldn't focus. His architectural practice had never been busier, his workload increased daily, but he couldn't get on top of his tasks.

On Saturday morning when Ryan met Louie at the museum, he'd thought their brief dialogue was wonderful. He'd genuinely wanted to join her tour and hear what she had to say about the architecture. She was smart and passionate and opinionated—there were so many things he liked about her. When she stood close to him, his heart warmed, and the feeling spread through his chest.

Earlier that morning, when he'd collected his takeaway coffee, he'd wondered how Louie might take hers—a cappuccino or a latte, with oat milk or soy? Then he thought about where they might go on a first date, assuming she'd agree to a date. A new Indian restaurant had opened close to his house; he wondered if she liked Indian food. It was at this point that Ryan decided he might be losing his mind.

He needed to see her again. He wanted to find out what

her favourite foods were, and how she took her coffee, and what type of books she liked, and what sort of dog she had. He needed to ask her about light and art. More than anything, he wanted to put his arms around her, look into her dark eyes, and kiss her. But they'd gotten off to a bad start—the confusion with the book. Somehow, he needed to fix this.

Now, sitting at his desk in his architectural firm, his computer in front of him, Louie's name had turned up in his inbox. He rested his elbows on the desktop and held his head in his hands. All weekend visions of Louie had been driving him crazy, and now she had followed him to his workplace.

He moved his cursor to the email and clicked on it. It was from the university.

An open invitation to all faculty members to attend a series of informal lectures by the PhD candidates. Louie Leon would be presenting her ideas on Wednesday at lunchtime in the auditorium. Everyone—students, faculty, and admin—were welcome.

Ryan marked the event in his diary. But he wouldn't forget; Wednesday was only two days away. It already felt like two weeks away.

Freddie paused at Ryan's desk. "Still mulling over the Chanel suit, I see. Did it have nice eyes?"

Ryan grinned. "Yes."

Work. Just focus on work, he told himself.

6

PISSARRO

STUDENT SERVICES WAS the collective name for all administration requirements and assistance at the university campus. As a casual lecturer, Louie's dealings with the student services team were a daily occurrence. Stationary requests, timetables, administration details, room changes, and IT equipment were all dealt with by the services team.

The services counter was on a raised, circular platform at the front of the administration wing. Louie thought this might be the crux of the problem. One group should never be raised above the masses—even if it was only three small steps above the masses. Height enabled the illusion of supremacy.

Their job was to provide customer service. They didn't have to sell anything, collect data, or validate parking, all they had to do was help a staff member or a student. That was the sole reason for their existence. Regrettably, student services looked upon the masses as if they were a problem that couldn't be solved. For decades, a culture of entitlement had been fostered within the ranks of the department, and this was transferred by osmosis to all new staff members when they joined the team.

On Wednesday morning, Louie approached the services desk. To make life as easy as possible for the staff, she had written her request for supplies on an oversized sticky note: *Whiteboard markers; one black and one green. Post-it notes; one pink and one blue.* She handed the note to the attendant at the desk. Her name tag read *Marissa.*

Marissa's dark curly hair was swept to one side, and large hoop earrings dangled from her earlobes. On the counter in front of her was a small mountain of gummy bears.

Reluctantly, Marissa took the note from Louie, and her eyes flicked over the list of supplies. She popped a gummy bear into her mouth, then she glanced across the counter at Louie.

Louie forced a smile.

Once again, Marissa studied the note, this time with more intensity. She popped another gummy bear into her mouth.

"I'm giving a lecture in twenty minutes," Louie prompted, hoping for haste.

Slowly, Marissa slid off her chair and headed toward the supply room. She returned several minutes later with a green marker and a pack of yellow Post-it notes. She passed the items over the counter to Louie, then popped a gummy bear into her mouth.

Louie considered the items on the counter. She had been specific about the colours because she was colour-coding a timeline diagram for her first-year students. She needed pink Post-it notes because the students would be in groups, and each group was allocated a different colour.

Briefly, Louie wondered if Marissa was colour-blind.

Louie pushed the supplies back across the counter. "If you could just change these to the colours on my list, that would be appreciated." She smiled, then added, "That's if you're not too busy." She glanced over her shoulder, the admin wing was almost empty.

Marissa glared. She ate two more gummy bears and considered the top of the counter for a long moment. Then, very slowly she slid off her stool and headed toward the supply cupboard. After a few minutes, she returned with the correct stationery.

"Any update on my staff card?" Louie asked. "We're in week three."

Marissa shook her head and shovelled a handful of gummy bears into her mouth.

"Okay, then I'm going to need a guest pass, so I can get into the building that I work in. And I'm giving a lecture in ten minutes?"

Marissa glared.

"Also, can you check my pigeonhole, because I'm expecting a late student submission and . . ." Louie paused.

Marissa had tilted her head to one side, and Louie realised this was a sign that Marissa was only half listening. Her attention was drawn to a conversation taking place behind her. Marissa held up a forefinger, indicating she'd just be a minute—she had to deal with something far more important than Louie's staff pass.

"I have a lecture in—" Louie's voice trailed away.

Marissa stepped back from the counter taking a handful of gummy bears with her. She joined two other staff members who were flicking through text messages on their phones. Shock and indignation plastered across their faces.

They had formed their own microcosm behind the counter, and it was pointless asking for anything once they were in a cluster like this. Piss one off, you piss them all off. Louie stepped away from the counter, content she'd managed to come away with her stationary because coming away with anything other than seething frustration was rare.

Ryan waited until a crowd had gathered in the university auditorium. Discreetly, he slipped into a seat at the very back. The stage was thirty metres away, there was no way she would notice him. The room catered for one thousand guests, and seats were quickly filling. It might even be a full house. The rows of chairs arced in a semicircle around the small stage at the front of the room and the floor rose steeply, allowing all attendees to see the speaker.

Louie walked onto the stage wearing a grey pinstriped suit over a white shirt. Her hair was pulled back into a pony-tail. She seemed small and fragile. His heart skipped a beat. He rubbed his palms over his thighs—he was nervous for her. Worried on her behalf. He wanted her to do well.

Louie stepped up to the podium. She picked up the wire-less presenter and flicked through the first series of slides, checking that the device worked and the sequence of images was correct.

A handful of female students in the front seats waved to Louie, and she smiled and wiggled her fingers toward them. When she slipped her hand into the pocket of her suit, Ryan recalled the stone he'd found in her pink jacket. She was nervous—of course she was nervous, there were one thou-sand people in the auditorium waiting to hear her talk.

At five minutes after twelve, Louie began by acknowledging the traditional Custodians of Country and honouring the Elders past and present of the First Nation's People. On behalf of the university, she recognised their deep and ongoing connection to their land since time immemorial and the richness of their cultural expression.

She introduced herself and explained that she was going to discuss one of the main aspects of her study, which was how sensory perceptions shaped aesthetic experiences in art, with particular reference to the effect of light and atmosphere in landscape paintings. Or why we like to look at pretty pictures of nature.

The audience tittered.

Ryan listened as Louie talked about how art shaped awareness of the natural world around us and how it enhanced emotional experiences. "When viewing art," she said, "it's possible to have a physiological experience and a psychological reaction, which can manifest in heightened feelings of love, astonishment, or even terror."

He listened as she discussed William Turner's hazy, expressive style of painting and the luminous, atmospheric quality of his work. When she showed an image of the *Fighting Temeraire Tugged to Her Last Berth to Be Broken Up*, she described the scene as a tragedy; the end of an age—wind power replaced by steam—he believed every word she said.

She talked about *Impression, Sunrise* by Monet, and she told the audience this was where it all began. She described the misty landscapes by Camille Pissarro, and how the artist rendered the ethereal elements of light, air, and atmosphere. She showed paintings of ships and vast oceans, sunsets and sunrises, rural scenes and cities, and she explained how they represented the voyage of humanity and the individual's vulnerability in the natural world.

Last, Louie explained how Van Gogh used the canvas as a sort of visual language that explored his emotional state. She said, "The work of Van Gogh moved beyond paint on a canvas, and he was able to capture some of the inexplicable qualities of human existence."

When Louie talked about Van Gogh, she took her hand out of her pocket. This small gesture caused Ryan's heart to race. In the very back row, where no one could see him, he smiled to himself.

Van Gogh was Ryan's favourite topic. Perhaps it was the quote about how drawing was the root of everything, which Louie had told him in the tutorial room, but Ryan found the images of his work, along with Louie's explanations, captivating.

At the end of the talk, Louie told the audience that in all the artwork she had shown, nature was the ultimate survivor. Then, she made a pointed reference to the consequences of climate change and the impact humans were having on the planet. "I think sometimes, without knowing it, we destroy the things we love," she stammered. Then, she thanked the audience for their time.

It was a wonderful, heartfelt presentation. Everything went smoothly; there were no glitches, the audience cooed when they were supposed to, and they laughed on cue at her subtle jokes. The images in her slide show were captivating. She stood out like a grey bird surrounded by sunsets and sunrises. But most of all, Ryan was fascinated by her ideas.

He thought she might be a hopeless romantic and a serious idealist, and they were the worst kind of idealists. Charming and earnest, often high-minded, but also frequently irrational and frustrating. Heaven help anyone who fell in love with someone like that. Still, he wanted to see her. He wanted to see her more than ever.

He also thought he might steal a few of her ideas about light—his post-grad students knew three different CAD systems. They could create 3D visualisations of buildings and interiors that looked like photographs, but they couldn't tell him which way was north. Some of them didn't know the direction the sun rose or where it set. Louie's slides made it evident.

As Ryan made his way out of the auditorium, he spied Max walking up the stairs toward the exit, and they met in the aisle, then continued their journey out of the hall together.

"Did you manage to catch all of it?" Max asked.

Ryan nodded.

"What did you think?"

"What did I think?" Ryan smiled to himself. "I think Pissarro is very underrated."

"So do I," Max agreed.

7
THE ORCHID

THE FOLLOWING MORNING, after his CrossFit class was over, Ryan began to wonder if Louie exercised. She looked athletic. He thought she might do yoga, or maybe she swam in the ocean pools. Ryan found CrossFit invigorating, and he wondered if she had ever taken a class. He could invite her to a session, show her a few upper body exercises, perhaps introduce her to the cardio equipment. When exercising, form was important, and he might give her some tips on flexing. Pointers on functional movement. Advice on properly warming up and cooling down. That sort of thing. Then, he decided he was being officious. He should leave the poor woman alone, but the classes were an excellent way to start the day.

As he sipped his morning coffee, he picked up his sketchbook and started to doodle. The sketchbook was his constant companion. Every day, he recorded images of the things he saw. If he was standing in a queue and an idea came to him, he would step aside, take out his sketchbook, and draw the concept. In the traffic, he would often pull the

Defender into a parking bay and do a rough sketch of a staircase, or an overhang—relevant to whatever project he was working on. His father was a builder, and when Ryan was young, there was an abundant supply of paper in their house. Ryan and his twin sister Kat could draw before they could talk.

After a few minutes, Ryan looked down at his drawing; he had sketched a picture of a woman who looked very much like Louie, wearing a cute two-piece suit, which may or may not have been Chanel. He pushed the sketchbook away and pressed his palms into his eyes. "I'm losing my mind."

He needed to talk to someone about how he felt, so he picked up his phone and called his sister. Kat lived in Melbourne, and if he had to choose a favourite person, just one friend to keep for the rest of his life, then it would be her. She was his soul mate, his confidant, his ally in all the things that life threw his way. No one made him laugh like she did, and she had an excellent bullshit filter.

She picked up immediately.

"Hey, Kat Girl, what are you doing?" Ryan collected a pen and slid his sketchbook toward him again. After opening a new page, he started to doodle.

"Eating a hot-cross bun—oh, my god, it's delicious. What are you doing?" Kat asked.

"I have a small problem—I pissed someone off, and I need to fix it."

"My advice, just forget about it—some people aren't worth it—move on."

"I've tried. I can't stop thinking about her. It's driving me crazy."

"Okay." Kat paused. "If it's relationship advice you need,

you might be asking the wrong person. My track record . . . well, you know my track record."

He stopped sketching. Kat hadn't dated anyone in years —she'd had terrible luck, and the memories of her past relationships squeezed his heart.

"I happen to think you're amazing." He spun his notebook around and continued to doodle on the other side of the page.

"Thank you. I presume you've apologised."

"It's more like I've tried to explain myself."

"She might not need an explanation. She might just need an apology. Also, if you're still pursuing her and she doesn't want anything to do with you, then it's probably because your ego's bruised. Where did you meet her?"

"I was doing the spontaneous thing—at your suggestion —and we kissed. Then we sort of made out in the tutorial room."

"Seriously?"

"Yes. What's the ticking noise in the background?"

"I'm toasting the other half of my bun. I was going to save it for later, but it wants to be eaten." She paused. "Oh, dear, I think it's stuck."

Again, Ryan paused his doodling. "Kat, do not put metal utensils in the toaster."

"Ouch. How did you know?"

"Intuition. Metal is an excellent conductor of electricity. Put down the knife."

"Okay, okay. I've turned the power off, and I'm armed with a wooden spoon. Back to the woman in the tutorial room."

"I think she was wearing a Chanel suit," he said dreamily. "But I don't think she knew it was a Chanel suit."

"More to the point—how did you, a thirty-eight-year-old straight man—know it was a Chanel suit?"

"*The Simpsons*—Marge finds one in the secondhand store. I remembered the episode and the buttons."

"Oh, yes. And she got it for like ninety-nine cents. Or was it ninety-nine dollars? I can't remember. What colour was it?"

"Pink. Checked. And she wore her hair up—on top of her head."

"Really? Hair on top of her head. Ryan, that's amazing," Kat chuckled.

He smiled.

"What colour were her eyes?"

Brown.

"You're not helping. Where did you get the hot-cross bun?" he asked.

"The place with the good coffee, the one on the corner that you like—*Flow*. Sadly, it's the last one. I've just sent you a picture—check it out."

Ryan put his pen down. He opened the message from Kat and found an image of a pink Chanel suit.

"That's it. But she was much prettier." Ryan grinned.

"Okay, my advice—write her a note. That's how George got Amal—and she was out of his league. Also, I forgot to tell you. I can't come to your gala thing. I have a site meeting the following morning at six a.m."

He paused. "So, you're not going to fly in after work, spend four hours listening to people talk about arts funding, then fly home, get a few hours of sleep, and go to work. Is that what you're saying?"

"You're right, I'm not. But I think you should ask Mum."

"Will she come?"

"I can't answer that. I'm not her. Why don't you ask her and find out?"

"Okay, I will—if you're sure she's up to it."

"I didn't say she was up to it—it will probably freak her out. Just don't leave her alone for too long. And don't let her catch public transport; collect her from the airport."

"I'm not twelve. You don't need to tell me that."

Ryan ended the call.

He placed his pen down and stared at his sketchbook—he had drawn a picture of Van Gogh's sunflowers. He pushed it aside and retrieved a copy of the book he'd edited on sustainable architecture from his bookcase. He placed it on the kitchen bench, opened the first page, and signed his name. Then, he pulled his laptop forward and straddled a stool.

Opening a Word document, he wrote *Louie* at the top of the page. Then, he continued to write, telling her about the conversation he'd had with the book publishers the morning she walked into his tutorial room. He explained about the changes they'd wanted to make to the profit share agreement. He told her that he regretted his actions—he should have signed the book for her, especially after what happened between them.

He left out the bit about confusing the word *cad*, with CAD. He thought that might make a funny story he could tell her in person. She might laugh or at least smile—he would like to see her smile. It was also slightly self-deprecating, which was never a bad thing.

After revising the draft until it was clear and succinct, he printed it out and put it to one side. It was good, but it was not enough. It didn't express the way he felt about her. The whole point of the apology was to ask her out. Then, he could talk to her about art and colour and Van Gough and Pissarro—because the man was underrated.

He also wanted to discuss neoclassical architecture in more detail, because he had other relevant points to make, and he was sure she'd be interested in his opinion. He wanted to see where she lived—what sort of house or apartment it was—if art graced her walls. She liked landscapes, she had told him so herself. He envisaged a large painting of the ocean in her living area. A field of flowers, blessed by dappled light—after all, light was her specialty—in her kitchen. More than anything, he wanted to talk to her about this amazing topic of light. He needed to tell her that she was right—light was everything, and on this, they both agreed. The suit that may or may not be Chanel also intrigued him. He wanted to take her jacket off, and then her skirt. Her shirt would follow, and then he would kiss every part of her body.

After opening another Word document, he took a deep breath, and typed, *Dear Louie, you have the most beautiful eyes. The way you look at me, it makes me want to take all your clothes off and* . . . He paused and rubbed his forehead. After highlighting the text, he selected delete.

He rubbed his hands together. "Okay, second attempt."

This time he typed, *Dear Louie, any chance of a date, followed by another kiss, and then you could come back to my place and we could* . . .

Again, he paused. Then, he deleted the text.

Pushing his laptop away, he stood up, walked into the kitchen, and stared at the wall. Maybe he should take a cold shower because he needed to clear his head. He spied a packet of hot-cross buns on the bench—Easter was a few weeks away. A toasted bun was a suitable distraction.

He opened the packet, cut a bun in half, and dropped it into the toaster. When it was cooked, he covered it in butter and returned to his laptop. Popping a slice of bun into his mouth, he licked the melted butter from his fingers. Kat was right—it was delicious.

"Okay, it shouldn't be this hard. I should write how I feel. Simple."

Facing another blank page, he wrote, *Dear Louie, I like you, and at some point, in the not-too-distant future, I'd like to lick your . . .*

He sat back on the stool. "Oh, my fucking god." He deleted the sentences and pushed his laptop away. He couldn't be trusted.

After a long moment, he realised there might be another way to approach this task. A way that expressed how he felt without inappropriate sexual innuendoes. A way that showed how he felt without the use of words. Drawing came from his heart.

His sketchbook was on the coffee table.

When he struggled to explain something, Ryan reached for pen and paper; drawing was the perfect medium to articulate his ideas. Clients never failed to understand what he meant if he drew the outcome. Perhaps a heartfelt drawing would be easier than a written message. He collected his sketchbook from the coffee table—there might be something inside—a note or a drawing—that would inspire him.

The pages of the book were filled with images of buildings—details of rooftops and rough sketches of façade treatments. But on every second page, was an image of a tree, a plant, blades of grass, a sketch of the harbour.

A few pages in, he found the drawing. It was the outline of an orchid—a native species. He had come across it last week while he was walking back to his Defender after his enchanting meeting with Louie at the museum. It was growing between the cracks in the pavement. An odd position for a flower, considering the parkland and the lush grass were only a few metres away. The flower was not a perfect specimen—it looked weary, like it was making a gallant struggle to stay alive in an inhospitable world, but it was a beautiful species, and he admired its persistence, so he took a few minutes to sketch it.

But his drawing of the orchid was just an outline, the suggestion of a flower. If he was going to give it to Louie, he would need to make it more tangible.

Carefully, he removed the page from his book. Then, he worked at the sketch, adding a few more petals and another flower, which gave it the illusion of boldness. He was careful not to overwork the picture—he wanted to keep the orchid's fragile quality. After a few minutes, he held up the drawing and considered it. He thought it was good, but it was not her. She was not an outline—the orchid needed colour.

From his office, he retrieved a set of well-used watercolours and several small brushes.

He painted the orchid mauve. He added leaves and grass to the foreground. He washed the background with a blend of translucent ochre and rust. The colours bled, the flower stood out, and the effect was luminous. He held up the picture again and considered it. This time, he smiled. It was colour and light. The perfect picture for her.

"Not bad." He grinned, excited about his gift.

Neatly, he signed his name in the bottom corner of the painting.

After it was dry, he turned it over and wrote, "I would really like to see you again. If you give me your number, I will call you." He wrote his phone number at the bottom. Then, placed the note and artwork inside the book. He wrapped it in yellow architectural sketch paper and tied it up with string.

The following morning, on his way to work, he stopped by the university and left the book wrapped in yellow tracing paper in her pigeonhole.

Louie decided the problem wasn't a staff shortage; there seemed to be dozens of people behind the student services counter. The problem was indifference and accountability. The first was at an all-time high, and the second at an all-time low. But it wasn't as if Louie could go somewhere else. Without a guest pass, she couldn't get into her classroom.

Marissa and her small mountain of gummy bears once again manned the services counter. As Louie approached, Marissa fixed her with a shrewd stare.

"Is it your birthday?" Marissa asked, popping a gummy bear into her mouth. "Is that why you're wearing that dress?"

Louie wore a wayfarer print dress with buttoned cuffs and a pleated skirt, which had once belonged to her nan.

"Because if it's your birthday we can order a cake," Marissa continued. "Even casuals get a cake."

"I'm sorry—my birthday?" Louie had no idea what Marissa was talking about.

Marissa took a long moment to consider Louie, then she asked, "How old are you?"

"I'm thirty-two. How old are you?"

Marissa popped another gummy bear into her mouth.

"It doesn't matter how old I am. Are you thirty-two now, or are you turning thirty-two?"

"I'm thirty-two now. Why are we even having this conversation?"

"Because of the cake—I'll need to order it this morning."

Oh, my god. "It's not my birthday."

"No need to raise your voice. If it's not your birthday, then why is there a present in your pigeonhole?"

"I have no idea what you're talking about."

Marissa held up a finger, indicating Louie should wait. After popping another gummy bear into her mouth, she slid off her stool and headed toward the lecturers' pigeonholes.

She returned a minute later with a package wrapped in yellow paper and tied with string. "There's no card," Marissa said. "We all checked." She ate two more gummy bears.

Louie took the package. "You're sure this is for me?"

Marissa rolled her eyes.

Louie tore the bottom corner off the wrapping, which revealed Ryan's name. It was his book on sustainable design. "Oh," was all she could manage.

Marissa leaned toward her.

Louie held the book to her chest. Slowly, she backed away from the counter, then she turned and scurried toward the exit. Outside, she found a bench seat at the edge of the Quadrangle. She sat down with the book in her lap, took a deep breath, and pulled at the string. It slipped off effortlessly and the yellow paper opened.

After running her hand over the cover, her fingers nervously touched Ryan's name.

Tentatively, she opened the book. Inside, there was a

note and a small painting—a purple flower in a field of golden light.

She picked up the picture and studied the flower. Tiny, almost undetectable dots covered the petals. And in the foreground, delicate grasses and leaves. The background wash was the perfect complement to the flower. The effect was stunning. His signature was at the bottom. He had painted this picture for her. A tingling sensation shot right through her.

After putting the painting to one side, she opened the note and read his apology and his explanation for not signing the book. Then, she folded it and stowed it in her bag. She picked up the painting again, turned it over, and read the message written on the back.

I would love to see you again. If you give me your number, I will call you.

As apologies go, it was an excellent one. On a scale of one to ten, she would rate it a solid nine, maybe even nine and a half. He could add excellent apologies to his list of skills, along with talented artist, good-looking, lovely green eyes, cute earlobes, and perseverance. Perhaps she had misjudged him. Going by the evidence at hand, he seemed to be a decent human, and he still had a tiny piece of her heart.

After her classes for the day were over, Louie knocked on Max Cabot's door and poked her head into his office. "Do you have a minute?"

"For you, always. Take a seat."

Louie entered. She sat down at the desk opposite Max. "What can I do for you?"

"I was wondering about someone. A casual lecturer who works here. Teaches architecture—or something like that. I think his name might be Ry—"

"Ryan McDermott. He teaches a post-grad micro-credential in architecture—ACT431—Social Design in Practice. He wrote the subject and agreed to teach it for a term—iron out any bugs."

"Social design?"

"Low-income housing—essentially housing for the homeless—that's his thing."

"Housing for homeless people is his thing?" She leaned forward, glaring at Max.

"Yes. He started a foundation."

"A foundation? Really? A foundation. What sort of foundation?"

"Stop saying the word *foundation*. It's a charity. A not-for-profit, where architectural firms donate a percentage of their profits at the end of the financial year. The proceeds fund projects for the homeless."

Nervously, Louie fiddled with a container of pens on Max's desk.

"Are you interested in donating?" Max asked.

"I would, if I could, but I'm already sponsoring Labradors, and I don't have any extra money right now. But it's a worthy cause, isn't it? It's very worthy."

"It is."

"You don't happen to know how old—"

"Thirty-eight."

"Gosh, that's getting up there." She covered her face with her hands, then spread her fingers and peeked at Max through the gaps. "Would you say he was a caring, kind sort of person?"

Max dipped his head and peered at Louie through her fingers. "Yes, I would say that."

Louie sat back in her chair and bit her lip.

"Is there anything else?" he prompted. "Would you like his timetable?"

Louie snorted. "Stop it."

"You're as subtle as a brick."

A long silence followed. Louie stared at the container of pencils, and then she looked at Max. "I don't have time. You know I don't have time."

Max nodded. He looked her in the eye. "He's a good man. He's also single. And just between you and me, he thinks Pissarro is underrated, and he talks about light all the bloody time. A combination that doesn't come along very often."

Louie nodded. "Okay, point taken." She paused. "There is something else. I was hoping I might pick up another subject or even two, next term. When that thing we're not talking about is finally over."

"I'll see what I can do. Your student feedback scores are amazing—the highest in the department."

She grinned. "Do I get something for that, like more money? Or a prize?"

"No. Now, send me an email—available days and times etcetera. Keep it official."

"Okay." She dug into her bag and retrieved a small book on Romanticism. "Can I do a swap? I'm finalising my section of the Sublime." Without waiting for an answer, she left her chair, stepped toward the bookshelf, and slipped the book back into its place.

The Sublime had its own section within Romanticism, and running her finger the length of the shelf, she scanned the titles until she found what she was looking for. She pulled out a copy and studied the picture on the front cover —a deep valley surrounded by sheer mountain ranges. In the background, the sun peeked through a dark cloud-filled sky. She traced her fingers over the shape of a bird descending into the valley.

"Can I borrow this?"

"Of course." Max glanced at the cover. "*A Philosophical Enquiry into the Sublime and the Beautiful* by Edmund Burke. You could also try *Shades of the Sublime and Beautiful* by John Kinsella."

Louie turned her attention back to the bookcase. She retrieved the second book and stowed both in her bag.

"How is the thing we aren't talking about going—how are you feeling?" he asked.

She met his gaze. "It's going very well. Do you know how close I am to finishing?"

"I do." He smiled. "Will I see you over the weekend?"

"No, I have to study." She lowered her voice. "But give Uncle Filip a big kiss from me. If his portrait makes the finals, he's going to be famous."

Until some hidden talent revealed itself, part-time teaching was a good way for Louie to earn a living. It paid well, but as a career, it was not her ideal vocation and certainly not a long-term prospect. She looked at teaching as a job for later in life. After she'd gained a few decades of industry experience, she could share her acquired knowledge and skills with the students. She didn't see it as a primary profession. She couldn't teach five or six subjects two or three times a year for the next forty years of her life. That would kill her. If that ever happened, she knew she wouldn't have a life. She could say the problem was the system—not the job. But it was both.

There were too many students, and too many assessments to mark. Plagiarism was rife, and the university was not equipped to deal with submissions created by Open AI models like chatbots.

The administration used phrases like student happiness, emotional learning, optimal challenges, forecasted growth, and proximal development. She wondered how these concepts were relevant to the time she spent in the classroom.

Student retention—keeping them in the system—was paramount, because if they left, so did their tuition fees. Louie feared that revenue eclipsed learning. Class sizes kept expanding. The subject content was constantly squeezed. The lack of funding made it impossible to update subjects or teaching aids or research or moderation or field trips or materials. Lecturer feedback scores mattered more than they should and at the end of every term they were scrutinised by the administration.

It was not just a profession; it was a life in service. Fine, if that's what you wanted, but Louie didn't. For now, however, it was a financial refuge for the next few years of her life.

8
THE ENVELOPE

'"NO HUMAN BEING IS HAPPY. Strike it rich and you are luckier than your neighbour—but never happy,'" Lila said as she folded her leg over the table on Louie's veranda, stretching her hip flexor. Then she added, "It's from *Medea*."

"Oh, that's the Greek play you have the lead in?" Louie sat on the edge of the veranda, hugging Eva. All three had just returned from a wet Sunday morning run in the park.

"Do you think that's true?" Lila asked. She changed sides, bending her opposite leg over the table.

Louie shook her head. "We must never believe that. Let's face it, neither of us have any money. But we're still happy, aren't we?"

"I guess so." Lila finished her stretch. "You do the dog, and I'll do the drinks." She headed inside.

Louie sent Eva into her kennel. After breaking food treats into pea-size pieces, Louie hid them in discreet places around the yard: on the chair rails, inside potted plants, behind the watering can, and in the woodpile. When Louie finished, she let Eva out of her kennel and commanded her to find the food. The dog loved a good hunt; she raced around the garden sniffing out the treats and devouring them.

"Better than the treasure hunt I went on," Louie told the dog. "At least you got some food."

Food is treasure, Eva agreed.

Lila returned with tall glasses of water filled with slices of lemon and a bowl of nuts. They sat down at the table together.

"Let me show you Tara's painting for the Portrait Prize," Louie said. She flicked through her phone. "She won the People's Choice in the 1990s for her portrait of our neighbour—a young chef. She painted him asleep in his chair by the fire wearing his chef's hat, and only his chef's hat. He's now a lot more famous. This year, she painted Filip." Louie showed Lila the picture on her phone.

The image showed Filip walking through a park. The background of the painting was a blur of grass and trees. Filip wore a salmon-coloured suit. His shoulders slouched and his hands were clasped behind his back. "She's completely captured his personality," Lila said. "You can see her affection for him."

"I know. He's such a lovely man. Sometimes too serious, but he would do anything to help anyone. He'd be my pick in a crisis."

"Do you think she'll win?"

"I doubt it; the judges always select paintings of celebrities, but she'll make the finals, for sure. How'd you go with the Born to Fish commercial?" Louie asked.

"Second again." Lila took out her phone and ran an internet search on Ryan McDermott. "He has a company—an architecture practice," she said. "SLD Projects, it stands for *Sustainability, Liveability, Diversity*. There's lots of stuff about social housing."

"Go to the *About Us* section," Louie prompted.

Lila scrolled through her phone. "Okay, Ryan McDermott is a multi-award-winning architect. His portfolio includes converted warehouses, heritage buildings, studio apartments, and mixed residential—I have no idea what that is. His style is described as unpretentious, elegant, functional, and liveable—you'd hope it's liveable. They're building houses for god's sake. He just won the Royal Architecture Medal for his commitment to affordable housing." She turned her phone toward Louie, showing her an image of Ryan.

"That's him," Louie confirmed.

"Cute. Throw-down factor of what? Eight?" Lila's term for a person's fuck-ability rating was their throw-down factor.

"Nine," Louie said. "Maybe nine and a half."

"Oh, my god, you're gone." Lila smiled. She continued scrolling through her phone. "What the hell? Principle architect fees are four hundred dollars an hour. That's more than I make in a day—with overtime."

Lila put her phone down. They sat in silence for a minute, sipping their drinks, and thinking about the housing market, their lack of career options, the future, hourly rates, and happiness.

Eventually, Lila said, "Do you think he'd take his shirt off and pose topless with Eva?"

Louie giggled.

"Well, he'll certainly have sex with you, which is good for your mental health, and you should be looking after your mental health."

Louie bit her fingernail. "He's like a proper grown-up man, isn't he?"

"Seems that way. Successful career. Probably has a nice house—since he's an architect. A reliable car, and a kitbag filled with life skills. Are you ready for all of that—is that what you want?"

"Life skills are admirable."

The bell on the side gate buzzed.

Louie jumped up and opened the gate for her mother. Tara carried in a box of seedlings—herbs and green-leaf vegetables. Louie took the box from her, while her mother grabbed a bag of gardening equipment—spades, gloves, fertiliser.

Louie liked to joke that her house came with a cook—Tara—and a gardener—also Tara. With no garden of her own, Tara happily pottered and weeded Louie's small court-yard when she found the time.

"Lovely to see you, darling." Tara kissed Lila on the cheek. "You're looking fit."

"I'm in a play—naked," Lila said.

"How naked? And for how long?" Tara asked.

"Very naked for most of the play."

Tara considered Lila for a moment. "You know, some-times a sheer fabric is a lot more sensual and evocative of sexuality than explicit nudity." Tara turned toward the sky. "The human body draped in a diaphanous or a gossamer textile is very suggestive, perhaps the director should consider dressing you in something translucent."

"It's *Medea*."

"God, no. You don't want diaphanous. Full nudity is the way to go. Now, pass me that box of seedlings, and I'll need some fertiliser and potting mix—good soil is the foundation for healthy plants."

Tara worked in the garden. She mulched the beds on the eastern side of the house, adding compost and blood and bone to improve the soil. She planted spinach, rocket, and lettuce seedlings and added a fine layer of wood chips to keep the young plants warm during the winter months. Externally busy, she thought about very little, enjoying the physical labour, the joy of productive work, and the respite from the rain.

Lila and Louie remained on the veranda, both internally industrious. Lila studied her lines for *Medea*, and Louie worked on her thesis. They sat at opposite ends of the outdoor table, which was covered with papers, highlighters, and well-thumbed books filled with coloured flags.

As far as Eva was concerned the more humans in the yard the better. Her favourite number was four. After that, they became a consolidated group, which could be hard to penetrate, although not impossible, but it required a concerted effort to pull one away, enticing them with a ball, a Frisbee, a stick, or a playful grin.

Eva worked her three humans in a clockwise direction. Starting with Lila, she dropped the ball at her feet exactly ten times. She then moved on to Tara and finally Louie. Targeting one individual at a time was an effective system and ensured the maximum number of throws. She would move onto the Frisbee next—she knew it was in the garden behind the lilly pilly trees.

When Tara had finished her gardening chores, she pulled off her gloves and asked, "Anyone for tea?"

Louie and Lila nodded.

Tara headed inside. She returned promptly, holding the picture of the purple flower that Ryan had painted.

"I found this on the fridge. Where did you get it? It's very sweet. Really, quite lovely." Tara turned it over and read the message on the back. "Oh, I see." She showed Lila the picture. "Have you seen this?"

"I have." Lila pointed at Louie. "The ball's in her court."

"Well, what's he like—does he have a job? I'm presuming the sender is a man. But of course, if—"

"Yes, *he* has a job," Louie said.

"That will make a nice change."

Louie crossed her arms. "Are you saying my past boyfriends were all no-hopers?"

"They were all lovely—I liked them very much—you have excellent taste in sensitive men, but they were a bit lost, weren't they?"

"Generally, aimless. I have to agree," Lila chimed.

They were just like me, Louie thought.

Tara took out her phone, opened it, and then squinted at the screen. "I don't have my glasses. Can't see a thing." She handed her phone to Lila. "Do an internet search on orchids. Native hyacinth orchids. Make sure you use the word *native*."

Lila swiped Tara's phone away. "I have a phone." She completed the search with her own phone. When she found the image, she showed Tara and Louie a purple flower, similar to the one in Ryan's painting.

"That's it. Such a beautiful flower," Tara cooed, "and very rare."

"It says here," Lila read from her screen. "*The hyacinth is a symbol of peace and beauty. And a purple flower means 'please forgive me.'*" Lila smiled at Louie. "I think we're way past that, aren't we?" She turned to Tara. "He has a throw-down factor of nine."

"And a half," Louie added.

"Inspiring," Tara said. "Have you penned a response?"

Louie shook her head.

"Don't you think you should? It's the polite thing to do," Tara said.

After Lila and Tara left, Louie walked around her house and considered the new artworks—so many pictures of flowers, fruits, and cakes. She was still unsure about the paintings. They were not delivering happiness as promised; they reminded her of domesticity and messy kitchens and women's work. She tried to think happy thoughts about the flowers, but she missed the serenity of the landscapes. She longed to stare at something vast and epic. The still-life paintings were closing in on her.

"They're not to be trusted," she told Eva. "But, god, those pears look good."

However, surrounded by so many delicious-looking cakes, she realised she hadn't made a cake in quite some time. Baking was a pleasurable task. Louie decided she would make a cake the following weekend, which was something positive, so maybe the paintings were having a subliminal affect on her. This made her suspicious. She knew the images that graced the walls of her home mattered. Quite a lot. What she looked at every day affected her outlook on the world, in fact, it became her outlook on the world. She decided the cake she would make needed to be bright—perhaps something with citrus.

She moved to her desk and ran another search on

useless PhD topics. She was overly pleased with the results, which included, *Pigeons can identify a Cézanne from a Monet.* Louie found this remarkable. Some of her students couldn't tell the difference.

Another topic was titled *Is the booty call the best of both worlds?* She thought about this for a while. The booty call lay somewhere between a one-night stand and a committed relationship. She'd been there; sex, pizza with a gluten-free base, wine, and a reality TV show.

Eventually, she said, "No. It's not the best of both worlds. It's really not. No need for a PhD."

The final topic she found was titled *Fruit bat fellatio—mating pairs copulated for longer if the female licked the male's penis.* Louie thought this was an obvious conclusion. Again, no need for a PhD.

"When it comes to painting landscapes, is light everything?" she asked. "Is it really all about the light?" She pondered the question for a long moment. Then she turned and looked out the window—rain was falling gently over the garden. "Yes, it is. It's absolutely everything. Again, no need for a PhD." She sighed. "Too late to stop now."

Searching for more distraction, she collected Ryan's sketch of the art museum from her fridge and stared at it. Ryan McDermott seemed to be a very complicated person. Someone who had lots of rules—*I'm not going to sign the book because I don't want to, and neoclassical architecture is terrible, and my opinion matters because I'm always right.*

Confident. Opinionated. Composed. He was nothing like her. She found his earnestness annoying. But he seemed nice . . . more than nice, actually. She recalled the feel of his hands on her skin, the way he'd laughed into her neck when she'd asked if she could lift his shirt. Then, the sweet kiss he had planted on her lips after he'd looked her in the eye. She imagined resting her head on his chest, holding his hand, lying next to him. Intimacy would be good; it had been a while, probably too long. But it was also fraught with anxiety—the risk of rejection was terrifying.

Briefly, she wondered how long sex with him might take. Time was not on her side, but surely, she could make one night of sex work. A booty call. A one-night stand. A movie, followed by sex. A dinner date, followed by sex. It was only a few hours out of her life. But in her heart, she knew time frames rarely reconciled with tasks. Everything always took longer than you thought it was going to. Time had a way of slipping away and hours evaporated into thin air.

She pinned the drawing back on the fridge, then opened the door, took out a bottle of wine, and poured herself a glass. Taking a large gulp, she consumed half the glass.

After grabbing a box of photos from the shelf in the sitting area, she sat down at the kitchen table with her wine. The box contained pictures of nature—mostly trees, shadows, and light—that she had taken over many years.

Louie flicked through the photos, searching for an image that reminded her of Ryan—one that would be suitable to use as a card. She thought this would add a personal touch to her response. It wouldn't compare to the painting he had made for her, but it was a more intimate gesture than a store-bought card.

It was a difficult choice, and she flicked through the photos, mulling over the possibilities.

After finishing her wine, she poured herself another. Soon, dozens of photos lay scattered over the table.

Finally, she found a series on autumn leaves, which were

silhouetted against a grey-blue sky. The leaves were ragged and weather-beaten, but the colours—rust and olive against the grey sky—were stunning.

Turning the photo over, she stared at the blank background.

"Dear Ryan. To Ryan. Hey, Ryan," she mumbled.

She wrote *Dear Ryan* at the top of the card.

Her wineglass was empty again, so she poured herself another, took a large gulp, and once again confronted the card.

She collected her pen and drew a love heart. Inside the heart, she wrote *Louie Leon loves Ryan McDermott*. She snorted. Giggling, she tossed the picture onto her unwanted pile.

She plucked another autumn-leaf photo from the box.

"Just write how you feel."

Taking a deep breath, she wrote, *Dear Ryan, I think about you constantly. I think about your lips, your hair, your eyes—I even think about your ears—which are very cute. Please never cut one off. I think about kissing you—everywhere.* She crossed out the word *everywhere* and rewrote it in capital letters—*EVERYWHERE*. Then she added three exclamation marks after the word.

She continued, *I think about your cock—which I'm sure is the size of a cannon. The way you kissed me made me want to take off all my clothes. For god's sake, just fuck me and put me out of my misery so I can get on with my stupid life.*

She put her pen down and dropped her head into her hands. "I can do this."

She took another photo out of the box—this was the last in her autumn-leaf series. She turned it over and wrote *Dear Ryan, thank you for the card and the book—both were lovely. If you would like to get coffee sometime, maybe even a drink or dinner, that would be . . .* She paused and looked up.

"That would be . . . fine, nice, great, marvellous, awesome." She paused again. "Great. That would be great. And let's hope it leads to great sex."

She finished the sentence using the word *great,* then wrote down her phone number and scrawled her name at the bottom.

Dozens of photos lay over the table, and many had slipped onto the floor. She held up an image of a ghostlike sun through the clouds. Another showed a beam of afternoon light streaming through her bedroom window. Again, she considered the picture she had chosen for Ryan and wondered if she was doing the right thing. Pursuing love. But the alternative seemed worse—the thought of not seeing him again made her uneasy. Besides, it was just a phone number. She gazed at the mess of photos scattered across the table and over the floor—all of this for just a phone number.

She finished her wine. Then she slipped the card to Ryan into an envelope and placed it in her handbag, which was sitting on the kitchen bench.

She fell into bed.

The following morning, Louie told herself a few small glasses of wine were not a lot, so why was her head pounding? Why had she had such a fitful night's sleep? Why did she feel nauseous and dehydrated? Then she opened the fridge to check the level of wine in the bottle. It was not there. It was in the recycling.

"Oh, that's why," she said to Eva. "Okay, we're only doing Frisbee this morning."

After half an hour in the park, a coffee, a Berocca, two glasses of water, two slices of gluten-free toast, a ten-minute rest on her bed, and a cool shower, Louie's brain fog began to shift.

Before she left for the university, she tidied up the photos that she hadn't used, piling them back into the box. Then she grabbed the autumn-leaf photo with her note on the back, slid it into an envelope, dropped it into her handbag, and headed out the door.

When Louie arrived at the university, she figured Ryan was not likely to check his pigeonhole—many contract lecturers didn't bother—so after her morning class, she headed toward the Quadrangle buildings, climbed the two flights of stairs, nervously walked down the long corridor, and slipped into his lecture room.

She placed the envelope in an obvious position in the middle of his desk. Then she left.

In the staff room, she began to critique draft essays from her first-year students. She couldn't read the entire essay—that would take days, and it was not her job to proofread—but she'd let the students submit an outline for feedback. As she pulled her laptop out of her bag, she noticed the envelope to Ryan tucked into the side pocket.

Confused, she lifted her head and stared across the room.

Her heart began to race, and her fingertips tingled. Was her alcohol-soaked brain seeing things? Had she slipped into a parallel universe? Perhaps this was just déjà vu?

She turned back to her handbag; the envelope was still

there. What then, was inside the envelope she'd left on Ryan's desk?

The envelope wasn't empty, it held one of her photos. Stiff and not easily bent, she had felt the weight of it in her hand. What was written on the back of the photo?

Her heart sank. She knew the chances were fifty-fifty. It could go either way. But the way the universe worked; the odds were against her.

Quickly, she plucked the envelope out of her bag. She slid the photo out, turned it over, and read her note.

Dear Ryan, thank you for the card and the book—both were lovely. If you would like to get a drink sometime or maybe dinner, that would be great.

She felt sick.

"Damn," she whispered. "I'm not that stupid. I can't be." Again, she lifted her head and stared across the room. "I am. I am that stupid."

Her heart raced. Her hands started to shake.

She checked the time—three minutes past one.

It was too late, all was lost. He would be in the lecture room, the room would be filled with students, and he would have seen the envelope and read her absurd, mortifying, soul-destroying message.

She thought she might puke into the nearby wastepaper basket.

But wait! He might not have opened it.

Maybe he was one of those lecturers who arrived late—always turning up a few minutes after the class had started, then racing into the topic for the day. In fact, she was sure he was one of those lecturers.

There might still be time—maybe all was not lost. He

might not even be in the room yet, and if he was, he might not have read the message.

Leaving her belongings where they were, she grabbed the envelope and sprinted out the door toward the Quadrangle. Six minutes later, she was flying down the long corridor and swinging into the last room on the right. Inside, two dozen students talked among themselves.

No sign of Ryan.

She rubbed her forehead. "Thank god."

A few inquisitive students turned toward her.

"I left something behind," she mumbled, dismissing their glances as she stalked to the front of the room.

His desk was empty.

She scanned the floor—nothing.

She peeked under a box of drawing equipment—no envelope.

Ryan's laptop was set up on a nearby table, next to a mouse and keyboard. She lifted all devices, checking underneath—no envelope.

Grabbing the trash, which was filled with crumpled sheets of paper, she emptied it onto the table and began rummaging through the debris—but again she found no sign of the envelope.

Placing her hands on her hips, she looked up and scanned the room. Her eyes came to rest on Ryan. He was standing in the doorway with Mike from IT, watching her.

Mike scooted past her and headed toward the audiovisual monitor. He dropped to one knee and began to unscrew the front cover from the unit.

Ryan dug his hands into his pockets and walked toward her, a smug expression on his face.

She stepped closer. "It was . . . it was the wrong one," she mumbled. "The card, it was, it was meant for my . . . my grandmother." She wrung her hands. "She's not been well, lately."

"I'm sorry to hear that," Ryan said.

"Yes, it's a death's doorstep situation." She cleared her throat. "Anyway, the one I gave you. It was a . . . a get-well card," Louie continued. "I got them confused." She dived into her bag, retrieved the correct envelope, and handed it to him. "This one is yours."

He took the envelope from her.

"If . . . if I could just have the other one back," she stammered.

"The get-well card for your grandmother?"

She nodded.

He collected a sketchbook from his laptop bag, which was resting on the windowsill—she had completely over-looked it, which was a shame because she wasn't above searching through it.

Ryan pulled out the envelope. He handed it to her, but he was a little reluctant to let it go, and she had to tug it firmly from his grip.

Holding the envelope tightly in her hand, she breathed. Then, she pointed at the monitor. "If it's a syncing issue—hold down the space bar and the command key at the same time. That usually works."

Ryan walked over to the keyboard. He held down the space bar and the command key. The monitor came to life, reflecting the image of a house from Ryan's laptop screen.

"Thank you," he said. Then he gave her an endearing look that went on for far too long. Way longer than it needed to. Way longer than the situation required.

Again, she felt sick, a weight in the pit of her stomach,

her heart racing. She glanced down at the envelope in her hand—the back flap was open.

Shit!

She couldn't recall if she'd tucked the flap in or left it out. But she was not the sort of person to leave the flap of an envelope untucked. Neatness mattered—she was a tucker. There was no doubt in her mind, she was a tucker. It was highly probable that she had tucked the flap of the envelope. Now, it was untucked, which could only mean one thing.

"I have to go." Nervously, she backed out of the room.

9

THE CATASTROPHE

AT HOME on Louie's bookshelf was a small picture of a young girl walking a dog, which Tara had painted many years ago. The girl was holding an envelope, and she was on her way to the post office. Louie knew that. She knew about the dog and the envelope, but she hadn't looked at the painting for some time, and so she had forgotten. But now as she studied the picture she recalled the detail—and the letter. It was odd when something like that happened. How the past could reveal something about the present. Louie thought that maybe it was her destiny to be a messenger, which was a shame because she wasn't very good at it.

Joyous laughter drew Louie's gaze away from the painting. She was in her sitting room, a wine bottle in her hand, and Lila and Henri were crying with laughter. She had just told them about her incident with Ryan and her misplaced note.

She turned her attention to her guests. "Then, I wrote . . . his dick was the size of a cannon."

Lila was spread out on the sofa. She held her head in her hands, laughing.

Henri was perched on the Thonet chair—his favourite place in the house. He had just taken a sip of his wine and managed to swallow half. The remainder he attempted to spit back into his glass, but the liquid dribbled down his chin. He wiped his mouth with the back of his hand.

Louie grabbed a tea towel from the kitchen and handed it to him. Then she stood beside his chair, like an attentive waiter, while he wiped himself down. He handed the tea towel back to her, and she returned it to the kitchen.

Louie waved the wine bottle in her hand toward Henri, who nodded. She filled his glass. The remainder of the wine she poured into her own glass.

It was early evening, and outside it was cold, dark, and wet. Inside the house, Louie had the fire roaring and a captive audience.

"Then . . . then I said I think about him all the time—and I even think about his . . . ears. I told him I wanted to kiss him everywhere, and for god's sake just fuck me, so I can get on with my pathetic life."

Another bout of laughter rose from her small, but enthralled audience.

"Oh, my god." Lila wiped the tears from her eyes with the palm of her hand.

"And you have no idea if he read it?" Henri asked.

"No."

"Just ask him?" Lila suggested.

"I can't." Louie shook her head. "I never want to see him again. Never. I'm so embarrassed."

Louie's phone rang—it was charging on her desk behind

Lila's seat. Lila glanced over her shoulder and scanned the screen. "No name, just a number."

"Does it end in four-eight-three-two?" Louie asked.

Lila nodded.

The phone beeped—a voice message.

"That's him," Louie said. "He's left two texts, and now this—a voice message! Unbelievable."

"Who leaves a voice message?" Henri quipped. "How old is this guy?"

"Old enough to know better."

Louie collected her phone and flicked it onto silent. She walked over to the fridge, opened the door, placed the phone inside, and firmly closed the door.

"You should at least listen to it," Lila said.

"No. My plan is to ignore him. Eventually, he'll go away. I've used this tactic before—very successfully. They give up. Sometimes, someone needs to take control—put the ball on the shelf." Louie turned to Eva, who was lying on her mat by the fire. "Isn't that right?"

A good ball should never be left on a shelf.

"He likes you, and he's keen," Henri pleaded.

"That's not my problem."

For two days, all Louie had thought about was Ryan and her note. Had he read the draft version? She had relived the moment with him in the classroom dozens of times. She had thought about the way he'd looked at her—was there pity in those green eyes? Did he think she was a hopeless idiot? Because she thought she was an idiot.

She had wasted her entire weekend obsessing about something that might not have happened. She had fritted away hours and hours of valuable study time, which was the one thing she didn't have to fritter. Ryan McDermott might have lovely green eyes, a throw-down factor of nine and a half, excellent drawing skills, and be very good at apologies, but Louie didn't have time for any of this romantic nonsense. She had a thesis to finish and a timeline with an end date that was looming. The incident with the letter confirmed what she already knew. Relationships didn't just devour time—they ate entire days.

Henri rose from his chair. "Well, I want to know what the message says." He strode over to the fridge and retrieved Louie's chilled phone. "What's your passcode?"

Louie shook her head.

"Four zeros," Lila volunteered.

Henri raised a disapproving eyebrow. "You can do better."

After typing four zeros into the phone, he opened it and read the message.

"Oh fuck!" he gasped and covered his mouth with his hand.

"What? What does it say?" Louie asked.

"It says, meet me at Kings Cross station at midnight and bring a vegan-friendly whip."

"For god's sake," Louie sighed.

Henri tossed the phone to Lila. She caught it and read the message. "Ahh." She smiled at Louie. "Do you want to know?"

"No," Louie snapped. Then she added, "Okay, I guess do." She held out her hand.

Lila placed the phone in Louie's hand. The first message said, *It was great seeing you yesterday. Thanks for the note and the tip about the projector. Are you free for dinner?*

Louie scrolled to the second message, which was sent

this morning. *Busy day yesterday? Maybe we could get dinner one night this week.*

Louie scratched her cheek. The messages were polite and well-intended. If he had read the draft version of her note, there was no indication.

She opened the voice messages, turned the volume up and selected *Play*. Ryan's voice filled the small sitting room.

"You know, someone once said something very profound about writing. They said, forgive yourself the catastrophe of the first draft. And just so you know, I also wrote a few . . . imaginative drafts about you."

Louie looked up.

Lila and Henri stared at her.

"No, this is not happening," Louie said.

Student services—they'd been so helpful lately—eagerly handing over the details of Louie's timetable and classrooms. Their enthusiasm to help Ryan caused him a moment of mild concern, considering the recent security crackdown. But they knew him, he did work in the building, so he dismissed their compliance.

Ryan figured Louie would be one of those lecturers who arrived early, so at 8:40 a.m. he parked his Defender in the university car park, and he set out toward the Arts Department, which was a ten-minute walk through a pedestrian laneway, surrounded by well-established gardens. With the changing season, the trees were losing their leaves. The gardeners were busy, and Ryan passed half a dozen men operating leaf blowers.

Louie's classroom was empty, but there were signs of

recent occupation. Dozens of small, laminated picture cards were laid out in a line across the tables.

Intrigued, he moved closer. On the front of each card was an image of a famous building. He selected a card with an image of the Eiffel Tower on the front and flipped it over —the rear side revealed the name of the structure and the date it had been built.

It was a timeline game.

The object was to put the cards in the correct chronological order.

Ryan placed a finger on a picture of the Great Pyramids. He slid the card all the way to the left-hand side of the table —he figured this had to be the earliest built structure and therefore the start of the game. Next to this, he placed Stonehenge, then the Parthenon, and then the Pantheon. He smiled, warming to the game, and continued moving through the centuries, and the art movements, placing the buildings in order.

"Crystal Palace comes before the Eiffel Tower, then the Barcelona Pavilion and then Frank Lloyd Wright—Falling Water," he mumbled, sliding the cards into place, confident his selections were correct. Then, in the mid-20th century, he stumbled.

"Does the Chrysler Building come before or after the Empire State—and do they both come after Villa Savoye?"

He stepped back and crossed his arms. "No idea."

"Would you like a hint?" Louie's voice, from behind him.

He turned. She was standing in the doorway, holding a mug. She wore dark jeans and a fitted, striped shirt. Her hair was loose, her fringe shorter. He had never seen her with her hair out, and he stared at her for a moment.

He shook his head and placed a finger on a card. "I'm

going with Villa Savoye, the Empire State, and then the Chrysler Building."

"Good try," she said.

"Damn!"

"Chrysler Building is 1930, the other two are 1931."

She left her post by the door and entered the room. Ryan leaned back on the table, watching her.

After putting her mug on the front desk, she turned to face him, nervously she folded her hands in front of her.

"Did you make this game?" He tilted his head at the line of cards on the table.

She nodded.

"It's great."

"Thank you. I also have one on chairs. Famous chairs."

"Famous chairs?"

"Yes. Like the wiggle chair and the swan chair. The bean bag—that sort of thing."

"Sounds hard. Who designed the bean bag?"

"It was a collaboration. But released by Zanotta in 1968." She looked at her hands and added, "Probably."

He suspected she was correct, and she knew she was right.

"I'm, I'm sorry," she stammered. "It was rude of me not to return your messages. I thought you might have read the first note, and obviously, you did. You did read it, and I kind of froze." She covered her face with her hands. "It was a stupid draft. I didn't mean for you to—"

"I know."

"I'm so embarrassed—"

"Don't be. I told you—I did the same." He tapped his finger in the air. "Delete button, very powerful. Typing is more efficient—and much safer."

She nodded. "Hindsight."

She sat on the edge of the desk next to him and crossed her ankles. "If you told me what you said in your first draft, it would make me feel so much better. I think that's only fair."

"Not a chance in hell. But I will say, my metaphors weren't as . . . inventive as yours. And your use of exclamation marks was excellent." He grinned.

Again, she covered her face with her hands. "Oh, god."

"Let's have dinner—Friday night."

She hung her head and turned away.

He knew what came next. He wanted her to look at him when she said it. If he caught her eyes, it might disarm her, and she might change her mind.

She continued to stare at the floor. "I'm, I'm going to opt out of this—whatever this is," she said. Tilting her head, she looked him in the eye. "It's not that I don't like you, because I do. And I love the drawings—both of them. I have them on my fridge. On the front part of the fridge, which is the . . . the door part." She nodded. "I see them every time I walk into my kitchen—about fifty times a day."

He smiled.

"It's a timing thing." She paused. "If this were to turn into something, I can't see how that would work. It wouldn't be fair on either of us."

He crossed his arms. "I understand."

"It's like there's this mountain I have to climb—a metaphorical mountain—and I'm almost at the top. If I get distracted, I might let go and plunge to a horrible death. I can't let that happen, not again. Right now, I'm so close to the top." She tilted her head back and looked up at her metaphorical mountain.

Ryan followed her gaze, staring at the ceiling. "I get it. I know how much work it takes."

She smiled at him. "Thank you."

"What for?"

"Everything—in capital letters with an exclamation mark."

Her comment hit him in the heart. She was thoughtful, clever, and funny. She had the most beautiful brown eyes he had ever seen. But he wouldn't pursue her. She was the gatekeeper of her heart and her emotions, and she had closed the gate on him—on them. If the timing wasn't right for her, then it wasn't right for them. Besides, he wanted her to succeed—nine years was a long time, and she deserved her success. Still, he wondered how one spontaneous moment, a few weeks ago in the tutorial room, had led to him feeling this sad. His chest hurt.

He peeled himself off the table. "If you change your mind, you know where to find me."

She bit her bottom lip.

A gesture that made him think she was unsure about her decision.

Six months was nothing. The time would pass quickly enough—he had a dozen projects that required his attention. Very soon, it would be winter, and after that, she would be finished. This thing between them was significant, and he knew she felt it too. A connection. A correlation of pheromones. A bridge between their personalities. But their timelines didn't align. In six months he might bump into her again. He could make that happen.

Looking at her he smiled. It wasn't over.

She pointed to the lanyard hanging around his neck,

which held his staff card. "How long have you had that?" she asked.

"A few weeks. Why?"

She crossed her arms. "Student services hates me."

"How could anyone hate you?" He took the lanyard from his neck and handed it to her. "Here, have mine."

"I can't take yours—then you won't have one. Obviously, you haven't watched the security videos. You're not supposed to give it to strangers."

"You're not a stranger. And I'm only here for one term— I'll manage. Besides, student services love me."

He slipped it around her neck. "Suits you."

10

A COCKTAIL DRESS

AFTER RYAN HAD LEFT, Louie turned around and bumped straight into the corner of her desk, bruising her thigh. Half an hour later, she tripped over a wastepaper basket and stumbled over a wayward chair. Not normally accident-prone, and generally sure-footed, she was good at navigating space. Making her way around solid objects had never been a problem—Eva had taught her that on their daily runs together. Somehow that morning, Louie lost her balance.

The planet did lean to one side—she knew this from her sun studies and her research on light. About four billion years ago, Earth was knocked off kilter by Theia, an ancient planet. Now the Earth's axial tilted 23.5 degrees, and Louie thought that felt about right, because she, too, had been knocked sideways. The effect was not only physical—she was also afflicted with a malaise of inattentiveness.

She confused the names of her favourite students— Bethany became Britney and Simon turned into Aiden. Halfway through a lecture on the Industrial Revolution, she forgot what she was talking about and started discussing a painting by Van Gogh, which depicted a steam train travelling through a sun-drenched field.

"Van Gogh was expressing how swiftly time passes," Louie told the class. "He was a risk-taker and should be commended for his emotional honesty."

When she finally realised she was on the wrong topic, she attempted to link the Industrial Revolution—the rapid growth of the railway system—with the rise of modern art. The connection had merit, but it was out of context. Several students sitting at the back of the class looked completely bewildered. She sympathised; she was also struggling to stay focused. All she could think about were Ryan's green eyes, the shape of his earlobes, and how he made her heart race.

As she drove home from the university, she couldn't shake the feeling she had made a terrible mistake. Spying a break in the traffic, she pulled the Elantra into a parking bay on the side of the street and gripped the steering wheel until her knuckles were white.

Saying no is sometimes the sensible, responsible thing to do. It showed control over her heart. It demonstrated power over her emotions. It confirmed she was a judicious human. Sex, dating, and a relationship were not going to work for her right now. Sometimes, the head overruled the heart, and this was one of those times. She was a wise and rational woman and she had made the right decision. This logic was galvanising. After starting the engine, she headed out into the traffic and continued her homeward journey. A few spots of rain appeared on the windscreen. Five minutes later, it started to pour. The closest parking space to her house was several blocks away. *Buckets,* she thought.

Her very good umbrella was not in the back seat of the car. It was still in the classroom, and she might never see it again. After plodding through the buckets of rain, she arrived at her front door soaking.

"I've had the worst day," she said to Eva. "An absolute shocker. Let's see if we can run it off."

Eva dropped her head. *This never works.*

From the onset, the pace of their run was sluggish. Louie had no stamina and her stride lacked rhythm. Her left knee felt tight and started to ache. Soon, the outing turned into a brisk wet walk, which became a meandering stroll through the park. Louie figured they couldn't get any wetter—the human body—and the kelpie coat—could only absorb so much water.

When they arrived at the duck pond, they found no ducks. Not one.

"They're out on a date," Louie told Eva. "Because that's what ducks do when it rains. They go on duck dates. They have all the time in the world. Bastards."

Louie and Eva did not have all the time in the world. They had a regular dinner booking at Tara's kitchen table— every second Wednesday at 6.30 p.m. The menu was on rotation, and this week, slow-cooked tomato and aubergine sauce with fresh pasta would be served at Tara's kitchen table. Her mother cooked for a crowd, and leftovers were expected.

Louie was starving.

It was a long, miserable walk back to the cottage.

An hour later, Eva forged her way through the front door of Tara's apartment. Louie followed. Eva searched for Tara in the kitchen, but they found no sign of her standing at the stove lovingly frying slices of aubergine or stirring a rich tomato sauce that had been simmering on the stove for hours. They checked in the living room—it was empty. Tara was not on the veranda reading a novel or consulting a vegetarian cookbook, nor was she in her art studio finishing a painting.

Eventually, they found Tara in the main bedroom lying on the bed. Her eyes were closed, and she still wore her purple suit, which she kept for special luncheon outings. She hadn't even bothered to remove her shoes. Her hair was a bird's nest. The air smelled faintly of liquor.

"Are you alive?" Louie inquired.

Tara stirred and opened her eyes—blurry and red-rimmed.

"Darling, what are you doing here?" Tara sounded drunk.

"It's Wednesday. Are you drunk?"

"I may have had some wine with *lunch*." She burped.

Louie stared at her mother. Lunch, midweek, with more than one glass of wine—a lot more. Where was the tomato sauce seasoned with fresh basil? What was going on? Who had Tara been to lunch with? Then, Louie remembered; it was the first week in April. The finalists for the Portrait Prize were announced that morning. Tara had not made the cut.

Louie considered her mother, and her heart tightened. Tara's expectations had been crushed by a group of judges who controversially selected portraits of celebrities and politicians. A little wine with lunch was to be expected. "I'm guessing you didn't make the finals?"

"It was not my year."

"It's just one prize—you're an amazing artist. The

judges must be idiots." Louie sat on the bed beside her mother.

"Yes, but it's the biggest." Tara sighed. "I was hoping . . . I really thought this might be my year—but I didn't even get through the first round." She paused and looked up at Louie. "You know, I'd be happy if I made enough money from my art to live for twelve months. Just one year. I don't think that's a lot to *ask*." She burped, again.

Louie agreed—she didn't think it was a lot to ask either.

"Did Vickie make the finals with that painting of a rabbit —the one that may or may not be a portrait?"

Tara nodded. She was turning green.

Louie helped Tara into a sitting position. She wrapped her arm around her mother's shoulders. "There's always next year."

Tara offered a resilient smile.

"Is there any food?" Louie asked.

"No. I'm introducing . . . *hic* . . . the Arts Medal *thing*. I told you."

"Told me what?"

"Intro . . . *hic* . . . ducing the Arts Medal recipient." Tara paused. "I don't feel well."

"Oh, god. Wait here."

Louie retrieved a bowl from the kitchen and handed it to Tara.

Tara hugged the bowl to her chest and puked. "God, I'm a mess."

Louie agreed; she didn't think her mother could get off the bed. "Whatever the art medal thing is, you can't do it. We'll say you're sick. I'll call Richard—he's still the head of the board?" Louie reached for her mother's phone, which was on the bedside table.

"Yes. But Richard has Covid, again. Mary and Tim are in . . . *hic* . . . Switzerland. I think they're having an affair. Actually, I know they're having an affair." Tara lay down on the bed, the bowl beside her.

Louie frowned. "Maybe you should have thought about the Art Medal *thing* before you got plastered at lunch."

Tara stared at the ceiling. "Everything is spinning." She hauled herself into a sitting position again.

"Okay, then Evin—Evin can do it. I have his number." Louie pulled her phone from her pocket.

"No." Tara shook her head. "He's the museum director—he's not on the Arts Council. It's highly political—the departments *never* mix." Tara raised her arms and made the sign of a cross. "But I have the power to . . . *hic* . . . nominate." She pointed her finger at Louie.

"No way."

"I can't see another option."

Louie rubbed her forehead. She could throw Tara under a cold shower, make a thermos of coffee, find something for her to wear—these things were usually formal so that would be an evening gown. Then drive her to the event, help her onto the podium, and watch as she catastrophically stuffed it up. She might lose her board membership, which would be a disaster because she couldn't support herself as a working artist.

Tara would do this for her. If Louie asked, Tara would do it in a heartbeat.

"Okay. Under protest I will do this for you," Louie said. "What do I have to say—for the introduction?"

"Ah." Tara held up five fingers. "Five things. Introduce yourself." She pointed to her thumb. "Then say three nice things about the winner." She pointed to her fingers. "That's it."

A long pause.

"That's only four things—is there something else?"

Tara shook her head.

Louie checked the time on her phone—6:30 p.m. She had an hour to change and get to the museum. "What's the dress code? Is it formal?"

"Black tie, but not formal." Tara fell sideways onto the bed. "But more formal than cocktail."

"What the fuck does that mean?"

Tara hauled herself up against the bed head. "Where do I start? Black tie is formal. A floor-length gown—you must never show your ankles." She glared at Louie. "Never."

"God forbid," Louie muttered.

"In winter, velvet is an excellent choice. In summer silk or satin something . . . *hic* . . . like that."

"It's autumn," Louie snapped. "What do I wear in autumn?"

"You need to . . . *hic* . . . settle down."

Louie narrowed her eyes. Her hands curled into fists. "It's six thirty; it starts in an hour."

"Actually, it starts at seven." Tara's shoulders jerked as she suppressed another hiccup. "With cocktail, it can be a wrap dress or a shorter style. These days, off-the-shoulder is also fine. But you must accessorise—makeup, hair, heels— the whole . . . *hic* . . . shebang."

"Christ." Louie massaged her temples.

"The wrap dress, with the embroidery. Mauve. Silk. Flowers. In the cupboard."

Louie knew the dress. It was part of the collection her nan had left behind.

From the wardrobe in the second bedroom, Louie retrieved the wrap dress; a full-length mauve gown embroidered with flowers and caught at the waist with a lattice belt. It was perfect.

Louie changed into the dress, which had a plunging neckline and revealed a thigh-length bare leg when she walked. It was comfortable, and the waist was adjustable. There would be food at the event—three courses—and she was starving. Free food was some consolation.

Louie considered her feet—she had no shoes to wear with the silk dress. Her mother's feet were larger than hers, and she didn't have time to go home and find a suitable pair of heels.

The black boots that she'd arrived in were her only option. There were far worse fashion faux pas than grunge meets luxe. Her boots were also comfortable, and she could run away in them after the event was over.

She stared at her shoes, which were lying on the bathroom floor. They were old, dirty, and scuffed. One of the laces was broken. Duct tape covered a hole in the toe. They were pitiful. They didn't do the dress justice. Barefoot would be a better alternative. She reasoned no one would be looking at her feet anyway, so perhaps shoes didn't matter. Then she realised she would be standing on the podium. Everyone would see her feet.

Louie checked the time again—6:45 p.m. If she didn't leave soon, she'd miss the entire event—and the food.

A lightbulb moment—she had an idea. Lila worked in hospitality. Her social network was wide and far-reaching— many of her friends also worked in the food industry. Like Lila, they relied on overtime pay rates because working in profit-share-theatre productions paid very little. After the production costs, there were no profits left to share. They made a living waiting tables at gala events that paid overtime rates.

Louie formulated a plan and sent a text to Lila.

A few minutes later, Lila responded—a suitable pair of shoes would be waiting for Louie at the museum.

"Bless her," Louie said. She headed into the bathroom. Scooping her hair back into a high ponytail, she fastened it into place. After rummaging through her mother's makeup, she applied eyeliner and painted her lips red.

She returned to the bedroom and threw a few items into a clutch. She dropped down on one knee and kissed Eva on the head. "You want to have a sleepover with Nan?"

Eva lifted her eyes to Louie. *We both know that's a rhetorical question.*

Louie roused Tara, who was still lying on the bed, her eyes closed. "Hey, wake up. Who's the winner?" Louie asked.

Tara half-opened her eyes. "Um . . . can't remember. God, don't tell them I have Covid—I used that excuse last month when I had to finish my painting."

"I'm leaving Eva with you. I'll pick her up later."

"I know this looks bad," Tara said.

Louie squeezed her mother's hand. "It's fine. It's one small thing. When I think about all the big things you've done for me, I owe you. Don't worry."

As she walked out the door, Louie ordered an Uber. On her way to the event, she would research the award winner. Pulling together five—or four—sentences about the recipient wouldn't be too difficult. She would make some notes on her phone, and then refer to the information while she was standing on the podium delivering her introduction. Hopefully, she would be wearing a reasonable pair of shoes and not her old boots. Her anxiety stone was in her clutch, and she would keep it close.

Difficult things build resilience, she told herself. "It's going to be fine. I'm going to be just fine," she whispered. But her stomach sank. Nervous anxiety pulsed through her. She had to navigate a room filled with people she didn't know, deliver a speech she hadn't yet written, and find a pair of shoes in her size.

First, things first, she opened her phone and ran a search on the award winner. In the back seat of the Uber, Louie froze. It couldn't be him.

She placed a call to the museum—just to make sure. She had been thinking about Ryan all day, and she'd thought she might have manifested the entire situation so she could see him one more time.

The museum confirmed the medal winner was Ryan McDermott. He was receiving the award for his ongoing commitment to social housing. Louie dropped her phone into her lap.

For the remainder of the trip, she stared out the window. The Uber glided slowly through the heavy peak-hour traffic and pouring rain as they headed toward the art museum. Toward Ryan McDermott.

11

THE GALA DINNER

AFTER TRAVERSING the marble steps of the National Art Museum, Ryan and his mother, Debra, entered the auditorium. Debra wore a silver pantsuit with a colourful silk stole, which Ryan had given her for her seventieth birthday last year. Ryan wore a velvet tuxedo—black jacket and matching bow tie—and the textile made him think of Louie. He couldn't get her out of his head, but the upcoming evening would be a good distraction.

The auditorium was buzzing. Guests had arrived early, despite the incessant rain. Most had come straight from work, and the waiters began serving drinks half an hour ago. Staff from Ryan's architectural practice, along with their partners, were already hoeing into the finger food like swooping seagulls. They waved to Ryan and Debra from the back of the room. The remainder of the guest list was eclectic and included past clients, close friends, and other prominent architects. Ryan recognised dozens of dignitaries, politicians, and board members from the Arts Council. In the background, a quartet began to play, and the smooth voice of the female vocalist crooned a familiar, lighthearted love song.

Debra placed her hand on Ryan's forearm. He turned and smiled at his mother. "Thank you for coming. It's good having you here."

"Thank you for asking me." She patted his arm. "I know you know this, but I'm proud of you. And your father would have been, too."

"As I recall, he wasn't very fond of architects."

"You're right, he wasn't. I've often wondered if that's why you became one, just to piss him off—posthumously."

Ryan stared at his mother.

"You've thought about that too, haven't you?" she said.

He wrapped an arm around Debra's shoulder, steering her into the room. "Now is probably not the time. We should mingle."

Debra pointed to Ryan's work colleagues. "Let's start with the fun people at the back, then we can rustle up some courage and work our way toward the boring people at the front."

Half an hour later, Ryan and Debra stood with a small group of board members and dignitaries, including the museum director Evin French and Ryan's friend from the university, Max Cabot. When Evin started talking about the internal politics of securing research funding for primary and secondary data sources, Debra placed two fingers on her temple and arched an eyebrow toward her son.

Ryan stifled a laugh. Spying a waiter with a tray of drinks, he called him over. The waiter promptly circled the group, and Ryan offered his mother a glass of champagne, then he took one for himself.

The waitstaff wore white shirts with black pants. Ryan

noticed their waiter had a shoe—a silver shoe—stuffed into the pocket of his pants. Tilting his head to one side, Ryan glanced at the man's other pocket—another shoe. The waiter had a pair of silver heels in his pockets.

The waiter, noticing Ryan's curiosity, said, "We're trapped in a fairy tale."

An out-of-work actor, Ryan thought.

Soon another waiter—this one was female—sidled up to the first waiter. "The butterfly has landed," she whispered in his ear. After plucking the shoes from his pockets, she headed for the entrance.

A woman, wearing a full-length cocktail dress was standing in the foyer. She had her back to Ryan, so he couldn't see her face, but he noticed her feet were bare. The female waiter sidled up to her and handed over the shoes. The woman in the cocktail dress slipped them on. The two of them embraced.

Ryan smiled; it was a charming scene.

"And they all lived happily ever after," the first waiter said to Ryan, then he promptly turned away and offered his tray of drinks to an adjacent group of thirsty guests.

Ryan's gaze returned to the woman in the colourful cocktail dress—a far more interesting diversion to Evin, who was still talking about university funding. Her presence was familiar. When she turned around, he realised it was Louie.

The dress had a plunging neckline and a thigh-high split in the skirt—his mouth dropped open. Had he manifested her? This woman had been on his mind for weeks, and now here she was at his event—looking like *that*.

He couldn't take his eyes off her. He watched, captivated, as she took a long slow breath to steady herself. Then, she smoothed down the front of her dress, checking that everything was in order, and holding her head high, she pulled her shoulders back and glided toward him on her borrowed silver heels. She looked like a goddess.

"Oh, my god," Ryan mumbled.

"Something wrong?" Debra asked.

Ryan continued to stare at Louie. "Do you need another drink?"

Debra considered her full glass of champagne, which she hadn't touched. "No. I don't."

When Evin spied Louie approaching, he paused mid-arts-funding conversation, and waving his hand in the air, called her over to their group. The gesture was unnecessary, she was headed straight for him.

"Louie," Evin cooed. "You look fabulous. Are you someone's plus one?"

Louie shook her head. "I'm alone."

"Lucky you. I'm free, and I'm yours forever—if you'll have me?"

Louie smiled. She took a small step in the opposite direction. Ignoring Evin's offer of eternal companionship, she circled the group of executives and board members—some of whom she knew. She exchanged pleasantries about the latest Chinese calligraphy exhibition and shared comments about the impediments of living under a constant storm cloud; there were never enough places to store wet umbrellas.

After completing a round of small talk, she could no longer avoid Ryan, so she turned to him and smiled.

Ryan smiled back. "Hello," he said.

"Hello." She held his gaze for a long moment. Then she stepped back and took in his velvet tuxedo. "You look very nice. Is that a new jacket?"

"No." He plucked a glass of champagne from a passing tray and handed it to her.

"Thank you," she said, then asked, "Is there water?" After witnessing the state of her mother, alcohol had lost its allure. She also needed to make a short introduction speech about the man standing in front of her, and she had no idea what she was going to say. Having spent her Uber trip in a state of shock, her research was incomplete and all four or five sentences remained unwritten.

Ryan replaced Louie's champagne with a glass of water. He introduced his mother, and Louie complimented her colourful stole.

"Thank you. It was a gift from my son. Lucky for me, he has excellent taste." Debra sipped her champagne.

Louie smiled.

Max Cabot had worked his way around the outside of the group of guests and sidled up to Louie. He slipped his arm through hers and pulled her aside. "Why are you here?" he asked.

"I heard there was free food. If you don't eat your dessert, and it's gluten-free can I have it?" She sipped her water.

"No. Where's your mother?"

"Tara is . . . unwell. Unfortunately, I'm her delegate. Why are you here?"

"I'm on the guest list. Ryan built my first house—we became friends."

"Which house? The new one on the north shore?"

"Yes, and the one before that, the one in the shire."

"I never knew you lived in the shire. That must have been a long time ago." Louie looked around the room, searching for Ryan as if to confirm Max was telling the truth —he had once lived in the shire.

Ryan was occupied. Evin was introducing him to a group of politicians. Identical-looking middle-aged men wearing homogenous dark suits and red and blue striped ties.

"Is Uncle Filip with you?" Again, Louie searched the room, this time looking for her uncle.

"No. He has a book launch. His second this week—it seems everyone's publishing something these days."

"Well, he is a book publisher. What's the book about?"

"I believe the title is *The Happiness of an Orange Cake.*" Max frowned. "Or maybe it was a lemon cake."

"I just had a thought." She grabbed his arm.

"About happiness or orange cakes?"

"Neither. Since you're on the guest list, and you know Ryan, you could do the introduction tonight. Trust me, Tara won't care." She peered into Max's face, blinking, pleading. "Please." She held up five fingers. "You only have to say five things." She folded down her thumb. "Or four things."

"Thank you for thinking of me." Max smiled. "I appreciate it." He patted her shoulder. "But it's not appropriate. The departments never mix. It's political." He turned and walked away.

Louie wasn't sure why it wasn't appropriate or how it was political. Max had an air of officialdom about him, and he held a title—assistant dean—and he also knew Ryan. Under the circumstances, Louie making the speech seemed far less appropriate.

Louie sighed. It had been worth a try.

Returning to her group, she realised Debra was not looking at all well. Rapid breathing and shaky hands, coupled with an anxious, fretful expression. Debra clutched her chest and swayed.

Louie grabbed her arm—she knew discussions about the value of public investment could unsettle a person. But she thought Debra might be having a panic attack. This was the second older woman (who also happened to be a mother) requiring Louie's help tonight—Debra also appeared to be overwhelmed by the world, and Louie suspected the condition might be spreading.

"Shall we get some air?" Louie suggested.

Debra nodded.

Louie guided Debra across the floor, through the rear auditorium doors to the terrace, which, due to the rain, was covered in a marquee. There were chairs, tables with imitation candles, and ropes of fairy lights scattered throughout the area. Other guests were milling, taking advantage of the fresh air and enchanting atmosphere.

At the far end of the marquee was a bench seat. They sat down.

"I think I had a panic attack," Debra said. She took several long, measured breaths, which appeared to calm her nerves.

Louie spied a waiter circling the balcony. After getting his attention, she signalled for a glass of water.

"I'm seventy-one," Debra continued. "And nothing like this has ever happened to me before. I've been a social worker for forty years—I know how to handle high-stress situations. Now I can't stand in a room with a hundred people for more than half an hour. I think the fear of having an attack triggers the attack."

Louie offered her a consoling smile.

"I'm not sure I can go back inside," Debra said.

"Stay here. We'll talk up."

Debra laughed.

"I used to get anxious," Louie said. "When it got bad, I would hold an ice cube between my fingers." After finishing the last of her water, Louie tipped her glass upside down and an ice cube landed in her palm. She handed it to Debra. "Worth a try," she said.

Debra held the ice cube between her thumb and index finger. "It's a distraction—it clears the head."

"Also works if you find yourself surrounded by idiots—not as effective as slapping someone, but a lot more humane."

"Might have to get an ice machine installed in my office." Debra smiled. She looked up and glanced back at the auditorium. "Ahh, finally, the waiter with my water."

Louie followed her gaze. Hovering at the terrace doors, holding a glass of water, was Ryan.

Under the enchanting ropes of fairy lights, he resembled a character in an old movie—confident and charismatic—the hero of his own story. Inside the auditorium, the band struck up another tune—a romantic and vaguely familiar love song.

As Ryan made his way toward them, Louie decided he might just be flawless. His velvet jacket was immaculate, and a perfectly fit—although his bow tie was slightly skewed. He looked like the archetype of an Arts Medal Award Winner. Talented and accomplished in his field, with a sense of responsibility, and a desire to help some of the most vulnerable people in society. In her mind, she married the image of him standing beside her under the marquee lit by strings of fairy lights, with the vague information she knew about him. Suddenly, she knew what she would say in her introduction.

Ryan approached and Louie stood up.

"Thank you for rescuing my mother," he said.

"Oh, of course." Louie clutched her empty glass.

"I'm surprised to see you here." He searched her face. "I don't recall seeing your name on the guest list."

You're about to be astonished, she thought.

"I'm equally surprised," Louie said. "And let me just say, I wish someone more distinguished, more accomplished, more appropriate—in fact, someone who wasn't me—was delivering the introduction tonight—but it seems . . ." She swallowed. "It seems the task has fallen to me."

"You're introducing *me*—tonight?" He looked astounded.

"Yes."

"Are you sure?"

"Yes."

A long pause. He appeared concerned.

"My mother is on the board, and she's . . . she's not well. I agreed to help her out, but I had no idea it was you." She took a breath. "Do you prefer Professor or Mister McDermott?"

"Just . . . Ryan."

"Okay." She looked him over. "How do you feel? Are you nervous?"

"I don't get nervous."

Surely, everyone gets nervous, she thought. "Are you going to mention the disparity in STEM in your speech?"

Ryan frowned.

"It's a hot topic right now, something all universities need to address." She raised an eyebrow.

"I wasn't going to . . . do you think I should?"

She smiled. "I'm kidding. It's architecture, not science."

He narrowed his eyes, but a smile hovered over his lips.

In the background, they heard the emcee calling people back to their seats.

"That's the five-minute signal," Louie said. "We should probably get back." She smiled at Debra. "It was very nice meeting you."

"Likewise," Debra said.

As Ryan watched Louie walk through the auditorium doors, he realised he'd forgotten to compliment her dress. He wanted to follow her inside and tell her how beautiful she looked. But it was not just her dress—it was her hair, her red lips, her eyes, her legs—she took his breath away. He made a mental note—the most important thing he had to do tonight, was tell her how beautiful she looked.

"I'm fine, by the way," Debra said.

"Oh, god." Ryan dragged his eyes away from Louie and turned to his mother. "I'm sorry. This was for you." He handed her the glass of water. "Are you okay?"

"Yes."

"I should never have left you."

Debra sipped her water. "What happened between you and Louie?"

"I did the wrong thing, by accident. She called me a cad —I thought she meant a software system."

Debra laughed. "Have you apologised?" She wiped a tear from the corner of her eye.

"Several times—but now, I'm not sure where we stand."

"You must hate that."

"I do."

"What does STEM mean?" Debra asked.

"Stands for fields in science, technology, engineering, and math—biased toward white males."

"Ah, and you walked right into that."

"I did, willingly."

"Come on, we should head inside. I think you're about to find out where you stand with her. And I for one, don't want to miss it. This is a lot more fun than I thought it was going to be."

Inside, after the guests were all finally seated, Louie stepped up to the podium and placed her phone on the lectern. In her left hand, she held her stone.

Her introduction began by acknowledging the traditional Custodians of Country and honouring the Elders past and present. This was a similar dedication to the one she'd made at her university presentation. After taking a deep breath, she dug into her resolve and looked at the crowd.

"Good evening. Some of you might be wondering what I'm doing up here—myself included. I'm not on the Board of Trustees. But Doctor Richard Wilson couldn't make it because he has Covid—for the third time. He's doing well—just a mild fever and some joint pain, but I think you'll all agree, thrice is not a charm."

The crowd laughed.

"Doctor Mary Bourke, the deputy director, and Doctor Timothy Mackenzie are both in Switzerland enjoying the fondu and also unable to make it tonight due to . . . conflicting travel issues."

"Doctor Tara Leon, my esteemed mother, was going to deliver the introduction this evening. Unfortunately, she had an unforeseen mishap and sprained her ankle."

The crowd wailed a chorus of concerns.

Louie dismissed the guests with a wave of her hand. "She's fine. Tucked up at home with a whisky sour. Mind you, just the one—she may have taken some wine with lunch."

Chuckles rose from the audience.

"So, the task of introducing tonight's Arts Medal winner has fallen to me." Louie tapped her phone and scanned the list of facts she'd managed to hastily compile on Ryan. "He's an extremely accomplished recipient. High school captain. He made the honour roll at university. Received a distinguished Fine Arts award and maintained a perfect attendance record." She paused. "I made the last bit up, but it's probably true." She smiled nervously.

The crowd laughed.

If she caught Ryan's eye, she might lose her nerve and freeze, so she avoided looking at him.

She continued, "It occurred to me after learning about all of Ryan's achievements that what we're celebrating is not so much an accomplishment of architectural talent, but a commitment of the heart. Because many can build, but very few people care enough to donate their time and energy to helping some of the most vulnerable people in society. Few people have the foresight to create a foundation to ensure a legacy that proposes a meaningful solution to homelessness. So, without delay, ladies and gentlemen, please welcome the recipient of this year's Arts Medal—a man who continually raises the bar with his commitment to social housing, Ryan McDermott."

Louie stepped back from the lectern.

The crowd rose to their feet and applauded.

Ryan made his way across the room and onto the podium.

Louie collected the medal from a side table—a silver star enclosed in crystal—and handed it to him.

"Thank you," he said, taking her hand.

She avoided his gaze. Her internal temperature had skyrocketed.

Her task for the evening was complete. She was about to walk away, but she realised his bow tie was still lopsided. She couldn't let him take the podium with a crooked bow tie.

She pointed. "May I?"

Without waiting for a response, she straightened his tie. "It was . . . wonky," she explained.

He caught her eye and smiled.

She froze. The effect those green eyes had on her.

Eventually, she pulled away and headed back to her seat.

Ryan stepped up to the lectern. He stacked his speech cards neatly to one side. He acknowledged the Traditional Owners of the Land and thanked the Arts Council for the award. He began his speech by saying, "Housing must always be a shelter before a commodity. It must have a social function before it has an investment purpose. Wealth inequality is nowhere more obvious than in the global and national housing markets."

He talked for the next twenty minutes about his vision for the future, discussing strategies for a social housing policy. He called it architecture for social good and said access to secure housing was not a privilege but a fundamental human right because a home is essential for survival. Without a house, people's ability to raise a family, pursue a job, and stay safe was compromised.

He concluded his speech with a dialogue on how academia should support diversity in the arts, especially architecture, which was a male-dominated field. He said the unique and diverse perspectives that LGBTQAI+ communities bring to the field, allow innovative solutions to real-world problems like homelessness.

When Ryan finished, Louie got to her feet, along with the other guests, and applauded. Ryan received a standing ovation, which Louie thought he deserved. It was a wonderful, heartfelt speech with a universal message of kindness. Ryan McDermott was a remarkable man, and Louie thought she might be falling in love with . . . his ideas. Although, his ideas didn't make her want to take all her clothes off. It was the man behind the ideas that she wanted to get naked with.

Realising she might be in trouble, she sat down, grabbed a nearby wineglass, and took a large gulp. The hot stone in her heart had flared up again. There was an indefinable thing between her and Ryan. Was it love, lust, or just like a lot? She had no idea, but she knew he felt it, too. Otherwise, he wouldn't have pursued her so ardently—the attention, the apology, the drawings. But hot stones in the heart come and go. The world was full of women and men who found each other attractive. What she didn't understand was why he was so interested in her. Why would a man like him—with a serious job and a company, accolades, and a vision for the future—pursue a woman like her? She had no proper job, no life savings—she lived week to week and her car was fifteen years old. She was also nine years into a PhD on possibly the most useless subject in the entire history of PhDs, except for fruit bat fellatio (even the woodpecker headache idea had some merit). She lived in a dilapidated, one-hundred-year-old house, and she had no vision for the future. She barely had a vision for next week.

She took another sip of wine. This thing between them was never going to work; they were at different stages of their life. You can't maintain a relationship on a hot stone, and while the thought of using him for sex was tempting—she had a vision of him licking her nipple, which made her gasp—it was also distracting. Sex was addictive, and the last thing she needed right now was an addiction. Maybe, in six months, when she was finally free, she would call him, and if he was not seeing anyone, she would ask him out, and they would have a very pleasant and civilised dinner discussing his worthy social causes, and she would try to make her dull life sound more interesting than it was. This would be followed by a weekend of sex, which she thought might leave her breathless and happy.

Or . . . she could tell him she'd made a terrible mistake. She'd known it the moment he'd walked out of her classroom. She decided it was now or never. Seize the day, or a fortuitous moment at a gala dinner. She was going to tell him that the hot stone in her heart meant something, and she'd changed her mind.

The music rose, and the female vocalist crooned the lyrics to another old-fashioned love song. Louie saw this as a sign. She had never asked anyone to dance before, but it couldn't be that hard. She would get out of her chair, walk across the room, and ask Ryan to dance. Then, she would tell him how she felt.

Ryan had returned to his table and was once again seated next to his mother.

Debra patted his arm. "Excellent speech, and I thought Louie's introduction was perfect. Heartfelt, even. Did you think it was heartfelt?"

"Honestly, I'm not the best judge."

"Well, you must like her dress because you haven't stopped looking at it."

"I like the woman inside the dress."

"Now might be a good time to ask the woman inside the dress to dance—then you can tell her how much you like her ... dress." She suppressed a laugh.

He held her gaze. "Mother."

"I'm sorry, but I don't often see you so distracted. Go ask her to dance. You'll remember how to do it when you get out there."

"Will you be okay?"

Debra took her empty water glass and tipped it upside down. An ice cube fell into her palm. "Yes, I'll be fine."

He pushed his chair back. "Wish me luck."

"Behave."

"I'd rather not." As Ryan turned, he saw Louie heading straight toward him. Perfect timing.

As Louie arrived at Ryan's table, she looked straight into his hopelessly handsome face and said, "Would ... would ..." Then no more words left her mouth and she bit her lip. Asking someone to dance was not as easy as she first thought. Gripping the rail of a nearby chair, she tried again. "Would ..." Still, the right words failed to come, so she tried a different tactic. "Do you think ..."

Ryan, sensing she was nervous, looked from her agonisingly beautiful face to her delicate hand gripping the top of the chair.

"Wood? No, it's cross-laminated timber," he replied.

Debra dropped her ice cube. She stared wide-eyed at Ryan. Then, she shifted her gaze and stared wide-eyed at Louie.

Max, sitting on the other side of Debra, watched the exchange and choked on his gluten-free bombe Alaska.

Louie frowned, confused. "I'm sorry. What?"

"You were asking about the chairs? They're made from cross-laminated timber," Ryan said.

Louie stared at her hand on the chair rail. "Cross-laminated timber?"

"Yes."

Louie pulled her hand away. "I was going to ask you to dance." She paused. "With me." She clarified.

Ryan grinned. "I'd love to dance with you."

Louie headed for the dance floor. Ryan followed. He took her hand and slipped his arm around her waist, holding her firmly, their hips almost touching.

She placed her hand on his shoulder, her stomach in knots and her heart racing. It took some effort not to think about kissing him, or resting her head on his shoulder, or staring into his green eyes. But before any of that could happen, she needed to tell him she had changed her mind. She would begin with some light-hearted banter, ease her way into the conversation and the fact that she wanted to take her clothes off and lie next to him.

Taking a deep breath, she said, "I thought your speech was wonderful. You didn't seem nervous at all, and I liked the ending, the bit about inclusion. I thought that was the perfect way—"

"You look stunning. I can't take my eyes off you."

"Oh, this dress, it belonged to my—"

"Not the dress—I mean you." He caught her eye.

Her stomach flipped. "Did . . . did I tell you I like your jacket?"

"Yes. Would you like to feel it?"

"Would I like to . . ."

"Don't you secretly love the feel of velvet—I believe it's the queen of textiles?"

"That's true. It is the queen."

Her hand found the edge of his lapel. She rubbed the fabric back and forth between her fingers. It felt supple and soft—a different sensation, depending on the way she rubbed it. The experience was soothing, and she felt calmer.

"There's nothing quite like it." She slipped her arm around his shoulder again.

Scanning the crowd, Louie noticed half the people in the room were watching them.

"People are looking at us," Louie said.

"That's because you handled my bow tie in public. And now, you've fondled my jacket." A smirk crossed his lips.

She frowned. "I think it wanted to be touched."

"I agree. It did."

Enough banter. She took a deep breath. "I wanted to tell you something."

"I'm listening."

"This morning when you came to my class, and then when you left my class . . . Well, not long after that, I realised I may have made a mistake. I would like to have dinner with you. I mean, if that's still an option. If you haven't changed your mind . . . since this morning."

"Let's go outside."

He guided her to the edge of the dance floor. Taking her hand, he led her onto the marque-covered terrace.

Outside, they sidled up to the edge of the railing, which overlooked the Botanic Gardens. Feeling his gaze on her, she turned away and considered the view over the parkland, which was bathed in the reflective light of the city. Several trees were illuminated with spotlights, their slivery branches distinct against the dark harbour in the distance.

"Do you know how much I want to kiss you again?" he asked.

She turned and looked at him. "I would like to kiss you, too. But if I do, I might not be able to stop. And this"—she ran her finger back and forth between them—"whatever this is, it's lovely. But it's happening very fast. If we could slow down, that would be helpful."

"I get it." He tucked a loose strand of hair behind her ear. "Whatever you want."

He slipped his arm around her waist, pulled her toward him and kissed her on the forehead. "Is that slow enough?"

"Oh, you're good at this, aren't you?" she said, breathless. She traced the side of his face with her fingertips. "You're also quite good-looking." She frowned.

"Is that a compliment?"

"No, I don't think it is."

He smiled. "You remember, I said I don't get nervous."

She nodded.

"Well, that's not entirely true. You make me nervous."

She took a long, slow breath and was very grateful for the dim light, hoping he couldn't see the apprehensive look on her face.

"Hey, I can do slow. I can't promise I'll be any good at it —I never do anything slow—but I'll try." He moved a little closer, his leg resting between her knees. "Let's have dinner. If you're lucky, I might kiss you again."

She swallowed. "Okay."

"Can I kiss you now?" he whispered.

"If you do, I'll have to take it off your date night tally."

Ryan stepped back and considered her. Kissing her now would be wonderful, and it might lead to many other tempting things—like her neck, her shoulders, her breasts —but he knew she was apprehensive, and he didn't want to lose her. In a strategic move, he passed the rule book to her.

"Let's do something this weekend. Why don't you call me when you're free?" he said.

12
PICK UP YOUR GAME

HENRI'S CAFÉ was in an unassuming warehouse at the edge of an industrial zone, on a disused laneway, in a quiet area on the southwestern side of the harbour. When he first started the business, it was the only place he could afford. *Build it and they will come,* he thought. Give people the best coffee in the neighbourhood and they will travel.

His coffee beans were hand-selected, and he roasted them onsite. A year later his cafe was included on the best coffee in Sydney lists. The café soon became a favourite haunt of the locals and a weekend destination for those who lived farther away. They came for the excellent coffee and the creamy Italian-style eggs made by his New Zealand chef.

The roaster and coffee machine sat on a raised platform surrounded by bar-style seating. Additional chairs and tables were available on the footpath outside the café. The place had a funky industrial vibe—mostly because Henri had no money for the fit-out—the colourful, nostalgic, secondhand furniture looked coordinated and some pieces masqueraded as custom-made. Most of it was picked up from footpaths and thrift stores.

After Louie, Lila, and Eva finished an early morning run around the bay area, they headed to Henri's café for breakfast.

"Once again, the ball is in your court," Lila said, placing the ball and Frisbee she was carrying in the centre of a table on the footpath.

At the mention of the word *ball*, Eva pricked her ears and tilted her head at Louie.

Louie caught Eva's eye. "No."

The women sat down at the table. Eva sat close to Louie's chair, unconvinced ball-play was not on the agenda.

"He made his intentions clear," Lila continued. "He apologised, drew a picture of your favourite building, painted you a purple flower, sent you the note, signed the book, and kissed your fucking forehead—I mean how cute is that. What more do you want? You either like him or you don't. Simple."

Louie dropped her head into her hands. "I hate this—he's driving me crazy. I want to curl up into a ball and hibernate."

Eva glanced from Louie to Lila. More ball-talk—this was a good sign. Every muscle in her body tensed. She was ready to pounce at the first sight of an airborne object.

Henri arrived at their table carrying a bowl of water for Eva, which he placed on the ground beside the dog.

Lila and Louie exchanged kisses and morning greetings with Henri.

"What can I get you?" Henri asked.

Lila ordered a three-quarter full cappuccino without

chocolate, explaining she was trying to cut back on her chocolate intake.

"You mean, like a latte," Henri said.

"Oh, yeah, I guess I do. But three-quarters—"

"Three-quarters full. I know," Henri said.

Louie ordered a soy cappuccino, extra hot. "Is that okay?" she asked. "When I ask for extra hot, sometimes I get a funny look."

"Extra hot is fine," Henri said. "Three-quarters full is fine. But froth on the side, no." He shook his head. "If your coffee order mentions more than three things, then that's a problem. It means you don't like coffee and you need to order something else." He gestured toward the menus on the table. "Are we eating?"

"Are the mushrooms good?" Lila asked. "I always have the eggs, but I've often wondered about the mushrooms."

"No, the mushrooms are terrible—the chef got up at five a.m. this morning and made terrible food."

"Great. I'll have the eggs." Lila handed her menu to Henri.

"Me, too, and no bread," Louie said.

Henri slid his pencil behind his ear and collected the menus. Behind him, a takeaway coffee order was called from the counter. A blonde woman with slicked-back hair, wearing dark glasses and a business suit, walked up and collected two takeaway coffee cups.

Henri turned and stalked toward the woman. "I'm so sorry, but that's not your coffee." He took the coffee cups from her. "You just ordered—one minute ago. There are fourteen people in front of you."

The woman pouted and stepped back into the line.

Henri handed the coffee cups to the people at the front

of the queue. Returning to Louie and Lila, he whispered, "She does this every day. Picks up a random order and just disappears. Customers can be so annoying." He disappeared into the café.

"I think he's out of my league," Louie continued. "He has a whole charity, foundation thing."

"I get it. You are practically a charity."

"He's like a proper grown-up man. A responsible adult. And I'm just getting started with life—I'm thirty-two, and I have nothing to show for it. I'm almost unemployable."

"That's complete crap. You have two very good jobs."

"Running tours is not a career—I make a few hundred dollars a week. I can't live on that. And I don't want to teach, at least not full-time."

"In case you haven't noticed, most of the population doesn't like their jobs. Get off that fat arse of yours and call him. And don't think about it. People go mad when they think about things too much. That's from *Medea*, and it's true."

"You think my arse is fat?" Louie asked.

"It's medium," Lila said. "But it is tight. And speaking of arses—buy yourself some decent underwear."

"What's wrong with my underwear?"

"It's old and full of holes. Pick up your game, Louie Leon."

Lila took the ball off the table and tossed it to Eva. The dog caught it on the full—she was more than ready.

"And while you're out shopping, pick yourself up some condoms." Lila glared at her friend.

. . .

That day, Louie's class on art history took a strange turn. This week's lecture covered some of the most famous moments in art, and someone—it was Carl—asked if Van Gogh had only sold one painting in his lifetime. The answer was yes, probably. At the most he sold two, Louie told the class. Then, Bethany said the Mona Lisa had her own mailbox at the Louvre because she received so many love letters, and Louie confirmed this was also true. The students started a discussion about whether Mona Lisa collected her own mail or if she had someone at the museum to do this for her, since she was famous.

This is why timelines are an important learning tool, Louie thought. She listened in amazement as the students formed opposing sides. Half of the class was adamant that someone else—like an assistant—collected the mail for Mona Lisa, and the other half was sure she collected it herself. Even when Louie reminded them it was painted by Leonardo da Vinci, it still didn't sink in.

Another student, Simon, asked if Salvador Dalí had a time machine. Then, Carl told the class that Yves Klein invented a blue colour, and he could fly.

Louie promptly told the class, "Time machines don't exist, and Yves only thought he could fly, but he couldn't fly because he was a human, and humans can't fly." She gave the class their essay topics for their next assessment.

When the class was over, and Carl was on his way out the door, he paused at her desk and with a sly grin asked, "What if Yves wasn't a human? What if he was from another planet? Then he might be able to fly."

Louie told him they would never know the truth, and she, for one, could live with that.

When Louie arrived home from work, she sat down at

her desk, opened her computer, and ran a search on her favourite retail outlets that had lingerie on sale. Scrolling through the styles—baby doll, bodysuits, corsets, suspenders, Brazilian, and vamp it up—she liked everything on offer. The colours were beautiful, the sheer fabrics and lace were gorgeous, the styles were sexy, and she thought all the models were extremely attractive. She ordered a handful of items that came in sets and a corset. Then, she did something she had never done before: she paid for express delivery.

Next, she placed an order at the online pharmacy for a box of ultra-thin condoms—surely any man would be happy with that. She patted herself on the back.

Once again, she wondered where her lost vibrator could be. For the third time, she checked the bathroom cabinets and the bedside drawers—this time she took out every item and conducted a more thorough search. Still no sign of the vibrator. She had an epiphany and checked under the bed, but it wasn't there either.

Eva placed her paw on Louie's knee. *We both need a run.*

On Friday morning, after his CrossFit class, Ryan arrived home with two takeaway coffees. He found Debra in the kitchen, scrolling through social media on her iPad.

"I don't understand how anyone has time for this," Debra said.

Ryan handed his mother a coffee. "What are you doing?"

"Uploading photos from the award thing to Facebook."

On Debra's iPad were a handful of photos from the Gala dinner. Most were of Ryan delivering his speech, but others showed Louie and Ryan together. A photo of her straightening his bow tie and a few pictures of her and Ryan dancing.

He paused, captivated by the images. God, she was beautiful.

"I could list hundreds of things that change as you get older. But that feeling never goes away," Debra said.

"And what feeling is that?" Ryan knew very well what his mother meant.

"Infatuation, love, lust—whatever you want to call it. A racing heart, sweaty palms, a knot in your stomach, the inability to speak. Then . . . the first kiss. There is nothing else like it—except maybe the second kiss . . . or the third. Shall I send you these photos?"

"Sure."

"Are you going to stare at them all day and get nothing done?"

He finished his coffee and tossed his empty cup into the trash. "Send me one photo."

Debra forwarded an image of Louie straightening Ryan's bow tie.

"I've been meaning to have a conversation with you about your father."

"Why?"

"Because you're a lot like him."

Ryan froze.

"I know you don't want to hear that, but it's the truth."

He leaned back against the kitchen bench and crossed his arms. "Okay, do your worst."

Debra smiled. "You have the same work ethic for a start, both driven, both stubborn, both people who like to get their own way and a little obsessive-compulsive at times."

Debra glanced around the neat kitchen; nothing was out of place.

Ryan looked at the floor.

"It feels like you're on the cusp of something, and I know you don't need relationship advice, but I've been around for a long time. I know you very well." She took a breath. "How do I put this? I've watched your past relationships end. I know it's not always your fault—god, that Jane woman was annoying." She raised an eyebrow.

Ryan nodded, confirming Jane was annoying.

"You don't have to be in control all the time." Debra continued. "Sometimes you can just let life happen. That's all I have to say."

"That was less painful than I thought it was going to be." Ryan paused. "And for the record, I know."

"Good." She checked the time. "Now, come on, chop chop—I need to be at the airport in an hour."

Hope was surprisingly disconcerting. Ryan was in his office reviewing shadow diagrams and solar plans for a new multilevel development when his phone rang. The sound startled him.

Two days had passed since he last saw Louie. He wasn't expecting her to call until the weekend, but every time his phone rang, it reminded him that he was expecting her to call. He felt like a kid the day before Christmas, knowing something wonderful might be just around the corner.

The call was not from Louie. It was from Kat.

"If it isn't Ryan the Lion," Kat said when he answered the call.

Ryan smiled; he knew what was coming. Kat always used his childhood nickname when she teased him.

"Kat Girl, what's up?"

"I'm looking at a picture of you at the gala dinner, on Facebook. You're with an attractive woman, but there's something else in the photo. It's a bit hard to make out, but I think it might be a . . . chair. Yes, it is a chair, but it's not a regular old wooden chair. It's made from . . ." Kat started to giggle. "It's made from cross-laminated timber." She laughed.

"Are you done?"

"I'm sorry. But you should know I'm wiping tears from my eyes. What were you thinking?"

"I don't know."

"This is the woman you kissed in the classroom, who may or may not own a Chanel suit, but she definitely called you a cad—and you thought she meant a software system?" Kat sniggered, sounding like a cartoon dog.

"Her name is Louie."

Ryan heard shuffling and rustling sounds in the background of the call. "Where are you?"

"I'm in my car—it's my new office."

"Are there Snakes Alive in your glove box?"

"Yes—emergency use only. Now, I'm calling for a reason. I need some drawings documented. We're doing renovations to an old boarding house. It's heritage listed, so we can't do much, but I thought you could work up a solution for the interiors—studios, apartments, that sort of thing—the rear faces north. I've done a spec drawing for a separate pavilion."

"Do you have an outline, a brief, a budget?"

"No, but we want something . . . *modern*."

"What does *modern* mean?"

"Use your imagination—that's what you get paid for."

"And who's paying for my *modern* imagination?"

A pause.

"Kat, who will I be billing for my *modern* imagination?"

"I owe this annoying client a favour. A big favour. Long story—anyway, I was hoping you might absorb the fees, for now. Maybe give the CAD work to a graduate to practice on."

A longer pause.

"Ryan, are you there?"

"Yep, I'm here. So, what you're saying is—I'm paying."

"It would be a favour to me."

"Kat, do you like this annoying client?"

Another long pause.

"Hey, I didn't mean anything by that—I'm just teasing you."

"I know. And for the record, no, I don't like him. Besides, I think he hates me, and you know me, I'm extremely likeable."

Ryan smiled. "Okay—but send me something to work with, even if you have to make it."

13
QUIVERING EYELIDS

Louie's new lingerie and the ultra-thin condoms arrived at the post office Friday afternoon, and she collected them on her way home from work.

Opening the condoms, she realised she had purchased a carton containing ten boxes. Each box contained thirty condoms—so she had three hundred. *It's always all or nothing,* she thought, *that's the way life works.* She was either going to have a lot of sex or absolutely none. She unpacked the boxes, stacking them in the bathroom cabinet. She would donate some to those in need.

The lingerie she opened in the bedroom, laying each piece out on the doona cover. She smiled at the sets of coloured bras and knickers—red, orange, purple—thinking they were all very beautiful.

She slipped on the black corset—it was the most evocative item of clothing she had ever owned—and walked back and forth across the bedroom. "No one can say I'm not prepared, because I am. I'm ready to have sex—with a man.

With Ryan, hopefully, it's Ryan. I am going to do this." She felt empowered and confident.

Still wearing her corset, she picked up her phone. She would call Ryan this instant and ask him out—immediacy was the key to her plan. There would be no thinking about the consequences, or letting her nerves get the better of her. And, she would call while she was wearing her new corset—it would be like manifesting their future sex life together. Corset ready and condoms stacked in the bathroom cabinet, she checked the time on her phone—6:35 p.m. She hesitated.

Six thirty-five on a Friday evening was widely considered to be a difficult time of the week. Universally, all over the world, people were busy at 6:35 p.m. on Friday evenings. It was the end of the working week; the roads would be clogged with traffic, which made life stressful. She glanced out the window—it was still raining. Extra stress.

Now was not the best time to call. She would wait for a more suitable timeslot, like tomorrow morning at ten thirty. Universally, all over the world, people were relaxed and content on Saturday mornings at ten thirty. She put the phone down and took off the corset. She would call him tomorrow.

The following morning, Louie followed her usual Saturday routine. She woke before dawn and sat at her computer studying for several hours. She made a green juice, changed into her running gear, and took Eva into the park. Her knee still hurt—a tight feeling that travelled up the back of her thigh. She picked up a coffee before returning home.

It was 9 a.m., and still too early to call Ryan, but she needed to keep busy and fill the next hour of her life. She laid out the utensils and ingredients for an orange and almond cake because that did sound like happiness. The cake was simple—only five ingredients—but she had to boil the oranges for an hour. She started the first stage of the recipe.

Tara called and once again apologised for the gala dinner disaster. Louie accepted her mother's fifth apology. The conversation soon switched to political topics from the weekend newspapers. Following that, they discussed cake recipes, recycling numbers, and the specifics of composting. Tara was adamant—onions, garlic, and citrus should not be included. Louie agreed, but she thought the conversation went on for far too long. After the call ended, Louie checked the time, it was now ten thirty.

She sat on the edge of the deck next to Eva and stared at Ryan's number in her phone. "It shouldn't be this hard," she said.

New things are scary, Eva agreed. *Food helps.*

"He's expecting me to call—he wants to see me. But my stomach is doing backflips, and look, my hands are shaking." Louie held a quivering hand in front of the dog.

Eat something, Eva suggested.

Louie had never asked anyone out before. She had never called an attractive man and organised a date. It was painstakingly difficult. Her admiration went out to anyone who had ever done this—particularly the male population. The inbuilt expectations were alarming, but she had no other option. She had to call him.

Louie dialled his number.

The phone rang. It switched to voicemail, something she wasn't expecting, and this threw her off guard. She left a stumbling, awkward message suggesting they meet for coffee or food or a drink, or maybe a walk in the park, if it wasn't raining, but it always seemed to be raining, so somewhere dry would be a better option. Yes, it might be best if they meet somewhere dry, out of the rain, she said, before hanging up.

She tossed her phone onto the veranda and draped herself over Eva. "That could have gone so much better."

Eva agreed. *Live and learn.*

A few minutes later, Louie's phone beeped. The message was from Ryan. He told her he was at work, and he would be a few more hours, but he would call her as soon as he was free.

"He's very good at this," she told Eva. "He knows what he's doing. Lucky one of us does."

Louie vowed to be more prepared when Ryan called back. She would suggest Henri's café for breakfast or brunch. She patted herself on the back—she had a plan.

The cake was calling, so she headed into the kitchen and finished her prep. The next few hours she spent working on her thesis. At 3:00 p.m., she still hadn't heard from Ryan.

After slicing herself a piece of cake, she sat down at the kitchen table with a cup of tea. She took a bite of her cake. It was excellent, better than she had hoped for. The citrus flavour was earthy and intense, but not too strong. The texture was perfectly moist. She gave Eva a taste.

Eva agreed. *Very satisfying and grain-free.*

It was so delicious she thought it might be a bad sign. A perfect cake like that, and the rest of the day was sure to go downhill. Unless, of course, a new type of domesticity was settling over her house. Louie glanced at the paintings on the walls—flowers and cakes and pears, everywhere she looked. Perhaps it was a sign—a new era of baking and home comforts was about to enter her life. It was not out of the question.

Louie had a second slice of cake—it was better than the first.

At 4:00 p.m., she decided to take Eva out for a walk in the park. She needed a distraction and Eva needed to chase something. She took her phone.

Earlier in the week, Sophie, a thirty-year-old graduate architect who worked with Ryan at SLD Projects, sat down at Ryan's desk. She dropped her head into her hands and rubbed her eyes. "I'm completely baffled," she said to him. "The client has a list of eighty-five items. I've just emailed it to you."

"That's a lot of defects on a *very small* renovation," Ryan replied.

"I know." Sophie yawed. "It's keeping me awake at night."

Ryan pulled up Sophie's email. He opened the list of defects and scanned through the items. "None of these are our problem. They're not defects. They're alterations."

"I know. He also wants to change the colour of the bathroom floor tiles. He says they feel cold. They're frigging tiles; they're supposed to feel cold." She wrung her hands.

Sophie looked exhausted. This was her first solo project and her first defects meeting. Ideally, Ryan wanted her to do this by herself. But halfway through the project, everyone realised the client was an annoying, antagonistic prick. Sophie was young and inexperienced, the client thought he could bully her into getting his own way. This pissed Ryan off. He didn't usually work for annoying, antagonistic pricks, but occasionally, one slipped through the net. It was a shame it had to be on Sophie's first project.

"Make a list of the issues that are our responsibility. I'll come to the meeting with you," Ryan said.

Sophie nodded. "It's on Saturday, at twelve." She stood up and patted Ryan on the shoulder. "Good boss."

On Saturday, Ryan's defects meeting with Sophie and the client finished at 4:00 p.m. when the client and the builder signed off on a smaller amended list of items that required fixing. Ryan had a way of saying, "That's not going to happen," and smiling at the same time until he got his own way.

Sliding into his Defender, Ryan picked up his phone and called Louie. Receiving her voice message earlier was a joy.

Louie answered. She suggested they meet for a coffee at her friend Henri's café—the place was in an industrial area, but the coffee and the food were great. She was free most mornings.

Ryan acknowledged her café request in an industrial area and trumped it by suggesting they have dinner tonight if she was free.

She was.

He was not.

He had dinner with his favourite clients—the Haigs. It had slipped his mind, and it was something he couldn't get out of. But he couldn't wait until next week to see her.

"What are you doing now?" he asked.

"I'm in the park, with my dog."

"I'm leaving work. I'll swing by."

"Now?"

"Is that okay?"

"Yes."

"Which park?"

"Near where I live."

Silence.

"Are you going to tell me where you live?"

"Sorry. It's Sydney Park. The northern side. There's a row of Norfolk pines; we'll be playing Frisbee close by."

He ended the call and cast his gaze skyward—dark grey clouds gathered overhead. It was about to pour. They were not meeting somewhere dry. He hoped she had her very good umbrella with her.

Ryan parked his car across the road from the park. After scanning the line of Norfolk pines, he spied Louie. She wore knee-length gum boots, a denim skirt, and a dark shirt. Her hair was loose. She didn't carry a raincoat and there was no sign of her very good umbrella. *Maybe she's immune to the elements,* he thought. Or maybe she didn't have a weather app on her phone. He had an excellent weather app that he could show her.

Ryan watched as Louie slipped behind a tree. She stood very still, with her hands behind her back. Cautiously, she peeked around the side and called out something, then she resumed her position. Soon, a black and tan kelpie came bounding over to her. It sat at her feet, and she gave it a treat from her pocket—she was playing hide-and-seek with her dog.

"Oh, my god, she has a working dog, a kelpie."

Ryan loved kelpies, and he knew the attributes of the breed. Boundless energy. Excitable. Devoted. Intelligent. Sweet natured.

Heavy drops of rain hit the Defender's windshield. Ryan grabbed his raincoat from the back seat and headed toward Louie and the dog.

Louie was soaked. Rain spots covered her shirt, and the soles of her boots were caked in mud. In her hand she held a slimy Frisbee, and by her side sat a wet kelpie.

Ryan grinned. "Looks like you two got caught in the rain."

"We did." Louie took a small step back. Self-consciously she tucked a strand of hair behind her ear.

Eva stepped forward and pawed Ryan's leg.

"This is Eva, she's three," Louie said. "The sweetest dog in the world."

"I've no doubt." Ryan squatted next to Eva, and with both hands, he scratched her neck and rubbed her behind the ears.

Eva leaned on his leg. *Firm hands, good technique, satisfactory duration—could have been longer. Nothing a few training sessions won't fix.*

"She's a bit wet," Louie said. "But she's dry underneath. She has a double coat, so she's rain resistant."

"Unlike you. Here, you want my raincoat?" He slipped it from his arm and handed it to her.

"No, no. You keep it. I'm already wet."

Ignoring her, he wrapped his raincoat around her shoulders.

She kept her hands fixed to her sides and shivered. Her lips were turning blue. "Thank you," she mumbled.

He held his hand out for the Frisbee, and she gave it to him. He tossed it low and long over the grass, and Eva took off after it.

"She'll go out in any weather," Louie continued, her eyes fixed on Eva. "She's oblivious to the rain. This is her favourite season—mine, too. She loves the cold. It makes her feel alive."

Above them, the sky rumbled. A few metres away, Eva dropped the Frisbee and hung her head. Her tail slipped between her legs, and she returned and cowered by Louie's side.

"She's scared." Ryan leaned down and looked Eva in the eye. Eva dipped her head. Gently, he stroked her back. "It's okay, princess."

Eve looked up. *You think I'm a princess?*

Ryan turned to Louie. "Does she ever run away?"

"No. She's a Velcro dog—they don't leave your side."

The sky rumbled again. Heavy drops of rain began to fall, and Eva cowered.

"I live over there; we could make a run for it," Louie suggested.

Ryan nodded.

Louie pulled the raincoat off her shoulders and handed it back to him. She gave Eva the signal to run, and she took off after the dog.

Ryan thought someone should stay dry, so he slipped on the raincoat. He collected the Frisbee from the ground, suspecting lost toys might be a common occurrence in Louie's life.

It was a two-minute sprint across the park for Louie and Ryan in the pouring rain. Eva did it in under a minute, still not her best time. Louie was limping by the time she arrived at the gate and punched in the key code.

After opening the gate, they fled across the yard to the shelter of the veranda.

Ryan scanned the red brickwork and the colonial details of the small house. "Caretaker's cottage?" he asked.

Louie nodded. "It's housing commission. Three years ago, the state government moved everyone out; they wanted to renovate and sell off the apartments. But there were protests, and the renovations stalled. The place was empty. My mother has connections. Here I am." She shrugged.

"Lucky you."

They pulled off their boots. Louie hung Ryan's raincoat over the back of a chair. She scanned the walls, searching for Harry, and spied him on the far wall between the kitchen and the foyer. The sight of the large spider sent an involuntary shiver through her.

As Ryan stepped inside, he perused the pictures of brightly coloured flowers and fruit on the walls. Then, he spied Harry. "That's a big one."

"Ryan, meet Harry. Harry, this is Ryan," Louie said. "Harry has outstayed his welcome—he needs to go."

Ryan rubbed his hands together. "It's like a fridge in here."

"The house faces south. It makes the winters long."

Eva followed them inside, and Louie turned to the dog. "Wet dogs are outside dogs."

Eva retreated. *It's always worth a try.*

"I'm going to rub Eva down. Can you light the fire? It's set—just around the corner." Louie pointed to the sitting area.

"Sure."

Louie headed outside. She grabbed a dry towel from a basket by the front door and rubbed the dog over, drying her off. Then she gave Eva a treat and sent her to her kennel.

In the sitting room, Ryan knelt in front of the master firebox and fed the stove logs of wood. When the flames took hold, he closed the glass door and cranked it shut. He opened the flu all the way. The air drew over the wood, and the fire raged. Ryan dusted his hands. Standing up, he gazed around the room, taking in the art, the bookcase, and the Thonet chair. It was an old house, with old furniture and a quaint and homely feel. He liked it a lot.

His gaze came full circle and rested on Louie, who was standing in the kitchen, her clothes soaked, her hair plastered to her head. She smiled at him. He thought she had no understanding of the effect she had on him.

An impatient burst of rain battered the cottage windows, and they turned toward the sound and watched as the deluge thrashed against the lilly pillies.

"I love the rain," Louie said.

"It's going to rain until August."

"I don't love it that much." She looked at him. "Would you like a drink—tea or coffee? Or water? There might be a couple of beers in the fridge."

He shook his head.

"If you're hungry, I made a cake—orange and almond— or I could make you something . . . else?"

Her nervousness was endearing. What was the appropriate etiquette when you had a man standing in your kitchen on a wet Saturday afternoon, who wanted to kiss you? A heightened sense of anticipation filled the room; they expected something from each other.

"I'm good," he said.

Without warning, she looked up at him and her eyelids quivered. A signal, quivering eyelids should be taken seriously. Stepping toward her, he took her face in his hands and kissed her. She wrapped her arms around his neck and kissed him back, her fingers trailing through his hair.

He felt the urgency in her mouth, her lips, and he pulled

her closer. Her body pressed against his; he felt the shape of her breasts through her damp shirt. His mouth slid down her throat, and he licked the drops of water running from her neck—her flowery scent caught on his tongue.

"Oh, god," she moaned, pulling at his shirt, her fingers finding his stomach.

He pushed her against the kitchen cabinet, his hands cupping her face as they continued to kiss.

Eventually, he pulled away and gazed at her. God, she was gorgeous; even soaking wet he found her mesmerising. Her hair, her eyes, her beautiful skin, the way she looked up at him—he was on fire, and the hot weight inside his chest was spreading through his body. He was burning up.

She shivered. He realised she must be cold. He pressed his hand against her cheek—her skin was icy. "You're freezing," he said.

"Am I?"

He looked into her eyes. "Yes, you are."

She nodded. "I should probably get out of these wet clothes. Maybe take a warm shower. Would you like to—"

"Yes."

"It's this way." She took his hand.

In the bathroom, he pushed her up against the wall and kissed her. She undid the buttons on his shirt and pulled it off his back. She ran her hands over his chest, feeling his skin. Then her hands moved to his belt. She pulled at the buckle of his trousers and tugged them down.

"Undressing someone is so much fun. Don't you think?" She panted.

"Absolutely." He kicked off his trousers and underwear. Then he pulled her shirt over her head and tossed it over his shoulder.

She reached behind her back and unclipped her bra. He took it from her and tossed it away. His hand gripped the zipper of her skirt.

She grabbed his wrists. "Wait."

He paused, concerned she might have changed her mind. They were not taking things slow—this was nothing like slow. This was sex in the shower on their first date. Fabulous and fantastic, and god, he wanted her, but this was not the brief. He needed a moment to get his head around her change of heart.

She looked him in the eye. "Just so you know—and it's not a complete shock—I don't shave or wax—just so you know."

He smiled. "Thanks for the heads-up."

She nodded. "It's neat."

Again, he pushed her against the wall and kissed her neck as he pulled down the zipper of her skirt. She shimmied out of it and slipped off her underwear.

"Also, I have much nicer underwear than this," she gasped.

"Yeah, me too." He ran his fingers through her fine pubic hair. "Very neat," he confirmed.

"Thank you," she mumbled.

He grabbed her wrists and pinned her to the wall, enjoying the control he had. He wanted to kiss every part of her body. He moved from her neck to her shoulders.

"Bare skin is the best, don't you think?" she panted.

"It absolutely is."

After reaching inside the shower cubical, he turned on the taps and adjusted the water temperature. He pulled her into the shower and kissed her as the warm water flowed over their bodies.

Her hands ran down his back, and she gripped his arse, pulling him closer. When his penis pressed against her, she moaned. It felt so good to be touched by her, to be desired by her.

"Contraception?" he whispered.

"Condoms. I bought some." She smiled.

"Where are they?"

"Oh, in the cabinet." She pointed. "On the right."

Dripping wet, Ryan stepped out of the shower. Opening the cabinet door, he spied the multiple boxes of condoms filling several shelves.

"Planning on a lot of sex?" He grabbed a box and tore open a packet.

"Online shopping. I ordered a box. Got a carton. We have three hundred—I mean I . . . I have three hundred."

He smiled.

Joining her in the shower again, he slipped on the condom. Once more, he adjusted the water temperature and held her against the wall. He felt like a rally driver, concentrating on multiple things at once, everything under his control.

She took a bottle of shower oil down from the caddy—the perfect lube—and rubbed it on his chest, over his arms, and across his stomach. She held his penis and her hand moved back and forth. The sweet, floral scent of the oil filled the shower cubical.

He spun her around and entered her from behind. She pushed back, and they found a rhythm.

His climax was loud. He shuddered and held her.

When he was done, he spun her around, pulled her into his arms and kissed her.

After turning off the shower, he wiped her face with a

towel and wrapped it around her. He wrapped another towel around his waist.

"Come with me." Taking her hand, he led her into the bedroom and gently pushed her onto the bed. He lay next to her, and opening her towel, he rubbed his hand up her thigh, over her hips, across her stomach.

She shivered.

"Cold?"

"No." She shook her head. "Overwhelmed." She draped an arm over her forehead. "I had no idea the day would turn out like this."

"Me either."

His fingers moved lower, trailing through her pubic hair. He found her clit and massaged her.

She moaned and bit her lower lip.

He pressed a little harder, and a shiver ran the length of her. She arched her back and tilted her pelvis toward him.

He smiled, his eyes flicking between her naked body and the rapt expression on her face.

With his free hand, he trailed his fingers around her areola, and then he licked her nipple. The sensation tipped her over the edge, and when she came, she wrapped her arm around his neck and whispered, "Kiss me."

His eyes met hers. He kissed her while she climaxed. His fingers didn't stop until she fell back onto the bed, completely done.

"God, I needed that." She sighed.

He smiled.

She snuggled into the side of his body, hooking her calf under his leg. She yawned and closed her eyes.

He traced her arm with his fingertips, a gentle rhythmic pattern, back and forth. She was content and comfortable, lying naked next to him, and this made him happy.

"I'm loving this version of slow," he said.

"I think we just had sex on our first date." She yawned, again.

"It doesn't feel like a first date." It felt like he'd known her for years.

After a few minutes, she fell asleep and pulled the bed covers over her. He couldn't sleep beside her because he had a dinner date with his clients—outside it was already dark. He would need to leave soon, but he figured he could arrive late and blame it on the rain. He had half an hour.

Quietly he slipped out of bed, the towel still tied around his waist.

On the chair in the corner of the bedroom, he spied Louie's new underwear, which was resting on a pile of tissue paper. He took a step closer, and with one finger, he picked up a purple lace bra with the tag still attached. He let it fall from his hand. She'd bought new underwear. And a carton of condoms.

Turning around, he watched her sleeping, her damp hair trailing over the pillow. He felt a deep well of affection for her.

Quietly, he retreated from the room.

In the bathroom, he dressed. Her clothes were on the floor, still wet from the rain. He hung them on the side of the shower screen.

In the kitchen, he checked the kettle for water and then switched it on. He found a cup draining on the sink and tea bags in the first cupboard he opened. While he waited for the kettle to boil, he noticed Harry the Huntsman had ventured into the kitchen and was crawling down the wall.

Taking a notebook and pen from the sitting room, he coaxed Harry onto the book, opened the door and flicked him into the garden—Harry would have to find a new haunt.

Ryan noticed the kitchen wall clock was crooked, which annoyed him, so he reached up and straightened it with a tap of his finger.

The rain was coming from the east, and water oozed under the side door in the sitting room. He used a tea towel from the stove rail to stem the flow. The door seals had perished. Under his feet, he could feel the floor sinking. He noticed the paint was peeling on the ceiling around a watermark—probably a cracked roof tile. He started to make a mental list of all the things that needed fixing: door seals, the sinking floors, the leaking ceiling in the kitchen—he stopped. There was no need to torture himself.

Still, he thought it was a fine house. It must have good ventilation because there was no sign of any mould. It was triple brick with no cavity. Once it heated up, it would stay warm, and he was heartened by the pile of firewood on the veranda. Although it was stacked on the wrong side of the house. Ideally, it should be on the eastern side, closer to the side door and the fire.

The fire was dying, so he poked the blackened logs until sparks flew. He threw on a few more logs, which restored the flames.

He poured his tea and considered the orange cake on the kitchen bench—she had offered, and it was already cut with a large piece missing. He found a plate and cut himself a thick slice. He took the Thonet cantilever armchair. Old, but beautifully made—a gorgeous piece of furniture. After pulling it closer to the fire, he sipped his mug of tea and ate his cake—which was excellent. He wondered if it was too soon to be in love . . . with all of this.

A scratching sound at the front door. It must be the dog.

When he opened the door, Eva was sitting patiently on the mat. She looked up at him with imploring eyes.

"You want to come inside?" he asked.

I live here. The dog slinked straight past him into the sitting room.

This time, Ryan took the sofa, and Eva sat at his feet, again staring at him with pleading eyes—an intense, unyielding look, which he found impossible to ignore.

He chuckled. "You want to sit up here with me?"

Eva jumped onto the sofa. She lay down, placing her paw on his thigh.

He scratched her neck. "You might be an eight out of ten dog."

Eight!

Eva was top of her class in puppy school. She could do better than an eight. She dropped her head into his lap and sighed.

"Okay, you're a nine."

Give me a week.

"I think your human might be a ten." Ryan scratched the dog under the chin. "Don't tell her I said that."

Got it.

The bookshelf on the wall beside Ryan was filled with dozens of novels, journals, and notebooks, as well as several houseplants and small paintings. He spied an open box of photographs and flicked through them. Some were blurry images—abstract photos of shadows and light—but most were pictures of landscapes. He realised the note that Louie had written him must have come from this box. He smiled, recalling the scene in the tutorial room and her terrified expression when she'd asked for the draft version of her note back. It felt like months ago.

He grabbed a notebook from the pile on the shelf and started to flick through it. Inside, he found the notes and ideas for her lecture on impressionism and light. He read a few passages, then he kept reading.

Twenty minutes later, Louie stumbled into the sitting area.

She wore a pair of boy-leg knickers, and she was pulling her arms through a checked flannel shirt. Her eyes scanned the foyer walls, searching for Harry, and when she didn't see him, her concerned gaze shifted to Ryan sitting by the fire with Eva.

"I . . . I thought you might have left," she said, fastening a button on her shirt. She pulled her hair out from under the collar and tied it back with a band.

"The opposite. I've made myself at home."

"I can see that." She gave him a smile that warmed his heart.

Louie's eyes met Eva's, and her expression shifted from delight to disapproval. "*Really?*" she said to the dog.

OMG. He offered.

Eva yawned. Slowly, she stretched and rose to her haunches. After slipping off the sofa, she walked with exaggerated slowness to a spot under the kitchen table.

"I did offer," Ryan said.

"She knows better."

Louie noticed the notebook in Ryan's hands and a similar disapproving expression to the one she just gave Eva crossed her face. "Really?"

"I was just flicking through."

She plucked the notebook from his hand and tossed it onto the bookcase. "Can I sit on your lap?"

"Sure." He took her hand and pulled her into his arms. She never had to ask. "You write very well—it's great to read."

Ignoring the compliment, she leaned her head on his shoulder.

"I had some cake—it's very good. I hope that's okay?" he said.

"Of course. I won't eat it all."

He kissed the side of her face and watched the fire.

She turned the other way and watched the rain batter the glass doors. "It's like we're at sea," she said. "Adrift."

He looked out the window. "It seems that way."

She glanced at the clock—six thirty. "You need to go?" she said, alarmed at the lateness of the hour.

"I do—a long night of substance abuse beckons."

She smiled. "You'll have fun."

"I will. What are you doing tonight?"

"I'm not leaving the boat—I need to study. And I'm only two ingredients away from an excellent pasta dish."

"Tomorrow?"

"Study—all day."

Together, they ambled toward the front door. As they entered the foyer, Louie again searched the walls for Harry.

"I put Harry outside."

"You did?" Her eyes lit up and she smiled. "Thank you."

Outside on the veranda, Ryan slipped on his raincoat. He pulled on his boots and tied the laces.

She waited inside the door, which was a step higher than the deck. When he faced her, their eyes met. He grabbed her waist, pulled her close, and kissed her again.

"I'll call you tomorrow," he said.

"Okay," she said. "But just to be clear. I'm not interested in just sex, as tempting as that may be. I've tried that, and it's never worked for me." Her fingers fumbled with the buttons on her shirt. "So, if that's what you want, then I get it, but I'm not that person." Taking a breath, she added, "So, what I'm trying to say is, if we're not on the same page, you don't need to call. I understand."

He studied her face. "I will call you."

After pulling up the hood of his raincoat, he fled into the downpour.

Louie turned and headed back inside. *Thank goodness the cake was excellent,* she thought. You never know with a new recipe; it could have gone either way.

14

PEARS AND TREATS

THE FOLLOWING DAY, Louie peered out her kitchen window. Outside, it was not a golden morning. The skies were grey, and rain continued to fall over the garden. She made herself a cup of green tea and looking into her mug, took in the earthy, floral aromas. After taking a sip she sighed; it tasted wonderful. It might just be the best cup of green tea she had ever made. She was giddy with happiness.

He would call—she knew he would call.

Passing through the foyer on her way to the bedroom, she paused and smiled at the artwork; flowers were the most beautiful living things on the planet. They were the perfect subject matter. It was no wonder artists painted them over and over. How could anyone resist the splendour of a bouquet? Ranunculus belonged in fairy tales. Daisies stood for happiness and joy. A bunch of roses said *I adore you*, but a single stem said *You have my heart*. Humans would be miserable without flowers. They brought colour to life. Colour and love.

The floral artworks on her walls were no longer passive,

frozen moments in time. They evoked smells, tastes, and activity: a morning baking cakes, an afternoon working the garden, flower arranging at the kitchen sink, and preparing pots of tea for guests.

Louie could feel the roundness of the apples and smell the sweet scent of the pears in the pictures. Turning to Eva, she said, "I think we should pick up some pears today."

Pears and treats.

Louie slipped into her running clothes. She grabbed Eva's lead and before heading out the door for the park, she collected her phone. It was still early, but she thought Ryan might call. He might be thinking about her because she was thinking of him. The way he touched her, the way he kissed her. The feel of his body against hers—she recalled all of it. When she remembered her orgasm, an involuntary tremor ran straight through her, and it took her a long moment to recover.

The park that morning was quietly colourful. Steeped in water, the trees were tranquil and the tall grasses were picturesque. In rare moments, when the sun managed to appear, it filtered softly through the branches and left atmospheric bursts of detail everywhere she looked.

"'*There is nothing more beautiful than nature early in the morning,*'" Louie said to Eva. "Van Gogh said that, and today, it's true."

It's three degrees, overcast, and raining. Are you sure you're not a kelpie?

After her run, Louie spent the day working on her thesis. In the afternoon, she cleaned and tidied her house. She set the fire and swept her front deck—activities of distraction. Ryan hadn't called.

At 4:00 p.m., she took Eva on a long walk. They stopped

at a café and shared a cappuccino—more distraction. On their way home, they called into the market and bought pears and apples and a few items Louie thought might never get eaten, but she couldn't resist because they looked so delicious—half a purple cabbage because she liked the colour, and a bunch of crisp asparagus that she had no idea what she would do with—again, more distraction.

After they arrived home, Louie sat at her desk. She opened her computer and stared at her thesis document. She moved a few sections around to see if the placement was better. It wasn't. She moved them back. She worked on her introduction for a few more hours, achieving nothing, unable to concentrate.

It was 7:00 p.m. No calls, messages, or emails. She snapped her laptop shut.

"This is why love sucks. I can't believe I'm still doing this. Waiting for the phone to ring. I'm thirty-two, and I'm still waiting for a man to call me. It's stupid. Completely stupid."

She poured herself a glass of wine, headed outside, and sat on the veranda to watch another storm pass over. A sombre melancholy mood swelled in her chest.

It was just one call; how hard could it be?

Yesterday, she was happy. This morning, she was elated, but now, she was close to despair. Love was dangerous territory. Boundless desire coupled with rejection and heartache. Still, people continued to dive right in. She thought humans might be idiots.

Soon, it became the longest day in the world.

She began to wonder why he hadn't called. He was keen, she was sure of it. Persistent and eager from the moment they met. But sex changed everything, it always did. Maybe she was too willing. Had that put him off? Had she said something stupid or embarrassing? Was it her all-or-nothing ultimatum? Yes, that was a mistake. It was too soon to be having a conversation about a relationship. Their liaison in the park wasn't even a proper date. It was a hookup. She'd ruined their future with her needy demands. She was an idiot, just like the rest of humanity. She took no comfort from the fact that she wasn't alone in her stupidity.

Her phone beeped.

She jumped. "Oh, god, I can't do this. It's too distracting."

Her phone beeped again.

Again, she jumped.

She glanced at the screen—there were two messages from Ryan.

The first was a photo—a blue and grey blurry image—she thought it might be a photo of rain falling over the ocean.

The second message said, "I've been at sea, adrift on a boat all day, and all I can think about is you."

She smiled and wrote back. "Were you kidnapped by pirates?"

"Something like that," he replied.

Ryan knew there were two stones in Louie's life. The small one she kept in her pocket, and a much larger stone—the weight of her study—which she carried in her heart. She had lugged this stone around for over a decade—a degree, a master's, and a PhD. He imagined it got heavier and heavier with every passing year. He could see the timeline—the past, the present, and the future. He knew what she had to do to finish. That was her priority. He could have easily spent Sunday with her, but she'd said she was studying, so he left her alone. He'd called her late in the day because he didn't want to distract her. She had said slow, and he put the brakes on.

Dinner on Saturday night with his favourite clients, Rebecca and David Haig, was followed by an invitation to spend Sunday on their boat—a luxury super yacht. Rebecca wanted to show Ryan the bathroom vanities, which had been designed in Italy. They had a holiday house on the north coast, and she wanted Ryan to use a similar design—if he could get his hands on the same marble. (He couldn't, but he had another idea.) The Haigs had generously offered Ryan the weekend use of their yacht next month. It slept eighteen and had a crew of eight. Ryan would ask the project architects and the graduates who'd worked on the Haigs' house, along with their partners, to come on the boat. If he was seeing Louie, he would also ask her to spend the weekend with him. God, he hoped something came of this.

Early Monday morning, he called her on his way to work.

She answered, and he could tell from the pitch of her voice she was happy to hear from him. His heart quickened. He told her about his weekend—the Haigs and their super yacht. He kept the future boating adventure to himself.

She told him she was lying on the damp grass with Eva, under a tree in the park. She thought it was a willow tree and asked, "Are willow trees native?"

He had no idea, but he made a mental note to look it up as soon as he got to work.

He asked about Eva. Louie told him she had chased the ducks—but it wasn't her fault; duck chasing was in her

DNA. She also thought the ducks enjoyed the chase. An elevated heart rate was not a bad way to start the day.

Ryan suggested a midweek dinner—any day was fine with him; he could move things around. But she was busy. She had commitments—she mentioned a study schedule that couldn't be compromised. A certain number of research and writing hours had to be completed every day, or she would fall behind. He understood. The conversation went back and forth. They decided on dinner Friday night—he would book the restaurant. He asked about her food preferences.

"Gluten-free, dairy-free, and vegetarian," she said.

"What food groups does that leave?" he asked with genuine concern.

"Honestly, I do eat cheese but not milk, and I quite like chicken schnitzel, and I love lasagne—with gluten-free pasta. If you've already bought the meat, then I'll eat it."

"I'm not following," he said. "Explain it to me again."

"I avoid meat and milk, but gluten is out. Wheat makes me depressed."

"How dare it."

She laughed.

Two minutes after Ryan ended the call, he received a message. It was from Louie. She had sent him a photo of a canopy of leaves—an insipid blue sky through dark green foliage. It was her view from where she lay underneath the tree in the park. He didn't think it was a willow tree. It took all his focus not to turn the Defender around and go find her in the park. He wanted to lie with her on the damp grass under the unidentifiable tree.

He didn't know how he would make it to Friday night. Five days felt like five weeks.

. . .

On Tuesday night, at around nine, Ryan parked his Defender on the street outside Louie's house.

Inside the house, Eva raised her head. She pricked her ears and growled.

Louie's hands paused over her computer.

The buzzer on the side gate rang.

Eva knew it was the man with the firm hands and good petting technique. The one who let her sit on the sofa. She dropped her head back onto her mat and sighed.

When Louie realised it was Ryan, and not a zombie attack or some axe-wielding murderer, she opened the gate and waited by the front door as he crossed the yard.

"Hello," she said, holding onto the edge of the door, feeling light-headed at the sight of him. "What are you doing here?"

"I was working late," he said. "I got in my car . . . and this is where I ended up." He looked bewildered, mentally unaware of how he got there.

"Oh, you have one of those cars that goes wherever it wants. Impressive." She raised an eyebrow. Then she let go of the door, grabbed the front of his shirt, pulled him close, and kissed him.

"When I kiss you, it makes me want to take all my clothes off." She sighed.

"That's the response I was hoping for."

His hands went to her waist, and he picked her up. She wrapped her legs around him, and he carried her into the bedroom. Belts and buckles were quickly undone. Sweaters and T-shirts were cast aside. Trousers were dropped, and underwear was hauled down and flicked away. In less than a minute, they were both naked.

Holding her wrists, he pinned her to the bed. *He likes to be in control,* she thought. And she liked being under his control.

Ryan kissed her mouth, her neck, and her shoulders.

He let go of her wrists, and his mouth dropped to her stomach. Farther down, she felt his tongue in her pubic hair. He licked her inner thighs. His mouth was between her legs, his tongue inside her. She moaned and writhed, and he held her down.

"Can you come at the same time as me?" she asked.

He looked up at her. "Tell me when you're close."

A few minutes later, she told him she was close.

He crawled onto her body, leaving a trail of kisses over her skin. He was about to guide his penis inside her when she yelled, "Condom!"

"Fuck!"

Lost in the moment, they almost forgot.

He kissed her quickly on the mouth. "Don't move." He headed out of the room, toward the bathroom.

When he returned, he paused in the doorway, taking in the shape of her naked body, her smoky eyes, and the way her dark hair fell over her bare shoulders.

"I haven't moved," she said, pretending to be a statue.

He laughed. "You are—" He paused, unable to find the words to describe how beautiful she looked.

She sat up boldly—like a statue—and stared back at him. "What? What am I?"

"Beautiful."

She bit her lip.

In his hand, he held a box of condoms. Taking one out,

he tossed the box onto the bedside table. He opened the packet and rolled the condom over his penis. She watched him, breathless, her teeth still nibbling her lower lip.

He couldn't wait any longer and neither could she. Hovering over her, he guided his penis inside her.

She dropped her head back. "Oh, god, you make me feel so good. I'm going to come . . . any . . . moment . . . now."

"Okay, give me a minute."

A minute was too long. She was past the point of no return. Arching her back, she held his shoulders and pushed her pelvis toward him.

The sight of her climaxing was the catalyst for him. A minute later, he shuddered. Closing his eyes, he said, "Oh, my fucking god!" He collapsed on top of her.

Hot and covered in sweat, pressed against one another, arms spread, legs tangled, they lay together. Neither moved.

Eventually, Ryan raised himself above her and kissed her forehead. He lay beside her side. His fingers traced patterns on her body: over her thigh, her bottom, her stomach, and around her breasts.

"You're very fit," he said. "Fit and furry. I'm going to call you Louie the Lynx."

She giggled. "Why am I a lynx?"

"From what I know so far—you're a runner. You have neat fur." He raised an eyebrow. "You're also solitary. You have amazing eyes, and you're very, very beautiful."

"The things you say." She smiled. "Solitary. What makes you think I'm solitary?"

His eyes flicked from her face to the trail his hand was leaving over her body. "You're a bit of an island. You have two jobs, you're finishing a PhD, you have a dog—a working dog—and you live alone."

"Are you saying there's no room left on my dance card?"

"You have a dance card?"

"We all have a dance card."

He paused. "That's true.

"Can you stay over?" she asked.

"Sure."

She yawned. "Which side of the bed—I can sleep on any side."

"Um, closer to the door. I need water. You want some?"

"No thanks." She yawned again. "Sex always makes me sleepy. Also, I get up at four-thirty."

"Every day!"

"Yes." Hugging a pillow, she closed her eyes.

He pulled the covers over her and climbed out of bed.

"Wait," she called. "My computer is open—can you control-save my documents?"

"Sure."

Early the following morning, Ryan, still half asleep, reached over to the other side of the bed, searching for Louie. His hand found her pubic hair, and he guided his fingers around the area, finding the sensation extremely erotic. Hoping to arouse her, he moved his hand in a wider arc, but he couldn't locate her inner thigh.

Suddenly, he froze. Something was not right. His desire faded. He pulled his hand back and opened his eyes. Two golden kelpie eyes stared back at him.

I'm as surprised as you are. But good technique.

Ryan chuckled and scratched Eva under the chin. He looked around the room. Louie was nowhere to be seen. He wondered if she'd gotten up to pee.

The semi-darkness outside the window confirmed it was still early, but the sunrise was not far away. After five minutes, she hadn't returned, so he got out of bed and went searching. The light on the rangehood in the kitchen signalled she was nearby. He found her around the corner in the sitting room, working in the blue glow of her computer screen.

Wearing warm socks, thick pants, and a fleecy jumper, she resembled a cuddly koala perched on her chair.

Hearing him enter the room, she turned and said, "Hey, how did you sleep?"

He frowned. "No, no, no. This is not what happens."

"It's not?"

He leaned over her shoulder and selected control-save on the keyboard of her laptop. Sliding one arm under her thighs, and the other under her arms, he picked up his koala and carried her back to bed.

Louie laughed into his shoulder. "I have to work," she protested.

"Ten minutes—come back to bed and listen to the rain with me."

She tilted her head, listening to the pitter-patter on the tin roof. After three years in the cottage, the sound had become background noise.

In bed, Ryan pulled her clothes off. She put up a fight over her warm socks, but he insisted, and she lost. They lay under the covers with Eva on the doona beside them. Ryan wrapped his arms around Louie, and they listened to the sound of the rain on the roof. After ten minutes, neither wanted to leave.

Ryan thought he might already be in love.

Louie knew she was going to fall hard.

Eva thought two humans in bed were not better than one human, and if this continued, she had legitimate concerns about the size of the bed.

The dog started her morning cleaning routine, licking her paws and her tail.

Ryan scratched Eva's head. "Hey, stop licking." He turned to Louie. "Not you—you can lick all you like."

"Okay, I will." She crawled under the bed covers.

An hour later, emerging from the shower, a towel wrapped around his waist, Ryan held up an orange egg-shaped vibrator. "You left this in the shower," he said.

Eva looked up from her mat. *Good man.*

"I've been looking for that," Louie said. She held out her hand for the device.

He withdrew his hand and held the vibrator close to his chest. "It was in the shower caddy, top shelf. Waterproof?"

Louie nodded.

"Bluetooth?"

She nodded again.

He grinned. "Hand me your phone."

"Oh, my god." She slapped her forehead. But she handed over her phone.

Ryan changed into the same clothes he'd worn the previous day—dark chino trousers and a retro shirt with a geometric print. While Louie showered and dressed for work, he wandered around her house and studied her belongings. The flower paintings on the wall caught his attention. From the shelves, he selected books and examined their titles. He picked up trinkets and vases and held them for a moment before replacing them. When he came across a calendar hanging above her desk, which was covered in different coloured stars, he paused and tried to work out the meaning of the colours.

"Inside, I'm still eight years old," she said from the kitchen. "Coffee?"

"Sure."

A small machine rested on the bench and she opened a bag of ground beans. He was tempted to tell her to keep the beans in the fridge, but he held his tongue. She laid out the cups and filled the head of the portafilter with coffee powder. The scent wafted through the small room.

He turned his attention back to the star chart. "What do the colours mean?"

"Silver stars are my thesis targets. Red is birthdays. Blue are my tours at the museum. Green are holidays, and gold is the stuff I look forward to."

He turned toward her. "There are no green stars."

"Not in my immediate future, no."

He pointed to a gold star. "What's happening next Wednesday?"

"Dinner at Tara's—my mother. She's an excellent cook." She paused. "I'm a visual person." It sounded like an apology.

He met her gaze. "Secretly, everyone wants a star calendar."

She handed him a mug, and they sat together on the sofa. He sipped his coffee; it was excellent. He placed his mug on the bookcase. "Is your knee still sore?" he asked.

"Yes."

"Which one?"

"My left."

Taking her left leg, he draped it over his thighs and massaged the area around her knee. "Does this hurt—"

"Ouch. Shit. Yes."

"It's not your knee. It's your hamstring." He considered her. "Do you ever stretch?"

She shook her head. "Not much."

"You might need to do less running and more stretching."

Eva's ears pricked at the sound of the word *run*. Her yellow eyes were fixed on Ryan. *Less running, the man can't be serious.*

"You don't understand. I need to run. I go insane if I don't, and so does Eva. We're kindred running spirits," Louie explained.

Eva wagged her tail. Running was life.

Ryan collected his phone and scrolled through several web pages. "I'm sending you a stretch program, with videos."

Louie pouted. "I don't have time."

"If you do less running, you'll have more time."

Her phone, which was on the kitchen counter, beeped— she had received the program. She looked at the floor.

An awkward silence followed.

He stiffened. He shouldn't be telling her how to exercise or sending her programs that she hadn't asked for. His intentions were good, he didn't want her to tear a hamstring, but he must have come across as an officious idiot.

He rubbed his forehead. "Sorry."

She looked at him. "You're right, and you're not the first person to tell me to stretch."

A short silence followed.

"I meant well," he said.

"I know."

Before Ryan left for work, he carried his mug to the dishwasher and opened the drawer. Spying the overloaded state of the shelves, he balked. Stepping back, he placed his hands on his hips and shook his head.

Louie squeezed past him and slipped her mug into the top shelf, covering a smaller glass.

"No, no, no. That's not happening," he said.

She looked at him. "It's not?"

"No." He plucked her mug from the shelf and handed it back to her. After unpacking the dishwasher, he restacked every item.

Ryan arrived at work two hours late, wearing the same clothes he had worn the previous day. The staff presumed he had an early site meeting, and no one recalled what he wore yesterday.

But Freddie knew Ryan's schedule.

Freddie also smelled something unfamiliar as Ryan walked through the front door of the office. Gardenias, or perhaps it was roses. He took a long, slow look at Ryan, letting the facts sink in: the floral scent, two hours late for work, and the man was wearing the same clothes he'd worn yesterday. Ryan had been on a sleepover.

Freddie plonked himself on the corner of Ryan's desk. "How was your night?" he asked.

"Good." Ryan smiled. His phone was on his desk. It was downloading an app. Freddie gazed at the screen. It was a *What plant is that?* app.

Freddie crossed his arms. "What time did you get out of here last night?"

"Around nine."

Freddie offered a thin-lipped smile. "I like that shirt on you."

"It's my lucky shirt."

"Is she a gardener? Because you smell nice—rose petals, I think?"

Ryan leaned back in his chair. He laced his fingers together and placed his hands behind his head. "No, she's not a gardener."

"It's the woman from the gala dinner, the one who introduced you. She touched your bow tie, and that's not the only thing she wanted to touch."

"Her name is Louie." Ryan couldn't wipe the smile from his face.

Later that day, Ryan caught Sophie staring at him from across the office. She squinted as she looked him over.

"Soph, is there something wrong?" Ryan asked.

Very slowly, Sophie shook her head. "Maybe. Maybe there is. But I can't put my finger on what it is. Wait! Did you get a haircut? It looks good."

15

CHAIRS MATTER

FRIDAY NIGHT DINNER at a restaurant that catered for gluten-free, sometimes vegetarians, who avoided dairy quickly turned into takeaway Italian food at Louie's house, followed by sex on the sofa in the sitting room.

For about three minutes, Louie wore her new lingerie, and for the remainder of the evening, she wore Ryan's bomber jacket and not much else. All evening, Ryan kept the fire stoked; he didn't want her to get cold, and he certainly didn't want her to put on any more clothes.

Ryan sat on the sofa. Louie reclined with her knees up and her head on his lap. They began a conversation about politics, both believed that the current political system was unfair and disadvantaged minorities. They thought that indigenous participation in the Constitution was important. They agreed that the minimum wage was too low and unemployment benefits didn't come close to covering the cost of living. Climate change was also a concern. Neither of them knew where the future of Open AI was headed. They quickly discovered they were politically and socially aligned. What else was there to talk about?

"Where do you stand on religion?" Louie asked.

"It's not my thing," Ryan said.

It wasn't Louie's thing either. "Okay, where do you stand on chairs?" she asked.

"I like them," Ryan confirmed. "I like them a lot."

Louie's favourite chair was the Transat Chair by Eileen Grey. The design was based on deck chairs from steamships. It was only her favourite because it was designed by a woman. Louie said it was a monumental feat to be a female designer in the 1920s, and for that alone, the chair should be recognised.

Ryan agreed. His favourite chair was the Eames lounge chair, and Louie complimented him on his good taste.

Ryan asked what Louie's grandparents did, specifically her grandmother, who seemed to be lingering in Louie's life —in the furniture, the artwork, and half of Louie's wardrobe.

"My dad left when I was young," she said. "I know nothing about his side of the family. They're a Great Mystery!"

He gazed down at her. "Well, that's a bit sad."

"Tara said my father was a professional alcoholic, so I didn't miss anything. I also have an excellent uncle for a male role model. My maternal grandparents were originally sheep farmers."

Ryan chuckled. "And you have a working dog. How apt."

"I know. Maybe it's in my blood. They were proper country people and quite successful—a nation built on the sheep's backs, that sort of thing. But after Gramps died, Nan sold the farm and moved to the city. She spent all her money on European clothes, Australian art, and fun times with attractive, insecure, continental men. What about yours?"

"Paternal. He was a wood-turner. She was a housewife —do we still say housewife?"

"Maybe homemaker—it sounds better than being married to a house."

"That depends on the house. On my mother's side, he was a mechanic, and she was a homemaker."

Eva lifted her head off her mat. *Herding dogs, originally from the Scottish smooth collie. Direct bloodline back to the King's kelpie—I really am a princess.*

"What about your father? What does he do?" Louie asked.

"He died, twentysomething years ago. He was a builder."

"Oh, that's why you became an architect?"

Ryan gazed into the fire. "Maybe. He walked out when I was fourteen. We didn't see a lot of him after that. Like you, I didn't miss much."

"Well, that's another sad story. Did you become the man of the house after he left?"

"I did."

"I bet you were good at it."

Ryan smiled. "I was."

She held his gaze for a long moment.

"I also have a sister, a twin sister," Ryan said.

"Really? What's she like?"

"She's great. Lives in Melbourne."

"Married? Kids?"

Ryan shook his head. He brushed the hair from Louie's eyes and gave her a melancholy look. "Tell me about your PhD," he asked. Without waiting for an answer, he fired off a round of questions. Had she covered other art movements besides Impressionism? Had she considered photography? Had she finished her first draft and how many words had she written? Was the conclusion done, and if so, what was the outcome?

When his enquiries finished, a short silence followed.

"In my opinion, light is everything," she said. "And that's all I'm going to say about the matter. I can't talk about it anymore. I'm sorry, I just can't. It exhausts me." Louie yawned. It was after midnight. In five hours, she would be sitting at her desk, working on her thesis.

After sending her to bed, Ryan cleaned the kitchen and restacked the dishwasher.

The following morning, Ryan once again found himself sharing the bed with Eva. There was no sign of Louie. As he made his way to the bathroom, he passed the vanity mirror and caught a glimpse of his reflection. He had to do a double take—his forehead was covered in gold stars. Louie must have put them there while he slept. He smiled, recalling her words—something to look forward to.

He found her at her desk.

Leaning over her shoulder, he kissed her neck. With his thumb and forefinger, he selected control-save on the keyboard. After picking her up, he threw her over his shoulder and carried her back to bed.

Knowing Louie had to study, Ryan disappeared for the remainder of the day, but he returned at 6:00 p.m. with wine, his laptop, and a small and unusual bunch of flowers.

"For me?" Louie grinned, taking the bouquet from him. It was an assortment of blossoms: dahlias, magnolias, gardenias, roses, and many more, but only one of each stem.

Her heart flipped. "Did you . . . get one of every flower?"

"I did."

"Because you couldn't decide?"

"No. It's what I wanted. I had a lot to compete with." He gestured toward the artwork covering the wall in the foyer.

"Did you personally select every flower?"

"I did."

"Did that drive the florist crazy?"

"It did."

Louie laughed. A pattern was forming.

A blue porcelain pitcher was the perfect vase. After placing the vase filled with flowers on the kitchen table, she stepped back and studied the arrangement. Her kitchen was turning into a work of art.

Ryan gave Eva a few minutes of focused eye gazing and intense patting, paying particular attention to the fur around her neck, which caused her ears to droop and her eyes to roll back in her head. When he called her princess, she rolled over, and he scratched her tummy. Then, he checked the fire, throwing on another log and adjusting the airflow. After that, he opened the wine, found glasses in the overhead cupboard, and poured them both a glass.

Louie was making pasta for dinner. A large pot of water simmered on the stove. "You have two choices," she said, "prawns or food prep." She waved her hand at the pile of ingredients gathered on the benchtop—garlic, chillies, lemons, rocket.

"Prawns." He grabbed a tea towel, threw it over his shoulder, and approached the colander of green prawns resting in the sink.

"I have tickets to a play next week." Louie plucked a flyer off the fridge and showed him. "*Medea*. A modern interpretation—you want to come with me? It's part of the fringe festival, so don't expect much in the way of ambience or comfort—bench seats, and it's three hours long."

"Bring your own cushion?"

She stuck the flyer back on the fridge. "Sure. If you're worried about your bony arse." She grabbed the tea towel from his shoulder and flicked it toward his arse—a direct hit.

He rinsed his hands. "You fool."

Swiping the tea towel from her, he spun it into a tight knot and flicked it several times in her direction. It cracked like a whip. Rodeo-style, he corralled her into the corner of the kitchen. With no means of escape, she was trapped. He slipped his arms around her waist, pulling her close. With both hands, he grabbed her bottom.

"You won't be needing a cushion, will you? I think there's ample padding here."

She narrowed her eyes. "How dare you. I'm a runner— my arse is my power source."

"Later tonight, I will tap this ample power source."

"I'm afraid it's going to need lots of compliments before that can happen."

"You want me to romance your arse?"

"I'm just saying . . ."

On the stove, the water boiled over. Louie shrieked. She wiggled out of his grip and turned the stove off.

With the prawns peeled and the food prep completed, Ryan set the table.

Louie served. They sat in the small kitchen opposite each other.

"Is *Medea* the play about the son who sleeps with his mother?" Ryan asked, stabbing a pink prawn with his fork.

He swirled it through the pasta sauce and took a bite. "This is good, by the way."

"I think that's *Oedipus*. *Medea*'s the story about a woman who kills her children to spite her husband, because he had an affair—he wants to marry someone else, someone younger and more beautiful." Louie shoved a fork full of pasta into her mouth.

"Sounds cheery."

"Honestly, you don't have to come. But my best friend has the lead. I have to support her."

"Okay, count me in."

"I must warn you—there will be full nudity—both male and female."

"Really? *Medea* . . . naked?"

"I know, what has the world come to?"

"I think I can handle it." He held his pasta-filled fork in the air. "I've had this dish dozens of times, it's one of my favourites—why is this so good?"

Slowly, Louie glanced at the artwork on the walls. Something was going on. This dish of pasta and prawns was part of her repertoire—but Ryan was right—tonight's dinner was way above par—one of the best she'd made in years.

"It might be the homegrown rocket," she said. "And you did an excellent job on the prawns."

He grinned. "I did, didn't I? Do I get a medal for that?"

"No. But you get to stack the dishwasher—I know how much you like doing it." She sipped her wine. "Was it your job to clean the kitchen and stack the dishwasher when you were a teenager?"

"It was."

. . .

At work on Monday morning, Ryan opened an email from Kat. It contained information about the old building she was working on, and a file of attachments was included. He sent the file to the printer, and Freddie delivered the pages to his desk. There were sketch ideas for the top-floor penthouse apartments. The levels below showed gallery spaces and retail outlets. Other drawings included information for a separate pavilion, which was to be a restaurant. Ryan liked this idea but thought it should be shifted to the northwest. Taking a closer look at the legend and the pencil notations on the side of the plans, he realised it was Kat's handwriting.

He picked up the phone and called his sister. When she answered, he said, "Kat Girl, you put on your architecture hat, didn't you?"

"I did," Kat said. "I also got out my HB pencils. I know how busy you are, so I sketched up a few ideas."

"These are great." Ryan flipped through the drawings. "Although, I'm not sure about the pitch of the roof on the main pavilion."

"I'm happy with it."

"And the central walkway, could—"

"It works."

Ryan grinned. "Okay, what do you want me to do?"

"Finalise the interior details. Then forward them to the client. And stop smiling. It's not what you think. As I said, I owe him a favour, and I don't like owing people anything."

"Well, now he's going to owe you."

"I can live with that."

· · ·

Early Thursday evening, after her shift at the art museum had finished, Louie sat outside on the marble steps of the building and sent Ryan a text with the address of Lila's play, which started in an hour. A few minutes later, he replied, saying no theatre existed at that address—it was an apartment block with shops on the ground floor. Louie explained it was a fringe production—the arts had no funding—so the venue would be makeshift—but there would be an improvised theatre somewhere in the building. She would meet him outside.

She sent Lila a good luck text, saying: *break a leg, break everything, you're going to be amazing,* and she couldn't wait to see her talented friend play the part of *Medea*—naked.

The fringe theatre was on Elizabeth Street in Surry Hills, not far from Central Station. The street, a main thoroughfare, was noisy and congested. As Louie ambled up the pavement, she spied Ryan waiting for her outside an African restaurant. He stood under an awning that said, "*Two for One.*"

He wore a patterned shirt with his dark bomber jacket and jeans. He looked very gown up. She wouldn't have called any of her past boyfriends men. But Ryan was a man. He had a profession and knew what he was doing with his life. He fitted comfortably into the world. A world that she often found complex and confusing.

Standing under the *Two for One* awning, he looked rock-solid—real and tangible—like a hard copy when she so often felt like a virtual imitation. She often felt incomplete, and she wondered if confidence came with age. She made a mental note to ask Tara that question. *Was there a point in life when you felt comfortable with who you were?*

As she approached Ryan, his eyes lit up. They stood

together for a moment, and neither spoke. They hadn't seen each other for three days.

"I've missed you," he said.

"I've missed you, too." She slid her arms inside his jacket and rested her head on his chest.

He wrapped his arms around her. "I'd like to take you home and have you all to myself."

"Then we'd miss the cultural event of the year. Come on." She grabbed his hand. They headed for a nearby door, which had a *Medea* flyer pinned to the front. This was the venue.

Ryan opened the door, and they entered a dark hallway. He flicked the light switch—nothing. There were high windows above the entrance, and dim, murky light filtered into the room. At the far end was the lift, and Louie headed down the corridor. Ryan followed. Pinned to the lift door was another *Medea* flyer indicating the performance was on level six. Louie pushed the button, and the doors opened. Half a dozen eclectic-looking people spilled into the hallway.

A middle-aged man wearing a business suit turned to Ryan. "Don't do it—the smell is utterly unbearable. Take the stairs." He pointed to the stairwell.

"Yeah, something funky happened in there last night." A woman wearing a leopard print dress said.

Ryan opened the stairwell door. Reaching inside, he flicked the light switch—it worked. They would be taking the stairs to level six.

Louie peeled the *Medea* flyer off the lift and stuck it onto the stairwell door.

As they scaled the stairs, Ryan looked around the interior of the building. "None of these doors are fire rated, the stairwell's not isolated, and the treads are way too high."

Deciding this didn't require a verbal response, Louie nodded, indicating she had taken the information on board.

When they reached level six, Ryan leaned over the thin, metal railing and peered into the bowels of the building below. "This railing is nine hundred high," he said.

"I'm sorry about that." Louie leaned over the railing, following Ryan's gaze into the void below.

"In fact, I think it's less. It might be eight fifty." He grabbed the top rail, dipped his head, and cast his gaze over the height of the balustrade. "Honestly, this is one of the worst buildings I've ever seen. Nothing is built to code. If a fire broke out, we'd probably die."

"It's raining outside. Hopefully, that will reduce any chance of spontaneous combustion," Louie consoled.

"It must get hotter than hell in summer." He turned to Louie. "Can you imagine?"

She could.

They entered a large open area, where dozens of people were gathered, all drinking red wine from small plastic cups. At one end was a makeshift box office that also offered an assortment of snacks and drinks. At the opposite end was an installation piece: a metal clothesline with hundreds of textile marsupials pinned to the wires. Louie spied Henri perusing the installation. She waved him over, and he scurried toward them, holding a half-filled plastic wineglass.

After their introductions were over, Ryan said, "I'd love a drink."

"They're not licenced," Henri advised. "They don't sell wine. But if you make a donation, they give you it for free."

Ryan headed for the ticket counter. He returned with two plastic cups filled to the brim with red wine.

"That must have been some donation," Henri said, comparing the level of the wine in his small plastic glass to theirs.

Ryan sipped his drink and balked. "Fruity."

"At least it's free." Louie smiled.

"It's not free," Ryan said.

"It tastes better when you pretend it is," Henri said.

Taking drinks into the theatre space was actively encouraged, and despite the poor quality of the wine, Ryan made another generous cash donation. Their glasses were filled to the brim.

The theatre was in an adjoining area, behind a curtain. The stage, in the centre of the space, was surrounded by temporary seating. The set resembled the interior of a small apartment—a messy domestic scene, with an unmade bed in the centre.

Louie, Ryan, and Henri had front-row seats. After they sat down, Ryan cast his gaze in a wide arc around the space, carefully scrutinising the aisles, the stage, and the narrow corridor behind the seats.

"What are you doing?" Louie whispered.

"Looking for an exit sign—in case of fire. If someone starts smoking, we're out of here."

"Thank god you're here." She rubbed his knee. Then she turned to Henri. "We're in safe hands."

The lights went down. The actors took to the stage.

In the modern version of the play, the young couple, Jason (played by Louie's friend Tom) and Medea (played by Lila) met at the local pub and fell in love. Jason worked at the bottle shop around the corner, and Medea was studying law. An awkward, slightly detached relationship developed between them. Then, Medea fell pregnant, and the couple had to decide what to do. As they discussed their future options, a completely naked Medea hovered above a semi-dressed Jason, who sat on the edge of the bed. When Jason rose to his feet, he cracked his head on Medea's nose. The noise of bone breaking resonated through the audience.

Stunned, Lila froze.

Tom looked at her in horror. His mouth dropped open and he covered it with his hand.

The audience gasped—Lila's nose was bleeding.

Slowly, Lila raised her hands and touched her nose. Then, she stared at the blood on her fingers. Looking around at the set, she searched for a cloth or a towel to stem the bleeding. The bedlinen was close, but she hesitated, not wanting to touch the props with her blood-soaked hands.

Blood poured out of Lila's nose. It flowed over her lips and dripped off the end of her chin. It ran down her bare breasts and onto her stomach.

"Oh my god," Louie muttered.

Ryan took his bomber jacket, which was wedged into the side of his seat, and handed it to Louie. He tilted his head toward Lila.

Louie jumped up. She walked onto the stage and covered Lila with the jacket.

The lights went down.

Backstage, in the small production office, Lila reclined in a chair with her head tilted back, and Ryan's jacket draped over her shoulders. Louie leaned over her and scrubbed the dried blood off Lila's body with paper towels and an old kitchen scourer. Nearby, the wastepaper basket was filled with more blood-soaked paper towels. Tom, wearing a bathrobe, sat to one side. He held his head in his hands.

The director, an agitated, bald man wearing jeans with a white shirt and tie, paced back and forth across the room. The producer, a slight woman with large glasses and pink hair, passed Louie handfuls of paper towels from an almost empty roll. The technical crew—lighting, sound, and props—waited anxiously by the door.

After Louie finished wiping Lila down, the crew entered the room. One by one, they took turns standing in front of Lila. Moving their heads from side to side, they scrutinised her facial features, assessing the damage—and the straightness—of her nose. No one said anything directly to Lila—a bad sign—but their frowns conveyed their dismay. Vickie, the prop woman shuddered before she turned and walked away.

Like Louie, the pink-haired producer had been staring at Lila's face for the past twenty minutes, and they both knew the appendage was no longer perpendicular. It looked like it was broken, two-thirds of the way up. Louie regretted the *break a leg, break everything* text message she'd sent to Lila before the performance.

"It's crooked," the producer confirmed. "Possibly broken—but we're not doctors . . ." Her voice trailed off.

"I'm so, so, so, sorry," Tom lamented from his seat in the corner of the room.

"It's not your fault," Lila said. "I think my mark was off."

"I think mine was off, too," Tom said.

"We should have rehearsed that scene a few more times," the director said.

The producer handed Lila three painkillers, which she scoffed with a glass of water.

"We're going to finish," Lila said, easing her way out of the chair. "I can do this."

"Are you sure?" The producer looked aghast. The director smiled.

"It's opening night. The critics are here, and they won't come again. We'll never get another chance," Lila said.

"The show must go on," the director said.

Louie didn't think the show should go on. She thought Lila should go to the hospital. "Maybe you should go to the hospital," Louie suggested.

"They can't do anything until the swelling goes down. Which will take a few days," Lila said.

"The pain is good, as long as you're not laughing," the director said.

Everyone laughed, except Louie.

"It's from the play," Lila explained.

Louie had no idea if Lila's comment about the swelling was true or what the best course of action might be. She was the only non-cast member in the room. The crew were a clique, and she didn't belong—this was not her world. Around her, the cast and crew were strengthening their resolve as they prepared to return to the stage, and the room buzzed with excitement.

Returning to the foyer, Louie found Henri and Ryan on their third glass of cheap red wine. Henri was outlining the plot of *Medea* to Ryan.

"In the traditional version of the play," Henri said. "Jason leaves his wife and children to marry the king's daughter—he believes this will advance his station in life. Medea has already killed her brother so she's emotionally unstable. Then, she plans her revenge, pledging to kill everyone—first the king and his daughter, and then Jason. Finally, she takes a knife to the kiddies."

"What's the message in all of this?" Ryan asked.

"Revenge," said Henri.

"Gender and power?" Louie said, taking a seat next to Ryan.

He passed her his plastic wineglass. She took the glass and sipped the wine.

"Lila's going back on," she announced before passing the plastic glass back to Ryan. Her hands trembled and she rested them in her lap.

Ryan placed his hand over hers, gently squeezing. Her tremors ceased.

After a thirty-minute interval, the actors returned to the stage, and the audience was back in their seats. Louie noted all the seats were filled; none of the critics had left.

The play continued.

After Medea fell pregnant, the unhappy couple decided to keep the child. Medea quit her law degree to take care of the baby. Jason began an affair with the daughter of a wealthy construction worker. Soon, he was making plans to leave Medea and take a job with his potential new father-in-law in the lucrative construction industry. In the final scene, Medea carries out her revenge by placing her hand over their baby's mouth, smothering it. Then, Lila delivered the final lines.

"Hate is a bottomless cup. I will pour and pour. The child is dead. I did this to make you suffer."

The lights went up.

A stunned silence settled over the audience and Louie scanned their faces, trying to gauge the public's reactions. People were holding their breath. The woman sitting next to her shook her head. A man on the other side of the room held his hand over his mouth. After a moment, a long collective sigh rose from the audience. A few people started to clap. Others followed. Everyone got to their feet, and a rousing applause filled the room.

Lila and Tom returned to the stage fully clothed and took their ovations—two more followed.

Eventually, the crowd gathered their belongings and began to file out of the theatre.

Ryan looked stunned. "Unbelievable?" he whispered.

"Oh, you didn't like it? I thought it was great," Louie said.

"It's the best thing I've seen. She was amazing. He was good, but she was outstanding. Why is this production on in *this place?*"

"They have no money—it's profit share."

"They don't get *paid?*"

"No. They work in hospitality—and sometimes in ticket sales—that's where they get paid."

"How can they be so talented and not get *paid?*"

"Welcome to the arts."

16
RYAN THE LION

ON WEDNESDAY MORNING, when the sunrise resembled the colour of Lila's black eyes—deep purple, red, and yellow—Louie knew they were in for more rain. She also knew Lila had a broken nose.

Lila had an x-ray booked that afternoon, and Louie had volunteered to drive her to the hospital. Sitting in the front seat of Louie's car, Lila looked like a panda.

"Does it hurt?" Louie asked, buckling her seatbelt.

"My ego hurts worse than my nose," Lila said as she wiped dog hair off the dash. "By the way, you need to clean this car."

"I know."

Louie started the engine and pulled the car out into the traffic. "I'm not sure I believe you. What's your take on Medea anyway? Do we like her?"

"No, of course, we don't like her. It's impossible to have empathy for the character. But I do feel sorry for her. She gets cornered, and to get out, she does something drastic.

It's her way of escaping the horror she's found herself in. I guess none of us know what we're capable of."

"Neither of us are going to kill our babies. I only have Eva, and I'd never hurt her."

"And I'm never having children. Although I might adopt one."

Louie considered her friend. "What's the worst part of all this?"

Lila paused, considering her options. "It's a toss-up between having to explain to people what happened—especially the medical staff—and putting on my makeup before the show—now that hurts."

"Ouch. It does look like someone hit you," Louie said.

Lila lowered her voice. "Domestic violence."

Louie took a deep breath. Neither of them wanted to talk about that topic.

"And the best part?" Louie asked. "Is there an upside?"

"I went back on and finished the play." Lila smiled.

Half an hour later, they were sitting on hard chairs in the hospital waiting room.

"People can't stop looking at you," Louie said.

"I know. It's made me realise I never want to be a celebrity."

Louie took out her phone and opened a folder. She had saved the *Medea* reviews so they could read them together. She glanced at Lila. "Ready?"

Lila nodded.

"Okay. *Time Out* says, *I was fortunate enough to see the opening night of* Medea." Louie paused. "*A captivating and profound performance. It reinvented the tragic form and achieved something rare on stage—the genuine shock of the new.*"

"They liked it." Lila let out a long, slow breath.

"They loved it." Louie flicked to the next review. "From the *Herald*. *Lila Montague delivered a profound and moving performance. Spectacular. Daring. Wonderful. She will be one to watch.*" Louie grinned. "Confirming what her friends already know—she's an incredibly talented actor."

"Oh, my god." Lila looked stunned.

"I made the last bit up," Louie confessed.

Lila's phone beeped—a text message. It was from the producer of the play—ticket sales had spiked, and the next three shows were sold out.

The x-rays confirmed what everyone already knew, Lila's nose was broken. She didn't have health coverage, so it would remain that way, slightly bent, three-quarters of the way up.

The following Friday evening, Louie packed her belongings into her Elantra and Eva jumped into the back seat. They headed north and drove over the Harbour Bridge. Louie took the first left turn off the freeway, circled under the bridge and headed toward Kirribilli. She parked the Elantra in Ryan's driveway.

Louie and Eva were having a weekend sleepover at Ryan's house. At first, she'd been reluctant—she didn't like changes to her routine. But Ryan had assured her she could study without any disruptions. Like a real estate agent, he promoted the desirable features of his property—the house had a garden, a driveway, and a king-size bed. He had also volunteered to cook dinner. The driveway was her weak point. She caved. Eva was looking forward to the king-size bed.

Eva jumped out of the Elantra, eager to see Ryan. Louie followed, hauling her bags, and Ryan met them at the front door. After patting Eva, he took Louie's bags, and they entered the house.

The front door opened to a long hallway. On the left were two large living rooms, one with a fireplace, and the other with a TV. On the right was a staircase that led to the upper levels. Ryan placed Louie's belongings at the bottom of the stairs, and she followed him through the house to the kitchen. Louie noticed a large wine rack and another unopened carton on the floor. There were two well-worn, leather armchairs, a modular sofa, and a bluestone coffee table. On the walls, were a few pieces of abstract art. The floors were polished timber covered in rugs.

The place was neat and tidy, nothing looked out of place.

The rear of the house had been extended, and the kitchen and dining areas were airy and open. The focal point was a feature wall of cement studded with stone. It ran behind the kitchen and extended outside to a covered deck. A large courtyard wrapped around two sides of the house— standing inside felt a bit like standing outside if the windows were clean. The glass was spotless.

A large island bench made from pale stone sat in the middle of the kitchen. Beyond this, timber cupboards. Open shelves along the back wall. The crockery and glasses were neatly stacked. Everything in order.

"You have an excellent house," Louie said, sliding onto a stool in the kitchen. "This might be the nicest house I've ever seen, except for Uncle Filip's, but you also designed that, didn't you? You must be a very good architect."

He smiled. "I try."

Louie swivelled on her stool and took in the rest of the room—the expansive glass, the covered deck and the garden, a dark-timber dining table. In the corner of the room, she spied a red chair—a nest of rope resting on three legs. She stared at it for a long moment, goosebumps shimmied up her arms. She turned to him. "You . . . you never said."

He was watching her, waiting for her reaction. "I wanted to surprise you."

Jumping off her stool, she headed toward the red chair. "You have a Vermelha chair."

The chair, made from metres of thick, red rope, looked like a pile of spaghetti on an aluminium base.

"Where in the world did you get this?" Louie asked.

"It was a gift from my friends when I opened the practice." Ryan ambled toward her, his hands were in his pockets.

Louie sat down in the chair and crossed her legs. It was a lot more comfortable than it looked. She changed her posture, leaning back and dropping her arms over the sides. Then she looked up at him and smiled. "Ask me; I know you want to."

"Designer and date."

"Fernando and Humberto Campana. 1993." She slapped the sides of the chair. "I never thought this would be your chair. I mean, it's lovely, and thank goodness it's comfortable because it sure doesn't look it—and that's the only thing that matters. But it doesn't seem like you. Like this would be *your* chair."

"It was a joke. To remind me that life was chaotic."

"Because the chair is so disorganised." She jumped up

and stood beside him. "That's so funny. Do you love it? Do you embrace the chaos?"

"No. I hate the chaos, but I love the chair."

She loved the chair, too.

Louie set up a study nook on a desk in a corner of the living area. Through the window, she could see Ryan giving Eva an extensive tour of the garden—he was talking to the dog, pointing out highlights that might interest her: the water bowl, the bird bath, a basket filled with balls and Frisbees.

Beside her, Ryan's phone rang. It was charging on the desk and the unanswered message went to voicemail. When he returned from his tour of the garden, he looked over at Louie and asked, "Who phoned?"

Louie glanced at the screen of his phone. "Someone called Kat Girl." She frowned at him. "Who is this Kat Girl?"

"My sister."

Louie beamed. "Kat Girl is your sister! That's so cute. Why is she called Kat Girl?"

"Childhood nickname."

"Do you have a childhood nickname?"

He hesitated. "She calls me . . . Ryan the Lion."

"Ahh, of course, that makes sense. Because you're . . ." She paused.

"Because I'm . . . ?"

She swallowed. "Because you're happiest when you're roaming on the savannah."

He moved closer, and his steely gaze pinned her to her seat. "Because I'm?"

She held his gaze. "Because you're handsome, like a lion. And you have a thick mane of hair."

He placed his hands on either side of her office chair and leaned toward her. "That's not what you were going to say."

She crossed her arms and sat back in her chair. "Okay, because sometimes you can be a bit bossy and you like doing things your way."

"That's because my way is the best way."

"It's the best way for you, and that's fine." She grabbed his earlobes and rubbed them between her forefinger and thumb. The sensation made her shiver.

Ryan collected his phone from the desk and headed outside with Eva. He took a Frisbee from the basket and tossed it across the garden for the dog while he returned Kat's phone call.

When she answered, Ryan told her he had received a carton of wine from her client—the man she did the free drawings for, Liam Wolf.

Kat seemed more annoyed than surprised.

Eva returned the Frisbee, and Ryan tossed it into the garden again. "It's Penfolds. Top shelf," Ryan said.

"Technically, that box is mine. I did the work on those drawings," Kat said.

"That's what I told him—when I called to thank him."

"Please tell me you didn't."

"I did."

"Worst brother of the year award for you, Ryan the Lion."

After dinner—fish grilled on the barbecue served with a green salad and baby potatoes—Ryan told Louie he had planned a weekend away—two days, one night—on a luxury super yacht.

"Two days!" Louie wiggled her nose. "On a boat. That's not going to work for me. And as far as surprises go, I've had better."

Ryan leaned against the kitchen bench and crossed his arms. He was expecting less hostility and more excitement. He thought her blockade would crumble once she realised it was a luxury super yacht with a pool, a spa, a chef, and eight staff.

It didn't. She looked horrified.

"Did you see any green holiday stars on my calendar?" she asked.

He shook his head.

"Let me show you something." She collected her laptop from the desk in the living room and opened it on the kitchen bench. After pulling up a spreadsheet, she spun the laptop around to show Ryan her colour-coded, time-management study plan. "This is my life for the next five months." She pointed at the screen. "See, from April to August, I have everything planned out." She gave an affirmative nod.

Ryan scanned the spreadsheet. "You have every hour of every day allocated."

"I do." Louie rubbed her nose. "It's the only way I get things done."

He dipped his head toward the computer. "You even have sleep time allocated."

"That's just a default," she dismissed. "It makes up the twenty-four-hour blocks of time so the formulas calculate. But see, there's no way I can fit in forty-eight hours on a boat."

Ryan scratched his head. He was a resourceful man; damage control was his forte, and he was sure he could make this work. "What if I pick you up late Saturday afternoon, then we come back Sunday morning? Eighteen hours —including sleep time." He considered her spreadsheet. "Maybe I can help you out with something. I could walk Eva." Ryan pointed to a grey-coloured cell on the sheet. "What this?"

"Grey is automotive."

He smirked.

Louie snapped her laptop shut. "You're being mean."

"I'm not . . ." He stifled a laugh.

She placed her hands on her hips. "I struggle with"—her voice cracked—"with time management."

Ryan covered his mouth with his hand, trying to suppress a smile.

"It's not funny. I get distracted easily, and I daydream. I daydream a lot. It's a problem."

"Daydreaming doesn't sound like a problem."

"Well, it is. I can stare at something and not even realise I'm doing it. I just look out the window and time evaporates. Afternoons slip by, which is why I have the spreadsheet."

"It's an excellent spreadsheet." Ryan cleared his throat and composed himself. "What's wrong with your car?"

"There's a weird noise and it needs a service. I've left it to the last minute."

"Let me do that for you. Then, shuffle things around. I'm sure you can make it work. It's an amazing boat. You'll love it."

"Will it be just the two of us on the amazing boat?"

"No. People from my work will also be there."

She frowned.

"Don't look so concerned. It'll be fun—I promise."

"Never take responsibility for someone else's fun. Meeting new people can be petrifying."

"You can stand on a stage and talk to a thousand people, but a few friends on a boat is petrifying?"

"Exactly."

"Well, you'll know me. I'm going to be very friendly."

She wasn't sure he'd be friendly enough.

The week before their boating adventure, Ryan skipped his CrossFit classes and took Eva for her morning runs through the park. Like Louie, he brought the Frisbee along, and when the run was over, they played together under the trees. Flicking the Frisbee over the grass and watching Eva catch it was a joy. Ryan thought he could do it forever until he realised Eva really could do it forever.

"If you were human, you'd be a workaholic," he told her.

Together, they made a handsome couple. Eva lapped up the attention she received from other park-goers and so did Ryan. He thought if he ever broke up with Louie and needed a date, all he had to do was get a dog, teach it to catch a Frisbee, and go to the park—although he knew Eva was special.

Eva loved the Defender. Ryan called it her chariot, but she was banned from the front seat and had to stay in the back. She didn't mind; Ryan tethered her lead to a hook, so she felt safe. When she jumped in the back, she held her head high.

Ryan took her to his early morning site meetings, then watched with amazement as Eva melted the hearts of the burly tradesmen, who, most mornings, he could barely get a grunt out of. The contractors lay on the floor next to Eva. They took selfies with their phones and sent the pictures to their kids and partners. Eva's behaviour on site was exemplary, which was more than Ryan could say for many of the contractors.

Ryan also sorted out the service and the noise in Louie's car—a loose guard on the muffler. He had the interior and exterior professionally cleaned. Returning from the garage, he dropped the keys into her hand and said, "You have excellent taste in chairs, dogs, and men . . . but your car! It drives like a piece of shit. The vision is appalling, the air-conditioning barely works, you need new tyres, and it was *covered* in dog hair."

He glanced at Eva. "It's not your fault, princess."

So, I shed a little; it's in my DNA.

"One day it will be a classic," Louie dismissed.

"No, it won't," Ryan said.

17
ONE BOAT

THE MOMENT EVA saw Louie's overnight bag open on the floor of the bedroom, her body stiffened; the item was vaguely familiar. After sniffing the bag, she walked around it a few times and sniffed it again. She lay down next to it and buried her head under her paws. Rejection hung in the air. She knew heartache was coming.

"You want to go to Tara's for a sleepover?" Louie asked.

Eva shook her head. *The overnight bag can go to Tara's.*

On the day of the boating adventure, the clouds vanished, and the temperature was unseasonably mild. Louie wore a mini dress covered in orange and yellow flowers. She slipped an amber rock into the front pocket.

It was not possible to board the boat outside the scheduled times. Guests were asked to arrive at 11:00 a.m., and they would depart the vessel on Sunday day at 4:00 p.m. Ryan inquired about a water taxi, but the boat would be at sea and too far away. The following week, Louie would need to amend her spreadsheet to allow for the lost hours.

Standing on the marina, Louie and Ryan gazed up at the

vessel. Louie's mouth dropped open. The boat was a fifty-metre luxury motor yacht—three levels high. She glanced at Ryan, then she looked back at the boat. "Some clients. How rich are these people?"

"I know," Ryan agreed. "It's extreme."

Ryan and Louie were the last to board. They were promptly shown to their cabin. A suite with oak-panelled walls, marble tiles in the bathroom, and a king-size bed with six pillows and half a dozen scatter cushions. There was also a private deck with lounge chairs, throw rugs, and more scatter cushions.

The staff from SLD Projects had gathered in the saloon: a cosy lounge area with navy and cream upholstery, marine-inspired art, and more scatter cushions than Louie had ever seen in one place. A dozen people were milling around, drinking cocktails.

As they entered the saloon, a thick-set, blonde-headed man wearing a cream linen suit approached Louie. "Hello, I'm Freddie," he said, taking her hand. "I work with Ryan. Obviously, I do. Everyone here works with Ryan. Why don't you come with me, and I'll introduce you."

Freddie escorted Louie around the room, introducing her to friendly groups of people who were eager to meet her. She shook hands with everyone, explaining several times that Louie was short for Elouise. She caught about half the other guests' names—Amy, Drake, Molly, Sam—and always kept one hand in the front pocket of her dress, clutching her stone.

When someone tapped her on the shoulder, she spun around. Two young women of similar height and age smiled at her. They introduced themselves as Sophie and Mia. Sophie had a pixie haircut. She wore a long navy skirt and a white top. A silky red scarf was tied around her neck. Mia had white-blonde hair and dark brown eyes. She wore a short, red and blue striped dress. Louie admired their nautical efforts.

"Forget about them." Sophie waved a dismissive hand at the other staff members. "We're the A-Team. You only need to remember our names."

"Great." Louie smiled. "Remind me again?"

Mia and Sophie laughed, but Louie was serious.

"We're as shocked as you are," Sophie said. "About the boat—it's beyond."

"There's also a gym and a spa," Mia said.

A dark-haired man wearing a straw hat was perched on a nearby sofa. He whipped out his phone and began scrolling. "They rent this out for a hundred thousand a week —in winter! Off-peak!" he said.

"They could give us the money," Sophie said. "To pay off our student loans."

"It wouldn't be enough." Mia laughed and slapped Sophie on the shoulder.

The concierge entered the room and announced lunch. The blue skies were holding, so they would be eating outside. A seafood buffet had been prepared. Guests began moving from the saloon to the outdoor dining area.

"I can get yours," Louie told Ryan. "Save me a seat." She headed toward the buffet tables, which held bowls of healthy-looking salads. The selection of seafood included prawns, oysters, and crayfish. Louie grinned on approach.

On the opposite side of the table, Sophie and Freddie were piling their plates with food.

Louie took two plates—one for Ryan—and joined them, making her way around the buffet.

"Hey, I'm Amos." The man wearing the straw hat sidled up to her holding an empty plate. "Ryan tells me you're a runner. Do you compete?"

"No." Louie scooped potato salad onto her plates and moved on to a beetroot dish. "I just run around the park with my dog."

"So, what, five or six Ks—that sort of thing?" He followed her lead and heaped potato salad onto his plate.

"A bit longer—"

"What? Ten Ks?"

"Something like that." She handed him a pair of tongs.

Amos nodded at a bowl of green herb sauce. "Try that; it looks good."

It did look good, and Louie added a generous amount to her plates. Then she offered a spoonful to Amos. He nodded. She obliged.

"What's your PB?" Amos asked.

Louie paused. "I have no idea. What's yours?"

"I did a ten-K fun run in forty-eight minutes. That's the fastest I've ever run—and I train. A lot." Amos rested his plate on the table and reached for his phone, which was stowed in the back pocket of his shorts. He pulled up a map of the city and turned the screen toward Louie. "Where do you live?"

"South Sydney." Louie leaned in and pointed at a spot on the map. "There, on the corner, next to the park."

"And you run to . . . ?"

"The art museum."

"Amos, put your bloody phone away," Sophie called from across the table.

"Settle down. I'm just trying to figure something out,"

he said, dismissing Sophie. He turned back to Louie. "How long does that take you?"

"Forty minutes," Louie said. "Maybe less."

"Maybe less!" He stared at her. "How much less?"

She stared back at him. "I have no idea. I run because it keeps me sane and because I need to exercise my dog. It gets me out of the house, and some days, it's better than taking the car."

"I've heard about your car." He frowned. Then he slipped his phone back into his pocket. "What sort of dog do you have?"

"A kelpie."

"My girlfriend loves kelpies. What colour?"

"Black and tan, with a white patch on her chest."

Amos frowned. "My girlfriend likes the red ones."

"Well, mine's a very shiny one."

Amos moved toward a bowl of salad. "She's in Denmark. I'm sorting out her citizenship visa. It's a nightmare. I miss her so much."

"That must be hard—being so far apart."

Louie could not fit any more food onto her plates, so she headed outside and took the spare seat that Ryan had saved for her. He was talking to a pregnant woman about working in indigenous communities.

Louie poured herself a glass of water with lots of ice, thinking very soon she might need to hold an ice cube.

Freddie, Sophie, Amos, and Mia joined them at the table. Ryan introduced Louie to another couple—Drake, a senior architect at the firm, and his wife Molly—who was pregnant.

"You should do a marathon," Amos said. "You can start with a half—entries open next month. Then you can build up to the full forty-two kilometres next year. I have a training program—I'll send it to you."

Louie forced a smile. "Thank you."

"Or you could do a triathlon," Mia suggested. She was peeling a large prawn. "We have three corporate teams—mixed—but we're always looking for more people."

Under the table, Louie's knee began to jiggle.

"I'll think about it," Louie said.

"We train three times a week. Tuesdays and Thursdays —Sunday is optional. We'd love to have you." Mia dipped her prawn into the green sauce. "This is bloody delicious," she said.

Under the table, Ryan reached for Louie's leg. He held his hand on her knee until her tremor passed.

"I hear you're doing a PhD on air or light—or something like that," Freddie said, smiling at her from across the table.

Louie reached for her wineglass and took a large gulp. *Here we go,* she thought, and her heart sank. She was expected to talk about her thesis. It was the last thing she wanted to talk about, but it was hard to avoid without sounding rude. These were Ryan's friends and work colleagues, and she didn't want to offend anyone.

She took a deep breath. "That's true, I am. It's about the intellectual and emotional responses we have to the representation of atmosphere in art. How the depiction of light and transparency affect us emotionally. Or why we're moved when we look at landscapes. My focus is on impressionism."

Freddie grinned. "Wow. That's amazing."

"I've been doing it for a while, so it's lost some of its amazingness."

"How much do you have to write?" Amos asked.

"Eighty thousand words."

"And how much have you written?" Amos took a swig from his beer bottle. He picked up his phone, which was on the table beside him, and started scrolling.

A collective sigh rose from the table. Sophie rolled her eyes.

"I'm still sorting out the final word count," Louie said.

"Only two percent of the world's population has a PhD," Amos said.

"There's a good reason for that," Louie mumbled.

"Who's your favourite painter?" Freddie asked.

"Um, today, it's probably Van Gogh—I might change my mind tomorrow."

"Because?"

"Honestly, there are so many great artists. It's impossible to narrow it down. I've had some intense relationships with dead painters over the last few years. I once had a sex dream about Renoir, and I dreamed that Frida Kahlo kissed me."

"She would be up for that," Sophie said. "Did she use tongue?"

Louie laughed. "I can't remember."

"So, why Van Gogh?" Freddie asked.

"Shouldn't we talk about something else?" Louie shovelled the potato salad into her mouth and scanned the faces around the table—all eyes were fixed on her.

"No," Freddie dismissed. "We work together. We know everything about each other. Let's talk about you."

They're just curious, Louie told herself. Curiosity is an important human trait. People are supposed to be inquisitive.

"It's his imagination," Louie continued. "The way he

took everything that was inside him and expressed it on the canvas as impassioned emotion."

Freddie smiled. "He's my favourite, too. He was lonely. But he wasn't crazy. He was depressed, and he drank too much, which affected his mental health. He was trapped in a cycle of loneliness and depression, so he hid from love and ran away from life. It was just too hard."

"I think we can all relate to that," Sophie said.

"He was only thirtysomething when he died." Freddie looked across the table at Louie.

"Yes," she confirmed. "He was thirty-seven. He went into a field and shot himself in the chest with a revolver. He died two days later in hospital. He was exhausted, and he thought he had failed. He once said, *'There is peace in every storm.'* I guess, at that moment, he forgot the storm would pass, as storms do."

No one spoke. People stared at their plates.

"Is it worth it?" Molly asked. "All the work."

Louie shook her head. "I wouldn't recommend it. Mental health issues are rife. About a third of students suffer from anxiety or depression. Fifty percent never finish. There's no financial benefit over a master's degree, and a third of graduates get jobs in unrelated fields."

"Shit!" Freddie balked. "Are you okay?"

Louie smiled and he caught her eye. "I'm almost done," she said.

"What will you do when you finish?" Sophie asked.

Louie cleared her throat. "I'm not sure. I might . . . teach."

A universal chorus of encouragement greeted her.

Amos reached for his phone. But Sophie's hand got there first, and as she swiped the device from the table, her elbow knocked Amos's beer bottle sideways. The liquid soaked the tablecloth.

Spare serviettes were passed between the guests, and Amos mopped up the spill. "Fuck. Sophie, give me my phone back," he said.

"No, we're having lunch." She passed the phone to Mia, and Mia dropped it into her bag. "No one else has their phone out."

A short silence. Then Amos scanned the crowd around the table. He sat down and turned to Louie. "What will you teach?"

"Something in the arts, I guess."

Across the table, Freddie offered a concerned smile.

God, please let's talk about something else.

"We saw your friend in *Medea*," Sophie said. "She was amazing. I was so impressed."

"You did?" Louie dropped her cutlery. She glanced around the table.

"We all saw it," Freddie said. "It came highly recommended."

"And did you all like it?" Louie asked.

"We loved it," Freddie said. "The building, however, is a death trap."

"Actually, it's a coffin," Amos said.

Louie placed her hand on Ryan's knee.

Louie discovered there was very little to do on a luxury super yacht filled with Ryan's work colleagues other than eat, drink, nap, and engage in late afternoon sex among the scatter cushions. When Louie and Ryan arrived half an hour late for dinner, she thought everyone would know the reason. And she was right, they did.

Dinner was followed by more wine and long conversations about architecture, annoying, arsehole clients, and the benefits of CLT beams, which Louie discovered meant *cross-laminated timber*. Everyone seemed impressed when she told them the chairs at the art museum were made from CLT and not solid wood.

Later, Ryan asked her if she wanted to go to the party room.

"What's in the party room?" she asked.

"Drugs. Knowing Freddie, anything you want."

"Bring me back something fun," she said.

Around midnight, Ryan and Louie left the group of revellers and headed back to their cabin. They lay together outside on a deckchair, covered by a throw rug. Millions of silver stars in the night sky shone down on them.

"What came first, architecture or a social conscience?" Louie asked.

"Architecture. But my mother thinks I chose it to piss my father off."

"Did you?"

"Yes, I think I did. I told you, he was a builder, hated working with architects, and complained about them all the time. The moment he walked out the door, I thought, *I'm going to be an architect*."

"That's a bit extreme. Remind me never to piss you off. What about homelessness? Where did that come from?"

"I have a friend, Griff—Griffin Reid. I met him at uni. During his second year, he slept in his car. Then he sold his car—because he needed the money—and he slept in a park for three months—until we found out. Then he slept on my couch or Freddie's couch. His mum died when he was eighteen. I think he was in a constant state of grief. He was always exhausted; I don't think he slept in a proper bed for about two years. His mental health wasn't great—he struggled with work, and you can't live on youth allowance in this country. It doesn't cover your rent. That was the moment I realised homelessness was just bad social policy."

"Do you still see Griffin Reid?"

"Yes, he has a charter in the gulf."

"We were homeless once—Tara and I. We walked out on my stepdad when I was about ten. Stayed in a hotel for a few days. Then my uncle Filip came and got us, and we stayed with him until we found a place of our own. I remember every detail. Packing the car. Driving away. The hotel room —it had bright green carpet, and a patchwork bedspread that wasn't real patchwork—it was just a printed pattern. The wall lights looked like shells, and the place smelled like cigarettes. It was scary, all of it, not just the decor."

"I'm sure it was."

They looked at the stars for a while, then Ryan asked, "Did something happen to you when you were working on your PhD?"

Louie nodded. "About five years ago, I came home from the museum and parked my car outside my house—which is rare because I never get a park outside my house, so I should have realised something was up." She paused for a short moment. "I couldn't get out of the car; I couldn't open the door. And yes, the door handle was working just fine, thank you."

"I believe you. Go on."

"I couldn't move. I froze. Then, a week later, I couldn't get out of my chair. Then one morning, I couldn't get out of bed. It lasted about six months—so I took some time off. But I knew I would go back—I had to finish."

He ran his fingers across her shoulder.

"You don't seem surprised," she said.

"I'm not. I know how anxious you get. And the dog—running is life—it keeps you sane. I get that. Your special stone, which you keep in your pocket."

Louie plucked the amber-coloured stone from her pocket and held it in the palm of her hand. "I've had this one a long time. It used to be much bigger." She grinned.

"Idiot." He smiled. "There's also your star chart—something to look forward to. The ice-cube trick, which you showed my mother."

"You're observant."

"I also have twenty-five staff. Two have been diagnosed with depression. Most days, someone cries in the office. Usually, it's Freddie."

Louie giggled.

"Did you do therapy?" Ryan asked.

"Yes. They said it was like a lie bundled up inside me. A deep truth that was trying to escape."

"Did you work out what that was?"

"Fear, probably. I want to succeed so badly. I want to do well." She paused. "But then what do I do when I'm done? What do I do with my thesis? I think I was scared of finishing because then I had to deal with the future."

"Is it worth it?"

"I have to believe it is. I tell myself words hold ideas, so they matter—just as much as experience matters."

"There can never be enough art in the world. And that's what you're doing, creating a piece of art."

She took a deep breath and rested her head on his chest.

It was late, she was tired, but she remembered something that she wanted to tell him.

"There's this quote by Cézanne," she said. "At least I think it's Cézanne, but it might be Van Gogh, or maybe it's Monet. I can't remember." She yawned. "Anyway, whoever it was said, *'There's a great fire in everyone's soul, but people never come inside to warm themselves by it. Passers by see nothing but a little smoke coming from the top of the chimney . . . and they go on their way.'* She paused. "It feels like you came inside and warmed my soul."

18

THREE BOATS

On Saturday morning, Tara entered the side gate of Louie's house, carrying a box of seedlings. She wanted to take advantage of the clear skies and spend an hour in the garden planting autumnal flowers and herbs. The remainder of the day she would spend in her studio, painting.

She expected to find both the garden and the house empty; Louie had a tour scheduled at the museum and Lila was walking Eva. On the veranda, she found a tall, attractive, dark-haired man stacking wood.

"Hello." Tara waved. "I thought you delivered on Fridays."

Ryan turned toward her. "You did?"

"Yes. I guess the rains messed your schedule up. It's certainly played havoc with mine." Tara placed the box of seedlings on the edge of the veranda and dusted the loose soil off her gardening jumper.

"You must be the gardener." Ryan pulled off his work gloves and jumped off the veranda.

Tara scanned his face. "You look . . . familiar. You're not the wood man, are you?"

"No, I'm not. It's Ryan. Ryan McDermott." He offered his hand and Tara took it.

"The architect? The Arts Medal recipient?" she asked.

"Yes."

"I see. Well, I'm Tara, and I am the gardener. Sometimes I'm also the cook. I'm sorry I called you the wood man. I guess the renovations are finally going ahead?"

Ryan frowned. "I'm not sure—"

"You'll need to take a good look at the foundations." Tara sidled up to him. "It's heritage listed—I suppose you know that already. There are sub-floor issues on the eastern side and the gutters leak—on all sides. But it's triple brick—they don't build them like this anymore."

"You're right, they don't."

"Still, it's a hell of a job."

Ryan smiled. "How can I say this—I'm not renovating the house, although, I agree it needs a lot of work. I'm seeing Louie."

"Oh." Tara paused. "I'm sorry—she didn't tell me your name. I just thought . . ."

Ryan crossed his arms over his chest and leaned back on his heels. "It's only been a few weeks."

She pointed a finger at him. "You met at the gala dinner —she introduced you?"

"Actually, we met before that, at the university."

She smiled to herself and looked away. "You drew the orchid."

"I did."

A short silence followed.

"Can I ask, what are you doing with the wood?" she asked.

"Moving it to the other side of the veranda. It was stacked behind the table. I thought if I moved the table this way, then the daybed could go on the far side, so it gets the winter sun."

"Perfect. I'll help." Tara pulled on her gardening gloves.

Half an hour later, Louie walked through the side gate of her house and found her veranda furniture rearranged. Tara and Ryan were sitting at the table, which was now on the opposite side of the deck. They shared a pot of tea and Tara was discussing the benefits of biodynamic gardening.

"They pack the cow horn tightly with manure, and they bury it," Tara explained. "The cosmic forces, that's the energy that drives the universe, are especially strong at this time of year, and it creates the most potent compost." Tara sipped her tea.

I'm so glad that conversation happened without me, Louie thought. She stepped onto the veranda and said, "So you two have met."

Before Tara left, she harvested the spinach and lettuce from the garden, which she had planted six weeks earlier. She sewed a new crop of seedlings: more spinach, kale, and spring onions. She made a mental note to include rocket in the next round of planting as this was Ryan's favourite. Lately, it had been hard to get—supplies of many herbs were scarce due to the rain—but she could raise the seedlings herself. It was more work, but it was his favourite.

After checking his weather app, Ryan told Louie it would start raining again on Sunday afternoon, and it was unlikely to stop for the foreseeable future. Keen to make the most of the remaining blue skies, they set out for a family outing with Eva in the park.

After a brisk walk, Louie spread a blanket over the damp grass. She lay down on her side, closed her eyes, and slept. Ryan took out his sketchbook and started to draw the long slender leaves from a nearby gum tree. Soon, he moved on to the gum nuts and spiky pink blossoms.

Eva had chased her ball twenty-four times, caught her Frisbee eighteen times, and received eleven pats from random strangers. She also had her two favourite humans by her side; this was her idea of a perfect day. She lay on the rug next to Louie, watching a motionless butterfly on the grass. The insect was either content—it was possible it had never seen sunshine—or paralysed with fear. When the insect refused to move, Eva became bored. She sat up and stretched, then she changed positions and lay beside Ryan, placing her head in his lap.

With one hand, he scratched the dog's neck, with the other, he sketched a seedpod. Twenty minutes later, he was still patting the dog. "Lucky for you, I can draw with one hand," he told her.

Louie opened her eyes. She rolled over and smiled at Ryan's drawings—the page covered in detailed sketches of flowers and leaves. "What kind of tree—"

Ryan passed her his phone. She opened the app and took a photograph of the tree.

"It's a Hakea. It flowers in winter, likes full sun, and is not suitable for pots. If the sun comes out again, we can use the bark for sunburn treatment." She rolled onto her back and looked up at the sky. "Why does it feel so good to be here, in the park?"

"I'm amazing company."

"Do you think nature is spiritual?"

"Yes. Biophilia."

"Biophilia?"

"It's the idea that humans need contact with nature—plants, animals, sunlight—for mental health." His gaze was fixed on his sketchbook.

"That makes so much sense."

"I omitted rain—on purpose."

"Good man."

"Although, I could add—the sound of water."

"Yes, and what about birds and butterflies?"

He smiled. "Sure."

"Do you teach that—designing with biophilia?"

"I do."

As she watched Ryan sketch with one hand and pat Eva with the other, Louie realised she was in love with this man. Ryan McDermott—architect, champion of low-income housing, lover of kelpies, painter of orchids, owner of a rope chair, and lover of light—was her man. He had burrowed under her skin, into her heart and claimed all of it, and she never wanted him to leave. He belonged to her, and she belonged to him.

Staring at the pale blue sky above, Louie said, "I've just realised something."

A long pause followed.

"Are you going to tell me what you just realised?"

"I'm sky-high in love with you. Did you know that?"

He froze, the point of his pencil fixed to the edge of the leaf he was drawing.

She turned over and stared into his eyes. "I had to tell you in case you didn't know." She turned away and gazed up at the sky again. "It's a good feeling, being in love with you."

Ryan smiled. He picked up her hand, which lay on the blanket next to him and kissed it. "You're the most beautiful person I've ever met."

Ryan loved everything about Louie. He loved the way she dressed, the way she walked around his house wearing only her underwear and thick socks. He loved hearing antidotes about her classes and students. He happily listened as she discussed her tours at the museum, the latest exploits of the wood duck family, what play Lila was rehearsing for, and Henri's disastrous dating endeavours. Ryan loved her house, and he loved her dog. He loved how open and honest she was—if she didn't like something, she told him. But even before that, he only had to glance at her face to know what she was thinking. He loved the way she saw the world. At times it was childlike, and she had not lost her sense of wonder. She hid nothing from him. Except for her thesis.

He had raised the topic of her study so many times, he'd lost count. He had offered to help, to read her drafts and check the references, but she refused. She didn't have time to explain it to fresh ears—even though his ears were lovely. So, he left her to it.

Lying beside Louie on the rug, he turned to her and said, "I love you, too." He would do anything for her, anything she asked.

"It's settled then. We're in love." After collecting her phone from her bag, she rolled onto her back and took a picture of the cloudless sky. Then she sent the photo to Ryan.

Ryan checked his phone. "Blue sky?"

"Is it though? I wonder if we both see the same blue—I

mean exactly the same. For all we know, your blue could be very different to my blue. Can we go to the museum on our way home? I want to show you something. My new favourite thing."

"Sure."

At the art museum, Louie and Ryan stood in front of three large canvases—a triptych—each one two metres by two metres.

"Three studies from the *Temeraire* by Cy Twombly. Oil on canvas," Louie said.

On the canvases, the artist had painted row boats. Three boats on the first canvas, two on the second picture, and one larger boat on the third.

The boats were empty, but they had oars and some of these were raised, while others hung over the side. There was no distinction between land, sky, or sea, so the boats appeared to float across the canvases.

"It's a tribute to Turner's *Fighting Temeraire*." She turned to him. "You remember it from my lecture?"

Ryan nodded.

"So, what do you think it means?" she asked.

"Maybe . . . the past, the present, and the future. Life's a journey," he said.

"Yes, I think so."

"It's melancholy."

"Yes," she agreed. "Life is inevitable. It just keeps going. Every day you get up and get on the boat." She paused. "And one day, we'll all be tugged to our last resting place."

He dug his hands into his pockets. "Depressing."

"Let's hope there's a sunset at the end."

He smiled.

She turned back to the paintings. "It's like a backdrop to

how we live. You can get on the boat and do nothing at all and still have a life. But what the journey needs is colour. It needs flowers and pears. And that's our job—it's what we bring to our own lives." She turned to him. "I'm not explaining it very well."

"I get it." He smiled.

Before they left the museum, Louie headed to the gift shop. She had a present in mind for Ryan. She disappeared into the store and returned a few minutes later with a pair of socks covered with cartoon images of Leonardo da Vinci. The words, *Leonardo Toe Vinci* were written under the elastic garter.

"I wanted to buy you something for no reason," she said. "I hope you wear them. They'll go very nicely with your disdain for the old masters."

Ryan considered the socks. He turned them over in his hand. "I'm keen to foster that relationship."

"Then you should put them on right now." She pointed to a bench.

He chuckled. Taking a seat, he changed into his *Leonardo Toe Vinci* socks.

Later that evening, Louie and Ryan were curled up on the sofa in Louie's sitting room. Louie gazed into the fire. A copy of *The Sublime and the Beautiful* lay open on her lap. Ryan sketched pictures of boats and oars in his notebook.

"Ex-girlfriends?" Louie asked.

Ryan frowned. He was shading the edge of an oar. "What about them?"

"Tell me about them. Who were they? Why did you end up as just good friends?"

"I'd rather not."

"But I want to know." She closed her book. "History is important. The past matters."

He scratched an eyebrow. "Why don't you tell me about yours, and we'll work forward from there."

"Okay." She sat up, warming to the subject. "In primary school, there was Alex—he played an air guitar and sang Nirvana songs to me. I found this extremely annoying. I just wanted him to leave me alone."

"You weren't ready to accept his love."

"No, I wasn't. Then, skipping forward ten years, Dominic Lawson. The first boy I had sex with at the tender age of sixteen. He left me because he found out Angela Boots liked him. And now they're married—to each other." She slapped her leg. "Can you believe it? It's a true story, but at the time, it broke my heart. I had planned our wedding and named our four children. I thought I would never recover."

"And surprisingly, you have."

"After that—David—he wanted to use me as a sex toy, which was okay at first, but then—"

Ryan raised his hand. "Please, no details." He continued to work on his oars.

Louie chuckled. "You're funny. Okay, then Jackson. Jackson wanted me to be a lot of things, but mostly he wanted me to be something I was not. He tried to make me fit into his life. It was never going to work." Louie paused. She stared out the window into the darkness.

Ryan caught her reflection in the glass.

She turned away.

"He left me when I needed him the most. I still have his cocktail shaker." Louie paused. "That's about it for the serious ones. What about you?"

"Same."

"You have your ex-boyfriend's cocktail shaker too? What a coincidence." Narrowing her eyes, she glared at him.

He refused to look up.

She sighed. Then she sighed again, for effect.

"I don't want to talk about it," Ryan said.

"You're being silly. Look, I have my serious face on, which means I'm very serious."

She did have her serious face on, which wasn't that serious. He glanced at her and smiled. Then he went back to his drawing.

"Eva also has her serious face on. You should be worried."

Ryan glanced at the dog. Eva's expression was grave, which concerned him.

You have a voice for a reason. Use it, Eva told him.

Ryan pulled a page from his sketchbook and handed the drawing to Louie. "This is for you. It's something I've been working on for a few days." He headed into the kitchen and filled the kettle.

Louie studied the drawing. It was a picture of an apartment block. She wondered what happened to the boats and oars. She was looking forward to his interpretation of life on the high seas in black and white.

The picture in her hand showed a large apartment with multiple levels and varying rooflines. Every rooftop had a little garden, and in one section, a woman and a dog were playing Frisbee. Across the front facades of the buildings were many small, irregular-shaped windows. In each window, Ryan had drawn a motif—hearts, arrows, circles, flowers. There were also letters. As Louie studied the drawing, she realised the letters were not randomly placed; they spelled out words. Ryan had written a message in the windows. Louie ran her finger over the letters. The message read. *Move in with me.*

"Oh, my god." The drawing fell from her hand and fluttered to the floor.

"Too fast?" Ryan queried from the kitchen.

"Two months. It's only been two months."

"I was just testing out an idea. Might not have been one of my best. But think about it—it would make life so much easier."

"I can't commit to anything until I finish my study."

He crossed his arms over his chest and leaned back against the cupboard. "I thought it might help with the time issue. I think it's worth considering."

"It's not." She collected the drawing from the floor and studied the picture for a long moment. Then she stood up, walked across the kitchen, and handed him the page. "Being in love with you hasn't helped so far. I don't see how living with you is going to make it any easier."

19
SUNFLOWERS

AT THE BEGINNING OF JUNE, Tara harvested the spinach, kale, and spring onions that she had planted in May. The constant rain had not been kind to the crops, and the vegetable yield was low. For the winter months ahead, she planted a selection of frost-tolerant seedlings, including more radishes, rainbow chard, leeks, and another round of rocket, which she'd raised from seedlings. The plants thrived on the windowsill of her studio.

Three months after Ryan received the Arts Medal, SLD Projects had more work than they could manage. Freddie hired two more project architects with excellent CAD skills and two more graduates. This helped with the production of drawings and documentation, but Ryan McDermott was the principal architect, the face of the company, and the winner of the Arts Medal. Despite Ryan's insistence that design was collaborative, and his firm employed many excellent architects, he was the only person a new client wanted to meet.

Freddie called Ryan into a crisis meeting. They could not

take on any more projects—at least not for the next six months.

"It's not a matter of more staff. I can barely manage the practice as it is," Freddie said, and he followed this with a small lecture about work-life balance.

Ryan agreed. The office was overflowing with projects and staff. This was never Ryan's intention. He didn't want to run a larger architecture firm—he wanted to work in a small niche practice with people he cared about. Bigger was not better.

They agreed. No new projects until summer.

Louie was also busy teaching at the university. The last few weeks of term were hectic. Her first-year students were not accustomed to the final assessment workload, and they had multiple submissions due at the same time. Many were short-tempered and moody. There were signs of physical exhaustion and often tears in class. She spent hours crafting long replies to students who were suffering from stress and anxiety. The on-campus student counsellors had long wait lists. It was a time-consuming and exhausting few weeks for faculty and students.

Ryan and Louie loved the reliable ritual of their routines. Over the cold winter months, their lives merged, and their schedules evolved without discussion. Ryan stayed at Louie's house two or three nights a week. He arrived early evening with red wine and his laptop. After Louie went to bed, he cleaned the kitchen and stacked the dishwasher. Then he spent several hours answering his emails, checking the status of projects, and reading site visit reports. Eva stayed up and kept him company.

"When it rains, it pours," Ryan said to the dog. "Do you have that problem with your job?" he asked.

Eva shook her head.

They knew the truth—most days she was operating at sixty percent capacity. She really could go all day, every day.

Louie cooked Italian—it was Ryan's favourite cuisine. Usually pasta with prawns, or aubergines, or mushroom, or courgettes, and sometimes caponata, and occasionally lasagne or cannelloni.

One afternoon, Henri stopped by and observed, "One day you're happily grazing on seeds and nuts, then suddenly, you find yourself in a relationship, and you're making lasagne—from scratch."

"With gluten-free pasta." Louie grinned.

Louie continued to wake between four and five in the morning to work on her PhD, but Ryan hadn't abandoned his habit of carrying her back to bed after first selecting control-save on her laptop.

On weekends, they alternated between their houses. One weekend they would spend at Louie's, and the next, they would stay at Ryan's. On Louie's sleepover weekends, she always forgot to pack an essential item—her laptop charger, her makeup, her running shoes, a favourite jumper, a notebook, or a textbook that she needed, gluten-free bread, warm socks, her sunglasses, which she wore even when it rained, or the athletic support for her knee, which still hurt.

Ryan kept a change of clothes, a spare charger, a tooth-brush, and a razor at Louie's house. He didn't need much else. Louie couldn't afford to buy two sets of belongings, and it often felt like she was living out of her car. But Ryan's house had a driveway, so she didn't need to endlessly search for a parking space.

The Defender continued to find the perfect parking spot right outside Louie's house.

Eva was content at both places. Ryan kept a ball and a Frisbee in the back of the Defender, and she knew there were treats in the top right-hand drawer in his kitchen. He also bought a special type of cheddar cheese they both liked. At Ryan's house, Eva was allowed to sleep on a blanket on the sofa, which caused Louie a small amount of internal anxiety. This was accompanied by a lot of sighing, eye rolling, and muttering about consistent parenting.

Eva ignored Louie's grumbles.

Ryan rebutted with, "You let her sleep on the bed, but not the sofa. Where's the consistency?"

"She comes on the bed for an hour, and only in the mornings," Louie retaliated.

"One hour, really?"

"Okay, maybe it's a little longer."

"I rest my case."

One Sunday morning when Ryan was staying over at Louie's house, Louie took Eva for a run and came home to find her kitchen benchtop covered in glassware. Ryan had removed every glass from her cupboard. He had washed and dried each one individually. Apparently, the dishwasher left a smudge.

Holding a wineglass up to the light, he checked for marks. "You might want to use a different brand of detergent. Or clean the filter," he suggested.

She nodded.

He cleaned the filter. It made a difference.

Ryan also insisted on packing the grocery bags at the market. Often shifting Louie out of the way, he would repack the bags like a game of Tetris. Louie became very familiar with the phrase, "No, that's not happening." Whenever he uttered these words, she stepped aside and left him to it.

Their weekend routine included breakfast at Henri's café. Many of the staff at SLD Projects were also frequent visitors. Louie attended office drinks at The Rocks every second week. Memorable cocktail themes included: An Evening in Paris where Freddie served overly sweet old-fashions; Island Holiday, which was quickly renamed Under the Sea—due to the rain—the featured drink was a pineapple piña colada; and an unforgettable James Bond night, where the drink selection included a Cherry Ripe martini, a Snickers martini, and a Bounty bar martini. Louie and Ryan skipped their exercise routines the following morning, blaming their lethargy on their excessive sugar intake from the previous evening.

On Sunday afternoon, after Ryan had washed and vacuumed the Defender and the Elantra, and after Louie had placed the vegetables in the slow cooker, they would often video-call Kat. After a few weeks, Louie and Kat were talking regularly during the week. Both busy, solitary females, neither had a large circle of like-minded friends, and their phone conversations included Kat's UTI and how Louie could avoid attending any more CrossFit classes with Ryan. Louie learned that Kat had kissed her annoying client. Kat discovered the Chanel suit was original. It was also her size. Sometimes on the phone, Louie and Kat would laugh like girls, which made Ryan smile—he loved their comradery.

Louie found exercising indoors at CrossFit claustrophobic and working out with a group of people intimidating. She liked the running machine, but she was happy to never pick up a weight again. She ran twice a day and figured that was all the exercise one woman ever needed. But she never wanted Ryan to stop training. For someone who spent long hours sitting at his desk, he was in great shape. Toned and finely muscled, his body was marvellous territory for her to explore. His biceps were round and firm, and his abs were taut. She admired his tight arse and the definition lines in his thighs. She loved resting her head on his broad chest and snuggling into his wide shoulders. Excellent stamina was also a direct outcome of his training sessions. She hoped he never stopped going to CrossFit.

Ryan bought Louie an excellent raincoat with four pockets on the outside—two were large enough to hold tennis balls—and two pockets on the inside, one of which was a secret pocket, which was where she kept her special stone.

Louie bought Ryan a pair of fluffy handcuffs because she thought he might like to tie her up, but if not, she would be very happy to tie him up. She was right the first time. Ryan was more than happy to tie her up, but he didn't want to entertain the idea of her tying him up. That made no sense to him. He bought her a new athletic strap for her injured hamstring, which continued to play havoc with her running routine, and a pair of black knee-high compression socks to keep her calf muscles warm on winter runs. The first time she wore the socks, he hauled her back inside the house. He couldn't deny it was a fuckable look on her.

At the outdoor store, Ryan also bought a beanie for Louie because she had complained about her ears getting cold when she ran. When she first wore it, he'd thought she looked hilarious. He had to bite his tongue to stop himself from laughing. But he told her she looked cute and encouraged her to wear the hat with her knee-high compression socks. The beanie might deter any possible suitors lurking in the park.

Secretly, he also purchased a second pair of sunglasses and a spare charger for her computer—saying it was a spare from work. Both items reduced the need for her to travel back and forth between their houses when she forgot something. He also kept a loaf of gluten-free bread in the freezer.

Ryan continued to give Louie flowers. Discovering her favourite colour was orange, she received an orange bouquet, and again, every flower was a different variety. One evening, he arrived with a single long-stemmed sunflower. He said it reminded him of Van Gogh, and that made him think of her. Two days later, he appeared with a bunch of fourteen sunflowers. Later that night, Louie kissed him in fifteen different places. There were two versions of the famous sunflower painting, one with fourteen flowers and another with fifteen.

In the background of their busy lives, Louie worked on her thesis. Instead of giving herself the whole weekend to study, she slotted in extra morning and evening times, so she could spend the weekends with Ryan. Some nights she fell asleep at her desk.

On weekdays, after arriving home from the museum or the university, she slept on the sofa for an hour, and then she took Eva for an evening run. The exercise and the outing were invigorating, and when she returned home, she would open her laptop, sit at her desk, and study. But the work was fitful and only marginally productive. Still, she crossed the hours off her study plan.

One morning, Louie jumped out of bed holding her laptop. Dodging Ryan, who was headed her way with mugs of coffee, she stammered, "Oh, no, no. Out the way, out the way, flat battery, flat battery." She scrambled toward the charger in the sitting room.

Ryan followed her into the sitting room and handed her a mug. "You just unplugged it." He sipped his coffee.

"Battery might be dead."

"We have spares at the office."

"Will they fit?"

"No idea. I'll get Freddie to email you."

A week later, on a blisteringly cold and rainy Friday evening, the cocktail theme at SLD was a cosy speakeasy, and the drink of choice was a bee's knees—gin, honey, and lemon. The cocktail appealed to Freddie's sweet tooth, but he selected it because everyone in the office had either a cold or the sniffles—which he found extremely annoying. When staff members had a cold, they stayed home, but with sniffles, they came to work, and then they sniffled—all day.

Freddie thought the medicinal effects of the cocktail ingredients might help ward off influenza A, which was scouring workplaces throughout the city—if it wasn't one dreadful virus, it was another.

At 6:00 p.m., Louie arrived with her laptop. Ryan met her at the door. He kissed her cheek, and as they walked inside, he took her hand. The thirty staff members were still at their desks, all diligently working through the backlog of projects. But they glanced up and smiled and waved at Louie. Sophie blew her a kiss from the far side of the room.

The office was an open-plan design. Concrete floors, exposed brick walls, and large, black-framed windows. It was a collaborative workspace, with rows of communal timber desks, which were stacked with folders, architectural drawings, and samples of tiles and textile fabrics. It looked chaotic. At either end of the space were two private conference rooms with glass partitions.

After dropping Louie's laptop at reception, Ryan shuffled her into a conference room. His laptop was set up on the boardroom table, and he was finishing an email. He told Louie it wouldn't take long. She didn't mind. She liked loitering in the office.

The far wall of the room held the scale models of houses the company had built, and Louie noted several new additions to the shelves.

Freddie entered holding a bee's knees cocktail in each hand. He passed one to Louie, kissed her cheek and placed the other drink on the table next to Ryan.

"Why are all the models white?" Louie asked. "Wouldn't they look better in colour?"

"Some architectural practices like their models to be *white* . . . or *white*." Freddie arched an eyebrow toward Ryan.

"Oh, I see. And this is one of *those* practices." She grinned and sipped her bee's knees.

Freddie nodded. "It's *tradition*."

"It's all about the form, and only the form," Ryan said without taking his eyes off his computer. "Also, competitions only accept white models, so we don't have to remake them, and it's cheaper."

"Really?" Freddie said.

"Yes." Ryan looked up. "Really."

"I never knew." Freddie turned to Louie. "Let's have a look at your machine."

"I have a machine?"

"Your laptop. I've fitted the new battery, but you need to start it up."

Carrying her drink, Louie followed Freddie to the reception. She opened her laptop, started it up, and entered her password.

"Did you have to order the battery?" she asked.

"I did."

The laptop came to life—files exactly where they should be.

"Thank you. I appreciate it." She lowered her voice. "Do I . . . do I need to pay because that's fine? Just tell me how much."

Freddie smiled. "It's on the house. Now, would it be okay if I took a little peek at your time-resourcing document?"

"I can't believe he told you about that. Is nothing sacred?"

"He tells me *everything*," Freddie said, sitting down at the reception desk and pulling out a spare chair for Louie.

Louie took a seat. "Hopefully not *everything*." She opened the spreadsheet and turned the screen to show Freddie.

"No, not everything. But he is my bestie, so it's my job to look out for him." Freddie scanned the spreadsheet.

"You make a great bestie. He's lucky to have you."

Freddie smiled. "Thank you." He turned back to the open document. "This is perfect. Do all the formulas work?"

"Yes. And you can just copy and paste to a new column." Louie glanced at the staff members sitting behind them. "Don't you already have some sort of resourcing system? How do you manage all these people?"

"We do, but it's confusing. It's linked to our WIPs. Don't tell anyone, but we fiddle with the work in progress, so it's not always accurate." He pointed at Louie's laptop screen. "This is visual, and it's colour-coded. I give everyone a colour and every project an acronym. With a glance, I'll know what everyone's working on or supposed to be working on."

"You're a visual learner, like me. You want me to send this to you?"

"I'd love for you to send it to me. If you don't mind." He cast his gaze over the spreadsheet, scrutinising the categories. "Funny, I don't see Ryan's name on your sheet."

Louie stared at the screen. "That's because we're taking things slow, at least that was the plan."

"And how's that working out?"

"It's not." She shook her head. "But we can't help it—it's official, we're in love."

"I heard—congratulations."

"Thank you." Louie smiled. "Now, I'm just trying to keep all of this"—she moved her hand in a circle over her screen —"from not turning to complete shit. So far, it's going okay . . . I think." She studied the document and frowned. "I need to update this." A shiver ran through her, and her hands began to shake.

Freddie shot her a concerned glance. "Are you okay?"

"I'm . . . I'm a bit behind." Her eyes flicked back and forth across the spreadsheet.

20

NO STICKS

By MID-JULY, Louie had finished checking the references for her thesis—all three hundred and twenty of them. She had edited her introduction down to twelve hundred words and she was happy with the way she'd framed her topic, but she was still struggling with the conclusion. What was the outcome of her research? She couldn't put her finger on the answer, or phrase it clearly and succinctly. She told herself that once the body of the work was complete, the conclusion would fall into place. A handful of chapters were also finished; the remaining were underway. Slowly, she was pulling the draft version of her work into shape, nibbling away at the task. Ideally, she needed a few weeks of uninterrupted time to tackle the remaining chapters, but she didn't have weeks. She had three-hour intervals at the beginning and the end of each workday. The final submission was due in four weeks.

Early Saturday morning in the first week of August, Louie updated her time management spreadsheet. The amount of work still required to finish was substantial. The final submission was due in two weeks. The date was not a surprise, but the workload was. For the last five months, she hadn't followed her time management plan. She had followed her heart.

Slowly, it dawned on her that she simply didn't have enough time to finish. The realisation was like a ticking time bomb, and suddenly, it exploded inside her. She was going to miss her deadline. Nine and a half years had passed, and she hadn't finished.

Sitting at her desk, she froze. Her eyes were fixed on her screen, her hands were paused over the keyboard, and she couldn't move. Another deadline had passed. The world stopped, and the room became unnervingly quiet. She had failed, again. How could she be so stupid?

She couldn't see a way to pull it together because it was impossible to finish in two weeks.

A tear rolled down her cheek and fell onto the keyboard.

She began to cry.

Half-asleep, wearing only his boxer briefs, Ryan wandered into the sitting room. He rested his hands on her shoulders and kissed the side of her face. "What's wrong?"

"I've left it too late." She wiped the tears from her cheeks. "It's due in two weeks, and I can't finish."

"Shit!" He scratched the side of his head. "I had no idea you were this close."

"I got . . . distracted."

"Okay, for the one-hundredth time—can I help?"

She shook her head.

"I could read something. Edit something."

Again, she shook her head.

He sighed and placed his hands on his hips. "Have you . . . have you written . . . *much*?"

"Have I written *much*?" she snapped. "You want to know how *much* I've written?"

He nodded. "Do you have a completed draft? I know you've been working on the references, and the introduction is done, but do you have an overall outline of what . . ."

Louie pushed her chair back. From the sideboard in the foyer, she retrieved a box containing a stack of A4 pages— over six hundred pages. The top page contained Louie's thesis statement.

She dropped the box on the kitchen table. It landed with a *thud*, which split the air.

Ryan took a step back.

Eva slinked out of the room and took shelter under the coffee table in the living room.

"I have three hundred and thirty-two thousand words," Louie barked. "That's how much I've written. That's the length of my draft."

"You've written . . . three hundred and thirty-two thousand words?" he stammered, surprised.

She nodded.

"I thought you were struggling to flesh out your ideas."

"Obviously, not."

"You only need eighty thousand words," he reminded her.

"I've been doing this for nine fucking years. I know how many words I need."

"I don't understand." He rubbed his forehead.

She stared at the floor. "I couldn't stop writing. I had so much to say, and once I started, I couldn't stop . . ." Her voice trailed.

"I see," he said, his eyes fixed on her face.

"My failure is not due to apathy. It's . . . it's a failure of excess. I have too much passion for the topic, I guess."

"I didn't say that—"

She held up her hand. "To be clear, this is the edited version. I wrote more, a lot more."

"Okay. I have an idea," he said. "You still have two weeks. We break this up into sections." He tapped the box. "Then, we tackle each section bit by bit. I can read one hundred and fifty thousand words in a week—if I have to. I can do that. Freddie can help."

Louie shook her head.

"Why won't you let me help you?"

"I don't know." She sighed and covered her face with her hands.

Ryan grabbed her shoulders.

She flinched.

"Honey, I have to ask this. Do you think you're self-sabotaging? Are you scared of success?"

She glared at him. "No. It's the exact opposite. I want to succeed." Her voice cracked. "You've no idea how much I want to achieve something. Something I can be proud of." She ran her hands through her hair. "I need to get out of here. I might go for a run. Alone. Maybe you should go."

Louie didn't run. She walked across the park to her local café and ordered a coffee. As she waited in the crowd, she wondered what the other patrons made of her. Did they see how hopeless she was, how badly she had failed? Did they know how humiliated she felt? She had spent three-quarters of her life in academia, a third of her life studying the one topic, and she had nothing, absolutely nothing to show for it. And it wasn't over. That was the worst part. It wasn't over because she hadn't finished.

A carved-out hollow space formed inside her chest. Inside, she was a shell, an empty vessel. *Where were all the words?* she thought. All the ideas and theories she had worked so hard to bring to life. Where was the light?

After her coffee arrived, she walked the long way home.

Filled with an acute sense of irony—love at what cost— she saw how her predicament was almost funny. She'd been so happy spending her time with Ryan. Naively she expected everything else to fall into place. And it hadn't. This was a soul-destroying realisation. Now, she would have to ask for another extension. She almost wanted her adviser to refuse, then she could punish herself for her stupidity because that was what she deserved.

Her thesis was absurd, academia was absurd, the Impressionists were stupid idiots, and as for light—she hated it. Darkness was her ally. Her balancing act had failed. She'd taken her eye off the ball. Now, all she wanted to do was crawl into her shell and hide from the world.

Finding a bench in the park, she sat down and stared at the line of Norfolk pines that bordered the fence line. She stayed on the seat, staring at the trees, watching the sun filter through the branches as it moved higher in the sky.

Two hours later, she walked through her side gate. Ryan had gone.

When Ryan heard Eva bark, he knew the Elantra had pulled into his driveway. He met Louie at the front door, hoping some of her pessimism had worn off on her run. Hoping she had formulated a plan. Another extension was disappointing, but it was not the end of the world. Some people took ten years, and that's just the way it went. He knew she could rally. Besides, she'd written everything she needed to write. It was just an edit—albeit a very large edit. Three hundred and thirty-two thousand was a lot of words to wrangle, to get your head around, to make sense of, but he thought she could do it.

As Louie stepped into the house, Ryan kissed her cheek. They headed through the living areas, past the kitchen to the back deck, and Eva followed.

Louie sat in a shaft of winter sunlight on the rear steps while Ryan made them both a coffee.

Eva sniffed at the edge of the garden, searching for a stick, but the maintenance man had recently cleaned the yard; the outdoor area was exceptionally neat and tidy. Eva had genuine concerns about the situation. What sort of yard had no sticks?

"I'm sorry I freaked out," Louie said, taking her coffee mug from Ryan. "It was a shock. It shouldn't have been, but it was. I'll sort it out."

He sat down on the step beside her and looked at her blotchy face. Her eyes were red and raw—he knew she was on the edge of tears again. It broke his heart to see her so upset. She'd worked so hard; she didn't deserve to feel this way. If he could have taken the burden on himself, he would have.

"It's fine, I'm going to be fine," she mumbled. "It's not like someone died." She rubbed her nose. "But I'm making some changes to get the thing finished."

"Good, that's good," he encouraged.

"I can't be with you and finish my PhD at the same time. It's just not going to happen. It's too much of a distraction."

He frowned. "Wait. Are you breaking up with me?"

"No," she said, alarmed. "I would never do that."

"Okay, good. Because I have another solution."

She sighed. "Ryan . . ."

"Hear me out." He paused. "Why don't you move in with me?"

She bit her lip.

"It would make life so much easier."

"I'm not ready. I like my house, and I like living alone with Eva."

"You could quit one job. I'm in the office ten hours a day. You'll have the place to yourself, undisturbed. You'll get so much done."

"It's a lovely offer. It really is, but if I move in with you, I may never move out."

"Is that so bad?"

Louie stared into her mug. "Let me spell it out for you. You're almost forty. You want a family?"

"We haven't talked about this." He gave her a sideways glance. "But yes, I do. I can see a future for us."

She swallowed. "The problem is, I have nothing to bring to this . . . to us . . . to our future. I'm not successful at anything. I don't own anything. I have no savings and no career, not really. What if I end up married to the house? What if the future you see for us . . . fails? I have nothing to fall back on."

He remained silent.

She glanced around the deck and the manicured garden.

"I want to be in your world. I mean who wouldn't? But I don't want to come empty-handed. And I'm not just talking about the disparity in our careers and good housekeeping. It's me. I feel like such a failure."

"You're just having a bad day." He paused. "Tell me something you like about yourself?"

She shook her head. "I don't want to."

"Anything."

"Um, honestly, I can't think of . . ."

"You're a great teacher."

"Ryan . . ."

"You're so smart. Come on, tell me one thing?" He stared into her face.

"Um . . . I don't know."

Eva wandered over and sat on the deck beside Louie, and she stroked the dog's paw. "I have an excellent dog," she said.

Ryan rallied. "Yes. You're also a great cook. A supportive friend. You can run a four-minute kilometre—actually, you can run ten in a row. You're kind, you recycle, and you don't eat meat—most of the time. You're an amazing photographer. The way you see the world is beautiful."

"This isn't helping."

"You have an excellent dog because you trained her. You have beautiful eyes. You're very, very kissable, not to mention extremely sexy. And I love you."

She sighed. "I love you, too—you know that. But I have a better chance of finishing alone. I just need some time. Maybe four or five weeks." She stared at her shoes.

Suddenly, he understood. "Oh . . ."

Eva slinked away from her spot on the deck and began once more to forage for a stick. She would use this to distract the two humans who were beginning to alarm her. Both were in desperate need of playtime. But the garden was spotless—not a stick insight. It made no sense for a yard not to have at least one stick. Not even a small one.

"Nothing matters more to me," Louie said. "I have to finish. I'll go insane if I don't, and I can't finish with you in my life. I love you so much, but you are my worst distraction. We didn't do the slow thing—we can't do the slow thing. It's all or nothing, so I'm opting for nothing, just for a few weeks—maybe six weeks." Her head felt like it was underwater.

"No, no, no. That's not going to happen. We either do this together or not at all."

"What do you mean . . . no? I would give you a few weeks if you needed it."

"And if I had a crisis, I would let you help. In fact, I would ask you to help."

Louie sighed. "We are worlds apart." She turned to him. "You don't have a choice. I don't want to see you for six weeks—I can't." She turned away. "Hopefully, it won't be that long."

"This is fucking crazy!"

She glared at him. "What did you just say?"

"I wasn't calling you crazy. I would never say that." He ran his hand through his hair. "I'm finding the situation frustrating, that's all. Just to be clear, I'm not doing this. I'm not waiting." He crossed his arms. "We're a team. We do this stuff together. It's all or nothing, and I'm serious."

The moment Eva picked up the rock, she knew it was a bad idea—no one was impressed.

Ryan looked Louie in the eye. He was not going to change his mind.

She stood up. "If you're going to be stubborn, I'm leaving. Goodbye."

"Oh, for god's sake." Ryan rolled his eyes. "Don't walk out."

Louie left.

Eva followed.

21

PRINCESS

On Monday morning, Louie rolled over in bed and stared into the semi-darkness outside her window. Her heart wrung with regret. For the first time in many years, she felt overwhelmed by the world. She didn't know why she had walked out on Ryan. Left him sitting on the back deck in his tidy garden, in his lovely house. But she knew fear gripped her heart—it still did. A deep and powerful familiar feeling that she had not felt with such intensity before.

She was afraid, and she didn't know why. Was it failure? Fear of the future? A career? She didn't know, but she knew she had to face it alone. Unaided and unaccompanied. She would cut herself out of Ryan's life for now because it was the safest thing to do, and she needed to protect herself.

Her thesis was a mass of words, an organised mayhem inside her head, and rationally, she knew what she had to do —buckle down and work twice as hard. But this seemed undoable. Her life, her brain, and her willpower were beginning to unravel. Winding it back into a tight ball would not be easy. Giving up and letting her thesis go seemed like the simpler option. But she couldn't let that happen. It would mean dismissing a decade of her life, and that was an unfathomable scenario.

The day always starts by getting out of bed. She had to get up and get on the boat. That's what she did.

During her morning run with Eva, it poured. The rain on her skin felt like knives falling from the sky. They paused, sheltering under a large tree in the park, waiting for the downpour to ease. Louie squatted beside Eva. She looked the dog in the eye and said, "I'm not sure if you realise, but things aren't going well."

The crying. The moping. The constant sighing and staring out the window. No run on Sunday, and the appallingly slow pace this morning. Eva knew things weren't going well. And where was Ryan?

With her hand, Louie cut a horizontal line through the damp air. "There's life up here," she said, and then she dropped her hand half a metre lower and made another line. "And then there's life down here. I don't want to be down there, ever again. I want to be up here." She moved her hand higher.

Eva nodded. She understood. A happy human was better than a sad human. She looked longingly into Louie's eyes. *Where's Ryan?*

"Ryan and I are having some time apart. Just a few weeks—it won't be long. The time will fly by. It will be like it was before we met Ryan. Just you and me. That wasn't so bad, was it?"

Eva stared deeply into Louie's eyes. *Trust me, two humans are better than one.* She turned her head and checked her tail —it was still there.

On their way home, they circled back past the duck

pond. The wood ducks always lifted Louie's spirits, and it was breeding season. Any day now, there would be baby wood ducks gliding across the water.

They approached the pond. Louie squatted beside Eva and surveyed the area. The wood duck couple were sheltering under a gum tree. The mature ducks peered up into the branches of the tree and made loud duck noises. Louie spied a fluffy bundle of ducklings clumped together in a hollow branch. The babies had hatched. Staying low in the grass, Louie pointed them out to Eva.

From their spot at the base of the tree, the wood duck parents continued their noisy quacking.

"They want the babies to fly," Louie whispered. They stepped back a few paces and crouched in the long grass, not wanting to scare the birds.

Soon, a fluffy baby wood duck threw itself out of the tree.

Louie held her breath, waiting for the bird to spread its wings and take to the air because that's what birds did; they flew. It was instinct. It was in their DNA.

But the duckling didn't open its wings. It fell, hitting a branch and bouncing off on its way to the ground.

"*Oh, my god?*"

Louie hugged Eva around the neck.

Another fluffy duck flung itself from the tree. This one didn't fly either; it missed the branch and fell straight to the ground. Another followed, and then another. Soon all the ducklings threw themselves from the nest and all fell straight to the ground.

"There's something wrong with them," Louie said to Eva. "Maybe it's climate change. Or the constant rain—they just can't take any more wet weather." She could understand that, but this was a severe reaction. None of them were flying. All were falling. Smashing to the ground. It was a mass suicide.

Louie's heart sank. She clutched her chest.

Commanding Eva to stay where she was, Louie crept closer and peered over the long grass, expecting to find a carnage of dead ducklings. Instead, she found the ducklings scurrying around among leaves. They were all alive, unperturbed by the fall.

Louie watched as the last few babies leapt from the tree and hit the ground. They bounced. The ducklings bounced —one, two, three times—then they shook themselves off, got to their feet, and scurried about.

Louie returned to Eva. "Ducklings bounce, who knew?" she whispered.

Eva shook her head; she'd never heard of such a thing.

Back at home, they found Harry the Huntsman had returned and taken up his usual haunt on the wall between the foyer and the bedroom.

"Come on in, snack away," Louie said. Then she opened her computer and stared at the screen.

Over the following days, the sky was in perpetual motion. Clouds constantly shifting and merging. Waves of rain fell at erratic and often inconvenient times: during lunch breaks, school pickups, and peak hour traffic. The short, heavy downpours were often followed by bursts of bright sunshine. Daily life became a standoff between rainstorms and luminous glare.

On the weekend, Louie received a call from Max Cabot. He wanted to discuss the teaching roster for next term. It was not good news; her application for more work had been denied. It was a timetabling issue, Max told her. Professor Fisher, a full-time staff member, needed another two classes to fill his quota of hours, and unfortunately, he would be taking two of Louie's classes. Max was powerless. Enrolments were down. Attempting to steer students into more skill-based courses, the government increased fees for many of the arts degrees hoping to deter enrolment.

Once upon a time, Max told her, an arts degree meant something. It got you somewhere. But in today's market, it doesn't have the same value. Louie asked what in the hell markets had to do with tertiary study. Max replied, "Exactly."

"We'll be okay. I'll get more work at the museum," Louie told Eva. "There are school holiday tours available, and they want someone to take a weekly tour on Glover—about perspective. Boring, but easy," she dismissed. "I can talk about perspective for hours. I wish the same were true of Mr. Glover—the man has no understanding of light. And weekly! What are they thinking?"

Our prime consideration should be food. Anyone for duck?

The following Monday morning, Freddie found Ryan lying on the boardroom table staring at the ceiling.

"What are you doing?" Freddie asked.

"Thinking," Ryan replied.

"It's not about the box gutter detail on the Mosman project, is it?"

"No, it's not. I was thinking about myself." Ryan turned his head toward Freddie, who was standing in the doorway. "Sometimes I can be a bit controlling, I know this. I like to do things my way. I have an office of thirty people to manage, and I was wondering if I transferred my work habits into my relationship with Louie."

Freddie closed the door and walked into the room. "I understand why you don't want to wait for her. Relationships don't split up every time someone has a crisis. There'd be no couples left on the planet."

Ryan sat up and swung his legs over the edge of the table. "A part of me wants to go to her house, pick her up and take her home with me. I can look after us. No problem at all. She can read or study or teach or do whatever she wants."

Freddie smiled.

"But I can't do that, can I?"

"No, I don't think you can," Freddie said. "She wants space, you need to respect that. She has to do her thing, without you."

Ryan lay back down on the table and his gaze returned to the ceiling. Freddie left, gently closing the door behind him. He returned a few minutes later with a cushion, which he tossed at Ryan.

Ryan caught the cushion and slipped it under his head. "Do you have any weed?" Ryan asked. "I need to lay off the red wine."

Freddie considered him. "I do, but it's never really been your drug."

"Thought it might help me sleep."

"I'll see what I can do."

Later, when Ryan dragged himself back to his desk, Sophie slunk across the room and sat opposite him.

"I've been there," she said. "I know how you feel. It's shit. Complete shit. The worst thing in the world." She slumped in her chair and stared at the back wall of the office.

Ryan slumped in his chair and stared in the opposite direction, toward the front desk.

After a while, Sophie got up and said, "Breathe." Then she returned to her desk.

The next day, Sophie brought Ryan a homemade brownie. She clarified it wasn't made by her but by someone at the café around the corner. The sign said homemade, and they looked like trustworthy people—one of them was wearing a badge that said, *I didn't stab anyone today.*

Ryan smiled.

Sophie said the homemade brownie would make no difference to the way he felt—not one bit—but she felt good buying it for him, so that was something.

He appreciated the gesture.

Kat called. When Ryan answered, she told him she had an uneasy feeling and wanted to make sure he was okay. Ryan told her he was not okay. Heartache was debilitating. He couldn't focus. He couldn't work. He couldn't sleep, and he couldn't stop thinking about Louie.

"I thought it was going so well. What happened?" Kat asked.

"She wants me to . . . give her some time."

"Oh, fuck. Ryan, I'm sorry. Did you tell her about Janie Minge?" Kat asked.

"Her name is Jane Minaj, and you know that," Ryan said.

"Okay, maybe I do. But did you tell Louie the Lynx you gave Miss Minge time to sort out her life? Lots of time. Then you lived through relationship hell. The never-ending it's on and then it's off, and then it's on again saga. Did you tell her that?"

"No."

"Why not?"

Silence.

"Ryan, why didn't you tell Louie about Miss Minge?"

"It didn't come up," he said. "Louie left and we haven't talked since, and now she's not answering my calls. She wants to be alone, so she can finish her study."

"You like to be in control, and I get that," Kat continued. "God knows someone has to be, and you're good at it, so it may as well be you. But being honest about your feelings is not a weakness. I think you should tell Louie about Janie."

"I know."

"Being vulnerable is hard. But the more you do it, the easier it gets. And I'll let you in on a secret. I'm kind of . . . almost . . . seeing someone. Sort of."

"Fuck. That's great. That's fantastic. How are you feeling?"

"Nervous. I've told him the truth . . . about everything. You need to tell Louie the truth about Janie Minge. It might give her some perspective."

"Please stop calling her that."

"I'm afraid I can't. Also, we need to address the elephant in the room."

Ryan frowned. "You're also hungover?"

"No. Our birthdays. We're forty next year. We should start planning."

"Okay, but can I turn thirty-nine first? Would that be okay?"

"Only if you have to."

They ended the call.

Ryan thought life without Louie would be like the sky without the sun or the stars without the moon. Being with her was the most natural thing in the world. Right from the start, she was on his team, and he was on hers. She had slipped so easily into his life and into his heart. None of his past relationships were like this. No one had ever made him feel the way she made him feel. He had envisaged a future together, a long and happy future.

He also missed Eva. He hoped she wasn't waiting for him. Expecting him to walk through the side gate two or three nights a week and stay over every second weekend. He wondered how she was coping without him because he was not coping without her. He missed her bright amber eyes, her paw on his calf, and her head on his thigh. He thought about her smile and the intense look that crossed her face when he mentioned the words *Frisbee* or *cheese*. She was the best dog he'd ever met. She was also his friend.

Ryan gave Louie two weeks of alone time, then he called her on the weekend—Saturday morning and again Sunday afternoon. She didn't answer. He sent her a *Let's talk, I'm sure we can work this out* text on Monday. Louie didn't respond. He thought she might have blocked him. Then he rejected the idea. She wouldn't go to that extreme. Would she?

No, she was ignoring him so she could work. Eventually, she would return his calls; he just needed to give her more time. After a few weeks, she'd miss him as much as he was missing her, and then she'd realise they should be together. That was the most important thing—being together—the two of them. Soon, she would be in his arms once again.

Four weeks later, Louie was not in his arms. She was still not answering Ryan's calls or texts. At work, Ryan cornered Freddie in the staff kitchen and said, "Do you think I should call the hospitals? Maybe she had an accident. Some sort of emergency. What do you think?" Anxiously, Ryan pulled at his earlobe. "Should I go to her house, and check if she's okay?"

Freddie took a deep breath. "I'm sure she's fine. She's probably inundated with work. Remember, she's had nine years of this, which is turning into ten. It's a lot to deal with. Wait until six weeks. I know it's hard, but let her do her thing. Besides, you've called her. She should be reaching out to you."

Ryan couldn't believe this was happening.

Freddie added, "Also, cut back on the weed, and stop playing with your ear. It's unnerving."

The six-week deadline came and went. She didn't contact him.

Ryan recalled a quote that Louie had mentioned when they were together on the boat. Something about a fire in everyone's soul that nobody came to warm themselves by. People passing saw only the smoke coming from the chimney and they went on their way. Ryan had seen the smoke. He had knocked on the door, and Louie let him inside. He warmed himself by the fire. He didn't realise there was a curfew.

By mid-October, it had stopped raining. Tara harvested the radishes, leeks, and rainbow chard she had planted two months earlier. She picked a few leaves of rocket and tasted it. Marvellous—peppery and pungent—you didn't get that from store-bought varieties purchased in plastic bags. She decided not to pick it yet; she would leave it right where it was and let it grow wild.

She sowed a new crop of spring seedlings, including lettuce, cucumbers, and peppers. She planted heirloom tomatoes in large pots, which she hoped would bear fruit by Christmas. She brought Louie an assortment of Tupperware containers filled with vegetarian food and a chicken cacciatore, which Louie thought was delicious and should be added to the round of fortnightly dinners.

One morning while lying on the grass in the park, Louie took a picture of the sky behind a patch of yellow flowers. It was so beautiful it made her smile, and she hadn't smiled in many weeks. She sent the photo to Ryan.

A row of oscillating dots appeared on her phone. A moment later, they vanished.

Louie turned to Eva who was lying beside her. "It feels like there's sand slipping through my hands."

Maddening, Eva agreed.

Two weeks later, after a sluggish morning run around Sydney Park, Louie, Lila, and Eva, gathered in Louie's kitchen for tea and yesterday's croissants, which were today's almond croissants.

"Does the house smell like a wet dog?" Louie asked.

Lila sniffed the air. "Yes."

They looked at Eva, and the dog dropped her head, confirming she was a very wet dog.

"Did you get the obesity commercial?" Louie asked, filling the kettle.

"No. But it's a good thing I didn't. They were going to superimpose someone's fat belly on my shoulders and make the obese person's stomach look like a face—no one would have recognised me anyway."

"That makes no sense."

"I didn't do an arts degree and then three years of acting for that."

Lila collected the mugs. Louie poured the tea, and they sat down at the kitchen table with their croissants. Eva busied herself, staring at a lizard in the corner of the room.

"Does ending your relationship with Ryan make sense?" Lila asked.

Louie paused. "I didn't end it. It's not over."

"You haven't seen him in two months. He never agreed to wait. I'm calling it. It's over."

"I just need a few more weeks. It's the most important thing in my life."

"Honestly, I'm sick of hearing about your PhD. We all are."

"I know."

"Maybe you should let it go."

"What?"

"Not every dream is going to come true. Do you think Henri wants to run a café? He studied to be a lighting designer. He had to make a difficult choice to give that up."

"I know."

"I go for five auditions every week. Sometimes I get a call back. Sometimes I get down to the last two. Most of the time I get nothing. Essentially, I've chosen a career in rejection, and that's not easy."

Louie stared at the tabletop.

"Sometimes you need to pivot. This might be one of those times." Noticing Eva standing in the corner staring at a spot where the wall meets the floor, Lila asked if the dog was okay.

"I'm hoping it's a lizard and she's not considering a leap

from the gap," Louie said. "She misses Ryan. I think she might be depressed. She keeps looking at her tail."

"Eva, sweety, come here," Lila called.

Eva ignored her.

"The dog's ruined," Louie said. "If she's in a mood, she only answers to princess or cheese."

"Cheese," Lila called.

Eva scooted over to Lila, sat next to her, and looked longingly into Lila's eyes—she was expecting a slice of cheddar cheese.

A terrible scent wafted through the air. Louie glared at Eva. "Was that you?"

It was, Eva confirmed.

"That'll be the hot dog you ate in the park this morning. It's playing havoc with your digestion."

It is, and it will happen again.

Later, Tara called Louie, and they discussed the need for winter colour in the garden. Flowering pansies, violas, and cyclamen, Tara suggested. The topic was short and one-sided, so they moved on and discussed the mining company that had blown up a sacred indigenous site. This led to a bleak discussion about the environment and ocean warming.

After a short pause, Louie asked, "Is there a point in life when you know what you should be doing? When you finally understand who you are?"

"Yes. I think there is," Tara replied.

Another pause followed.

"Do you want to elaborate?" Louie asked.

"Not right now because I have news. How are you feeling?"

"Fine, thank you."

"Good. You must always do what you feel is right, you know that, don't you?"

"I do."

"Good, because I'm taking my own advice."

"About winter colour?"

"No—"

"You're going to plant a horn filled with manure in my garden?"

"It's the wrong time of year for the horn. My own advice about painting."

"I'm not following."

"It's not working—my art. I thought about painting landscapes, but they're not me, and I'm never going to paint floral displays. I want to paint people, so I'm going on the road. I've decided to rent out my apartment for a year and travel—probably to the outback. Talk to people, find out their stories. Take a load of photos, paint a few portraits, and maybe open an exhibition the following year."

Louie smiled. "That's the best idea I've heard in my entire life."

"Well, you're the best daughter in the world."

After eight weeks, Ryan still had not heard from Louie. He thought she was an idiot. Beautiful and sweet-natured, but still an idiot. Honestly, who did this? How could she let go of what they had? Six months wasn't a long time to be with someone, but they fit together like two pieces of a puzzle, and that didn't come along very often.

It was over. He drew a line and said no more. He couldn't continue wondering about their future. Wondering if she'd finished her thesis, wondering if he would ever see her again. If he'd known what she was like, he would never have started something with her in the first place.

The following morning, Louie sent Ryan another photo —raindrops on a leaf.

He ignored it.

22
THE OPERA

At six on Sunday evening, Louie slid into the ticket booth at the Opera House foyer. Lila had a migraine, and Louie had agreed to cover her shift. (Lila had confirmed that Louie was the last person she had called. The situation was desperate, they were shorthanded, and half the staff had called in sick with influenza A, including her supervisor.)

Louie had worked at the Opera House a few years ago, so she knew the ticketing procedure and the computer system. She had Lila's staff card, and her identity badge—shaped like the sails of the Opera House—was pinned to Louie's shirt. The venue was celebrating its fiftieth birthday, and the program was packed with gala events and every show was sold out.

She entered the ticket booth, which smelled like disinfectant, and she wondered if the smell masked something worse. Opening the computer, she signed in as Lila, then downloaded and printed hard copies of the requested tickets for the evening's events. There were three shows, with staggered start times, including the first performance in the newly renovated opera hall, which was a black-tie event.

The tickets were printed in alphabetical order, and Louie filed them into boxes. She switched the lights on and opened the security screen.

A queue quickly formed. The first couple was elderly, in their mid-eighties. He wore a black suit with a red bow tie, and his wife wore a floor-length black gown with a red wrap. They were an adorable couple, and Louie hoped one of them was wearing red underwear, or at least red socks.

Their surname was Webster, and Louie checked the ticket boxes but found no tickets for the Websters. Her heart sank—she knew what came next.

"Perhaps they are under another name?" Louie asked, knowing they were not.

The couple shook their heads; they had been married for fifty-five years.

After undertaking a search, Louie confirmed what she already knew—the Websters had booked the matinee, which had finished two hours ago. A round of self-fluctuation ensued, and Mrs. Webster said she must be losing her mind. She apologised to Louie, to her husband, and to the people behind them in the queue. Her embarrassment was plastered across her face, and it tugged at Louie's heart to see the woman so upset. Frantically, she searched the floor plan for empty seats for the next performance.

A man wearing a tartan bow tie stepped out of the queue and glared at Louie. "Is there someone else serving?" he snapped.

Louie tucked a loose strand of hair behind her ear. "No, there is just me."

"If there's a problem, perhaps they should get to the back of the queue," the man quipped.

"There's no problem." Louie smiled.

The man glared and moved back into the queue.

An attractive blonde woman wearing an ice-blue gown was standing behind the Websters, and she had taken a keen interest in the unfortunate ticketing debacle. Slipping to the front, she placed a gentle hand on Mrs. Webster's arm. "It's an easy mistake to make," the woman consoled. "It happened to me last week, and I was booking international flights—can you imagine?"

The Websters chuckled, reassured.

Louie continued her search for seats, but she was having no luck, the performance was sold out. The only seats she could find were in the box, but the price difference was considerable.

"Perhaps . . . a box?" Louie stammered.

Alarmed, the Websters shook their heads.

The woman in the blue dress covertly slipped her credit card across the counter and made eye contact with Louie. "It's on me," she whispered.

Louie took the card and booked two tickets in the box. The Websters showered Louie with gratitude and promptly departed for their upgraded seats.

The woman in the ice-blue gown once again stepped up to the counter. Louie gave her outfit an appraising glance— the dress was floor-length, tapered at the waist, with shoe-string straps, and she wore delicate pearl drop earrings.

"You look like a fairy godmother," Louie said. "I love your dress."

"Thank you." The woman smiled. "You don't think the colour's a bit Queen Mother circa 1980s?"

"Not at all." Louie shook her head. "It's more like Grace Kelly in the 1950s. Like in *To Catch a Thief* or that murder thing."

"Oh, I love that!" The woman grinned.

"Can I have your name?" Louie asked.

"It's under McDermott, probably under Mr. and Mrs." The woman rolled her eyes, and added, "Knowing this place."

Louie's heart contracted.

There must be millions of McDermotts in the world. The name was a coincidence. She took a breath and focused on her task.

"I'm sure we're not that archaic." Louie plucked two tickets from her box. The name printed across the bottom was Mrs. and Mr. Ryan McDermott. Slowly, she lifted her eyes to the woman.

"I told you—Mr. and Mrs."

Louie paused.

Ryan sidled up to the blonde woman and asked, "Red or white?"

"Prosecco," she replied.

Ryan turned, his gaze resting on Louie's face. "Oh, god," he said.

"Hello," Louie said, her heart racing. A knot tightened in her stomach. She was surprised to see him.

Ryan nodded.

He wore a dark suit and tie—the perfect accompaniment to the tall blonde in the blue gown. Louie wondered if he was always meant to be with a tall blonde, because they looked like the perfect couple.

Louie was dressed in her opera house uniform, taupe pants, and black shirt one size too large. Separated by the ticket booth counter—less than a meter of laminate—two people could not have been further apart—socially or economically.

"How, how have you been?" Louie asked, barely able to get the words out of her mouth.

"I've . . . I've been good." Ryan stared at her, then he remembered the woman standing next to him. "Louie, this is Charlotte."

Louie turned toward Charlotte, her heart aching. "Charlotte, that's a lovely name," she said.

"Thank you." Charlotte smiled.

Louie took a deep breath. It looked to all the world like Ryan was with this woman. Like they were here together. The two of them. On a date. But there must be some mistake. How could he be on a date—with someone else? Glassy eyed, she bit her lip. She didn't understand what was going on. Why was Ryan here with Charlotte?

"Sorry. I didn't expect to see you," Ryan said.

Louie couldn't look at him. She stared at the counter.

"Lila's not well. I'm a stand-in," she mumbled.

"Oh, is she—"

"She's fine," Louie whispered, unable to raise her voice.

The man wearing a tartan bow tie tapped Charlotte on the shoulder. "I'm kind of in a rush."

"We won't be much longer," Charlotte said brightly. She appeared interested but not concerned about the interaction between Louie and Ryan.

"And . . . how are you?" Ryan asked.

Louie didn't answer. Inside she was dying.

The man wearing a tartan bow tie tapped Charlotte on the shoulder again. "How much longer?" he said.

Charlotte glared at him. "There's plenty of time. The

show doesn't start for forty minutes. Wait your turn. It's called a queue for a reason," she snapped.

"It seems to be taking longer than it should," the man lamented. "It's not the time or the place for a catch-up, you know."

"Jeez, some people," Charlotte muttered.

As Louie passed over their tickets, her hand trembled. She willed it to stop, but concentrating on the tremor made it worse.

Ryan couldn't take his eyes off her, and his hand moved toward hers.

She shook her head. "Please don't." She looked past him and gestured to the man in the tartan bow tie. "Next."

The man stepped forward, nudging Ryan out of the way.

"Sorry to keep you waiting," Louie said. "It's a busy time."

After her shift was over, Louie changed her clothes. She left the Opera House by the side door and walked across the promenade toward the water and stopped by the railing. Behind her, the illuminated sails of the building cast a radiant glow over the surrounding area.

It was a beautiful evening with just the hint of a gentle breeze. The sun had set behind the bridge hours ago, but a rising moon lit the promenade. The water in the harbour was glassy and still, but boats and ferries flitted back and forth, carrying the early rises home, and returning to the city with the night owls. The towering arch of the Harbour Bridge hovered in the distance.

She looked up at the clear, star-filled sky, wishing it would rain. The cold, wet weather had been a constant companion to her relationship with Ryan, and right now, she wanted it back. Closing her eyes, she breathed in the night air. She told herself not to cry. She had cried enough already.

Then, glancing to her left, she saw him leaning on the railing about ten metres away. He was watching her. His position now revealed, he walked toward her.

"I didn't think you liked opera?" she said.

"I don't."

"Then why . . . oh . . . she likes opera."

Ryan smelt faintly of red wine.

Louie turned away and stared at the water. "I can't believe you went on a date." The pain in her heart now filled her entire chest. Her brain was foggy, and she couldn't get her breath. "I suppose you thought . . ." Her voice trailed off. She swallowed. "I don't know what you thought. Why were you on a date?"

"I'm trying to move on."

"I see." She stared at the harbour for a moment. Then she turned back to Ryan. "She seems very nice, and she has a . . . a lovely name. But I thought we . . ." Her voice trailed off.

"It's been months. What did you expect me to do—wait forever?"

"No, of course not." She shook her head. "I guess I lost track of the time."

He reached for her hand.

She slapped his arm away. "Go away. You're breaking my heart."

"Really? I'm breaking your heart. For the record, I didn't leave, remember? You're the one who stood up and walked out. I'm the one who wanted to be with you, the one who said we should work it out together. The one who sent you all the texts and calls, which you never answered. What the fuck did you think would happen?"

"You make me so angry." She narrowed her eyes. "I couldn't answer them because I had to work—you knew that. Why haven't you replied to my pictures?"

"Because they confused me. Out of the blue, pictures of the light. What the fuck does that mean?" He ran his hand through his hair. "Fuck. This was a bad idea." He looked up at the night sky. "Tell me one thing—have you finished the damn thing?"

Her lips quivered. "Not yet."

Their eyes met, and his gaze softened.

She looked at her hands. "I'm sorry, I've really stuffed this up—made a huge mess of it. I'm . . . I'm just realising this now." She paused, then added, "I mean us, not the thesis—although I think I might have stuffed that up, too."

He stared at her.

She tried her hardest not to cry, but tears were leaking from her eyes, rolling down her cheeks.

"I'm going to go." She wiped her face with the back of her hand. "Eva is waiting for me." She looked straight at him. "I can't say it was good seeing you because it wasn't. It was awful." She rubbed her nose. "And I don't want to see you ever again."

Unconditional love, Louie thought. *How do you find that in a human?*

Later that night, Ryan dropped onto the sofa in his living room. He kicked off his shoes and undid his tie. His conversation with Louie could not have gone any worse. Did she really think they were still together? And why did she have to mention the dog? He was just getting used to not having Eva in his life. God, the encounter was awful.

He shook his head. Why did he have to say, "What the fuck does that mean?" about her pictures of the light. He knew exactly what that meant to her . . . and to them. It was a mean thing to say. He went on a date with someone else, then he said a terrible thing to Louie. He didn't know why he'd done either of those things. Maybe he needed to see a therapist.

After pulling a bottle of Penfolds off the wine rack, he opened it and poured himself a glass. He needed to talk to someone, but it was late, almost midnight. Collecting his phone, he called the only person he was allowed to call at this time—Kat Girl.

"Why are you awake at this hour?" Ryan asked when Kat answered his call.

"Can't sleep. Too much stuff going through my head. Why are you awake?"

"Because I made a monumental fuck up. I was on a date, and I ran into Louie."

"Oh, god. Who were you on a date with?" Kat stifled a yawn.

"My favourite client's niece."

"The Haigs. I've always liked them, and not just because they're ridiculously rich. Why were you on a date with their niece?"

"She put me on the spot. We were on their boat, halfway through a work lunch with Freddie and Sophie, and she asked me out. In front of everyone. Hard to say no."

Ryan sipped his wine, recalling Freddie's alarmed expression when Charlotte had suggested they go to the opera. When he glanced across the table at Sophie, she had mouthed the word *no* while slowly shaking her head. The moment was surreal, like he was in a dream. Still, Ryan had agreed. Charlotte was attractive, and she seemed pleasant. A date might be a good distraction.

"You hate opera. What are you drinking?"

"Red. I hate opera even more now."

"Wait a moment, I'm pouring myself a glass of wine."

A short silence.

"Okay, from the beginning, tell me what happened," Kat said.

Ryan recalled the details of his meeting with Louie at the ticket booth and their conversation at the edge of the harbour.

Another short silence followed.

"You have two choices," Kat said. "Either kill yourselves or each other—I can't take it anymore. Sort it out. It's not that hard. Tell her about Jane?" Kat yawned, again. She sounded weary.

"It's not that simple. I've realised something else. When Louie said goodbye and walked out, it reminded me of Dad leaving."

"Oh, god, Ryan."

He could hear Kat shuffling in the background. "Are you pacing across your newly polished floors with a glass of red wine?"

"I won't spill a drop. I'm an excellent pacer—it's my default position for thinking. Listen, Dad leaving was awful —not as bad as him dying, but still awful. I don't want to talk about that now, but sometimes I think that's why you feel the need to control everything in your life, and, spoiler alert, you can't."

"I know."

"How did she look?"

"She looked lost." Ryan paused. "Could you put your wine down while you do the backward and forward thing? It's making me anxious." He rubbed his forehead.

"Okay. I'm sitting down now. Are you going to fix this— is that what you want?"

"I don't know."

Kat sighed. "I'm sorry this is so shit for you. I really am." Her voice cracked.

He hesitated. "Kat Girl, are you okay?

"No, not really. The relationship thing didn't work out for me either."

"Oh, god, I'm so sorry. You want to talk about it?"

"Not now."

"Okay, I love you," Ryan said.

He ended the call.

23
A BALL CHAIR

HENRI GLANCED AT LILA, she was sitting in the passenger seat of his car. "I'll be back in ten minutes," he said. After opening the door, he sprinted down the road toward the local bottle shop.

They were parked in Ryan's driveway. Lila climbed out, headed toward the house, and knocked on the front door.

Ryan greeted her. "Hey, come in. I'll be one minute," he said and disappeared upstairs.

Lila entered and stood in the hallway. "Henri came with me," she called. "He's just gone to get a bottle of wine— hope that's okay. It was a last-minute decision. We weren't sure if you had any." She looked around the room—leather sofa, timber floors, stone tables, nothing out of place. "But we both need a drink," she mumbled. She wandered into the living room and sat on the edge of the sofa. "He won't be long."

Spying a wine rack in the corner, she stood and headed toward it. She pulled out a bottle of red wine and studied the Penfolds label.

Ryan entered holding a bag of Louie's belongings.

"My parents drink this wine. Is it nice?" Lila asked.

"I like it." Ryan offered her the bag.

"Just leave it at the front door. We'll get it on the way out." Lila replaced the bottle.

Ryan took the bag to the front door, just as Henri, panting and carrying a bottle of red wine, a tub of dip, and a bag of sea salt chips, entered.

Ryan was confused about the plan—they were there to collect Louie's belonging, he hadn't realised this was a social occasion.

Henri squeezed past Ryan. "Why don't you sit down and relax? I'll manage."

Ryan sat on the sofa opposite Lila. He noticed something vaguely familiar about her. She wore jeans with a T-shirt and an oversized bomber jacket with the sleeves rolled up. It was the jacket—it was his. Louie had used it to cover Lila when she broke her nose during *Medea*. She had kept it. It was too big for her, but she looked cute—it suited her.

Lila tilted her head to one side and looked at Ryan. "So, how are you doing?"

"Terrible."

Lila nodded. "Who can stop grief's avalanche once it starts to roll."

"Shakespeare?"

"*Medea*."

"Of course. Did you get the hand sanitiser commercial?"

"Yes! I can't believe it! They loved my hands." She held out her hands for Ryan to inspect.

"Charming," he confirmed.

"I know." Lila stared at her hands. "Print, TV, and social media. I'm buying a secondhand car."

"Good for you."

In the kitchen, they heard Henri making himself at home as he opened cupboards and searched for glasses and bowls. "Are you happy with this brand of wine fridge?" he called.

"Very," Ryan replied.

"My parents have the exact same one—although it doesn't hold as much wine as yours. They must have the mini version."

Henri entered the living area and placed the snacks and glasses on the coffee table. He poured the wine, and the three of them settled into their seats. "This is nice," Henri said, holding up his wineglass. "Cheers."

Lila and Ryan raised their glasses and sipped their wine.

Ryan rubbed his lips together—it was good. He was pleasantly surprised.

"You know she loves you," Lila blurted.

"She just got scared," Henri said. "She has a strong fight and flight instinct. When that happens, she doesn't handle life very well."

"I know," Ryan said.

"It's a self-esteem issue—which makes no sense because she's so smart," Henri continued. "You know about the last time—when this happened before? Her anxiety got so bad she had to take time off from life."

"Yes. She told me."

"I guess you also know about her ex," Henri said.

Ryan nodded. "Yes."

"He was such a dick," Lila said.

Henri grabbed the wine bottle and topped up their glasses.

"He was an idiot—" Lila began.

"You already said that," Henri interrupted.

"I said he was a dick, but I guess it's the same thing. He was an idiot dick."

"Their relationship was already on the rocks, but when she had the meltdown, he walked out. She never heard from him again. Not one call or text. That was it," Henri said.

"That's not entirely true," Lila said. "He came and got his things."

"Oh yeah, that's right, he did," Henri agreed.

"And they had dinner, remember the dinner?" Lila said. "At that fancy place—Sorento? There was nothing on the menu she could eat."

Henri shook his head. "I don't recall. Anyway, what we're trying to say is she *almost* had no contact with him. She *almost* never heard from him again."

"I see." Ryan rubbed his temple.

"We stalked his social media," Lila said. "He was seeing someone else while he was also seeing Louie."

"You don't know that for sure," Henri said.

"But it's possible," Lila said. "More than possible."

"Highly probable," Henri agreed. "Anyway, we think Louie leaving you was a form of self-sabotage. She got out because she was scared you might leave her."

"Are you going to leave her?" Lila asked.

Ryan placed his elbows on his knees, leaned forward, and rubbed his eyes. "We're not together. She doesn't want me in her life. What do you expect me to do?"

"Wait for her," Henri said.

"I don't want to wait for her," Ryan said.

"Why not?"

"Because she's never going to finish."

Henri pouted. "That's not fair, she might."

Lila shook her head. "No. Ryan's right. She said the final

edit would take four weeks. Now she says three months, but it could be six months. It could be a year. And where does that leave Ry?"

Ry?

A long pause.

"I guess that leaves Ry on a date," Henri said.

"Not my finest moment," Ryan said.

"Which is why we're here," Henri said. "It tipped her over the edge."

"I get it," Ryan said.

Lila and Henri finished their wine.

"Well, I guess that's about it from us," Lila stood up. "Henri has a date, and he doesn't want to be late." She teased.

"You do?" Ryan grinned.

"Yes." Henri cleared his throat. "With Freddie."

Ryan stared at him. "With ... *my* Freddie?"

"Yes. He's been coming to the café. I made him a mocha cookie Frappuccino with extra cream and wafers." Henri tilted his head to the side. "Turns out he was really into it."

"I'm not surprised," Ryan said.

"I might even see you for Friday cocktails at the office." Henri peeled himself off the sofa. "Also, did you hear Louie lost her classes at the university?"

Ryan sighed. "Oh, god."

"But she's got more work at the museum," Henri said.

"That's good," Ryan said. "I've been meaning to ask— how's Eva?"

Lila rubbed her eyebrow. "She's okay, but Louie tore her hamstring. She had to cut back on the running. We're helping out, taking shifts walking Eva." She turned to Henri. "I think I'm drunk. Who's driving?"

"It's my car and I'm driving," Henri said.

Lila and Henri left with their arms around each other.

A few days later, Ryan leaned on the doorframe of Max Cabot's office.

Max looked up, and they made eye contact. He was on the phone, but he gave Ryan a look that said, "Don't go anywhere."

Ryan waited, half inside, half outside the room.

Max cajoled his caller with a series of "Sounds interesting," "Fine by me," and "Why don't you take three, instead of two" remarks. Then he ended the call.

"So, how'd you go? Any major subject changes?" Max asked.

Ryan entered. "No. But I have a few updates. I'll send them through. I enjoyed teaching, but it's not for me. You'll need to find someone else next year." He stood in front of Max's desk, placed his hands on his hips, and looked Max in the eye. "Can you get her classes back?"

Max sighed. "Believe me, I've tried. Given a choice between Louie and George Fisher, who do you think I want teaching first-year art history? And the students want her back more than I do. Her retention levels are the highest in the department. Her feedback scores are exemplary, but it's not about that."

"It's about money."

"That's right. University funding is at an all-time low. Support for the arts is not a priority for the government."

"Has it ever been?"

"Yes, it has. Why don't you sit down and let me tell you a

little story." Max feigned the eloquent voice of a discerning narrator.

Ryan pulled out a chair and sat down. "Will this take long?"

"No. Once upon a time, many decades ago, education was free. Can you believe it—people could learn anything they wanted, and they didn't have to pay a cent." Max raised an eyebrow. "I know what you're thinking."

"I was thinking you might want to speed this up."

"People undertook arts degrees—partly to find out what they wanted to do with their lives but also to discover what they were good at. They did this for the sheer love of learning. Then, suddenly, someone decided that higher education would no longer be free, students would have to pay—a lot of money."

"I get the—"

"I'm not finished. Then, big businesses got involved in the education system, and they decided that students should learn business skills, and it was the universities' job to teach them business skills. Subjects and courses should be rewritten with this in mind."

"That actually makes sense."

"Hear me out. Students used to take photography, not because they wanted to become a photographer, but because they genuinely wanted to learn a skill—a life skill that wasn't related to their job."

"Photography is not a life skill."

"They took Modernism because their Aunt Elsie had a ball chair by Eero Aarnio, and they wanted to know more about these things. Not because it was going to get them a job, but because it made them a more interesting person. A person invested in self-growth."

"Is this a very long way of saying times have changed and there's nothing you can do about it? Because I don't buy it."

"Louie is Filip's niece. Therefore, she's my niece, and nepotism is a delicate subject in academia. I can't be seen to favour her."

"So, you do the opposite, is that what you're saying?"

"I do everything I can, and I'm doing my best to sort it out."

Ryan ran his hand through his hair. "But—"

"You care, I know. We all care, and we've been doing it longer than you have." He paused. "We have a plan. It will work itself out. Trust me on this."

Ryan eased his way out of the chair. "I hope so." He headed toward the door, then turned and asked, "Do you have a ball chair by Eero Aarnio?"

"My parents had one. White moulded fibreglass with a red interior." Max's eyes lit up. "As a kid, I used to sit inside and spin it around and around. I loved that chair."

"Those were the days." Ryan closed the door behind him.

24

BOUNCE

LOUIE LAY on the floor in her sitting room with Eva. It was 8:00 p.m., and she had stoked the fire until it was blazing— it was going to be a long night. The A4 box of pages that held her thesis was on the floor next to her. She plucked a random page from the carton and read through it. When she finished, she placed it beside her and selected another page, again reading it through. She continued like this, plucking random pages from the box and reading them. She was hoping to find some clarity. A thread that would help her consolidate 600 pages into 150.

"It's like digging a hole when the sides keep falling in," Louie told Eva. "But I keep digging. Every day I get up and I dig some more, and I get nowhere."

I know the feeling. You can't help it; it's in your DNA.

Three hours later, the fire was slowly dying, and Louie had read dozens of pages. Finally, she had realised something. It wasn't failure she was scared of—although it sort of was—the problem was her thesis wasn't very good. It was a convoluted expanse of words and phrases and ideas. It wasn't clear. It wasn't concise. It was still a draft and nowhere near finished, but it needed more than an edit because the underlying meaning was obscure.

She had buried her ideas in hyperbole. Her writing didn't feel authentic. She was trying to make it fit into a structure, an academic outline, and it simply wasn't working.

After rereading dozens of pages of her draft, she realised she'd lost sight of her main idea. The concept—light is everything—had become pretentious, exaggerated, and buried in lengthy descriptions and metaphors. If she couldn't grasp the meaning of her work, then no one else would.

What she felt was shame, because in her heart she had known this for some time. No one could read it. Especially not Ryan. He had loved her. He thought she was smart. She could never let him see how bad this was. Her thesis was a confusing mess with no direction, like a boat with a broken mast in a stormy sea. It was far from perfect. And to be loved, she thought she needed perfection.

She stared at the box of A4 pages and wondered if the draft was fixable, whether that was still a possibility. A complete rewrite. Start again from the beginning. Write a clear outline and stick to it. Don't try anything creative or unique. Stay focused and edit the work down to 80,000 words.

But she had just done that—over the last six months. She wasn't going to try again. Sometimes you had to stop digging, and this was one of those times. Two percent of the population completes a PhD and she wasn't going to be one of them.

She turned to Eva. "I can't dig anymore. It's not in my DNA." She could see no merciful way out of this mess.

Louie grabbed the carton—600 pages—332,000 words of her thesis—and dragged it closer to the fire. The master fire box was dwindling; it needed fuel. Louie opened the door and gradually fed the fire. "Forgive yourself the catastrophe of the first draft," she said.

When it was done, she broke the carton into pieces and threw them into the fire.

She had backups of her work—on multiple systems. But she wanted to make an offering, a ritual of the end.

Then, she lay down on the floor with Eva. "I think I just killed my baby," she said. A part of her wanted to follow the 600 pages into the fire.

What was the point of living? The world had become an unhappy place. She had lost Ryan, and she had killed her thesis. Eva was the only joy in her life. She ran her hand through the dog's fur, but it wasn't enough. Once again, Louie felt herself sinking, and she knew what followed. The downward spiral, and then the fear. The immobilisation that gripped her body and fogged her brain. What she suffered was a monumental failure of imagination because she couldn't see a future for herself. What was the alternative to lying on the floor in her cottage? She didn't know. She couldn't understand how her life—her future—could ever be bearable again.

Beside her, Eva stretched, then rolled onto her back.

As Louie tilted her head and her gaze shifted from the fire to a painting that hung above the mantel. A picture of nasturtiums and magnolias with a dragonfly, against a sky-blue background. The picture had been on the wall for the last nine months, and she had barely looked at it—the image was small and above her eye level. It had to compete for attention with the colourful still-life paintings that covered the other walls. But now, from her vantage point on the floor, she saw how exquisite the painting was. How soft and subtle the colour. The beauty of everyday things like dragonflies and magnolias.

The answer to her predicament hit her like a revelation, and she shook herself out of complacency. Her imagination might have failed, but it was only a momentary collapse. She knew what she needed to do. She had to bounce—like a duckling.

How easily life turned, how easily it went downhill, but then it rose again. She picked herself up off the floor and grabbed her phone. She needed to call Uncle Filip back.

Three days later, Louie had an early meeting scheduled with Uncle Filip at his office in the city. A cold snap had hit that morning, and Louie left home wearing a summer dress and no jacket. As she boarded her bus, the driver took one look at her outfit and informed her the heating was on the blink.

She took a seat. After a few minutes, an icy chill bled from the floor of the bus and seeped into her shoes—her toes were so cold they hurt. It travelled up her legs and it worked its way into her bones. Already filled with apprehension about her meeting, it was not a good start to her day.

To distract herself from the cold, she looked out the window and watched the sun rise over the city. Leaning her head against the window, she reeled off her data bank of adjectives. "Luminous, radiant, delicate, ambient, warm, cold, hard, heavy, drab." Life seemed to be going downhill.

Filip's office was in Kings Cross, an exclusive part of

town that was once—fifty years ago—the most disreputable part of town. He waited for Louie outside a 1940s Art Deco building. Standing against the façade, he resembled the picture Tara had painted of him. He wore a long camel-coloured coat and a navy scarf. His physique was slightly stooped, hands behind his back.

Filip greeted Louie with a hug. His gentle, contemplative dark eyes smiled at her. He took her frozen hands in his and rubbed them to get the blood flowing. He pulled off his scarf and looped it around her neck, attempting to keep her warm.

"Let's walk around the block, one full circle," he said. "I'll explain how this works."

Together, they set off down the pavement. They passed a bookstore, then an Algerian café, and a homewares store. They strolled in front of the house plant shop and passed two wine shops, several restaurants, a few more cafés, and finally, a gym, while Filip explained how it worked. Then, once again, they were standing outside the Art Deco building. The brisk walk had warmed Louie's heart.

Filip told her she didn't need to say anything in the meeting. He would do all the talking. He also said it was fine to cry. Most people shed a few tears. It came with the territory.

"Thank you," she said. "You've saved my life."

"Nonsense," he dismissed. "This is what I do." Then he added, "You assume that because we walk about on two legs we're a balanced species. The truth is we're all a little off-balance, at least some of the time. We're all looking for something to keep us perpendicular." He looped his arm through hers. "Ready?"

Louie nodded.

There were four people in the meeting, including Louie. She took the same chair on the same side of the table as her last meeting in Filip's office, which took place ten months ago. But the people who joined them were not the same. These people were different. A woman called Jill wore a beige pantsuit with a vest and tie. And a man called Nathan who wore a corduroy suit and retro glasses. Jill might have beamed in from the 1990s and Nathan from the 1960s.

At her first meeting, ten months ago, Louie had cried a lot. No one seemed to mind. They just kept handing her tissues, patting her hand, fetching water and tea, and offering her hard, unpleasant ginger biscuits.

But this time she didn't cry. She remained silent. She listened, as Filip had told her to do. She nodded when she was supposed to nod and smiled at the appropriate moments. She understood everything that was happening. The person who sat in the same room ten months ago, in the same chair on the same side of the table was no longer her. That person was gone, forever. She'd grown up because that's what life did—it forced you to adapt. To survive, she had to change.

When Louie left the meeting, she felt lighter. The heaviness inside her heart had vanished. The rock was still in her pocket, but she could breathe.

As she walked out the front doors of the building and onto the street, she realised her dream was over, but she wasn't sad, because now she had a different dream.

25

GLOVER

LOUIE'S WORKLOAD at the art museum had increased. Her roster now included six tours a week. She also managed the reading room and worked in the archives when they needed additional support. Her tour of the building still ran on Saturday mornings, and if the weather was good, she brought Eva along. Everyone agreed the dog's behaviour was exceptional. Louie's tips doubled. No one would be eating the wood ducks.

Louie's favourite tours were the ones on Conceptual Art and Colour Through the Ages, which ran every second week. Her Glover tour on early colonial art had dropped to once a month, and she was hoping it would soon slide off the calendar altogether and become permanently filed in the archives—she would make sure it was buried where no one would ever find it. Interest in the tour had waned and attendance had steadily declined. If this continued, the museum would replace Glover with something more relevant.

Early colonial art was not Louie's favourite period. She thought Mr Glover's naturalistic and romantic landscapes looked more like Leicester than Hobart; essentially, he had moved thousands of kilometres across land and sea and continued to paint the English countryside under a pale and insipid sky. He might be the father of Australian landscape painting, but Louie didn't think he had any understanding of the southern light, which was warmer, brighter, and richer than his homeland.

"Sometimes you have to get outside of your own head," she told Eva. "Mr Glover needs a lesson in perspective."

On the first day of summer, Louie wore her sundress with the orange and yellow flowers to work at the museum. The bandage around her knee was a bother, but she conceded it helped with the pain, and she could almost walk without a limp.

"Is it painful? Can you stand?" Evin asked her in the staff room.

"I am standing, so yes, I can stand," Louie said. She slapped a tour guide sticker onto her dress.

Evin stepped back and considered her. "You're not happy, are you?"

Louie sighed. "No. I'm not happy. It's summer, and I don't like the heat. I always get a rash. It's a prickly month, don't you think?" She scratched her neck.

"In the tropics, perhaps. But the heat is much dryer here, don't you think?"

"No. Not since climate change. My hands are clammy. Are your hands clammy?"

Evin looked at his giant bearlike hands. "They were clammy when I was outside, but they're not clammy now."

He dipped his head, peered into her face, and smiled. "I've got good news for you. The Glover tour is sold out. That should cheer you up."

"Seriously?"

Louie was surprised. Were there really twenty people who wanted to hear about Glover when, outside, the sun was shining and it was a glorious afternoon? Why look at drab landscapes when you could walk through the sun-drenched park and feel the rays on your face or lay on a picnic rug and watch the light filter through the trees?

"Just when we were about to cancel the thing." Evin grinned.

Ryan waited by a small, bronze sculpture of a naked woman standing on a bearskin. It sat on a pedestal near the entrance to the Colonial Gallery, and this was his meeting point.

"Are you here for Glover?" A grey-haired woman sidled up to him. She wore a two-piece black and white checked suit. A large black holdall, like a doctor's bag, hung from her forearm. Ryan thought she must be at least eighty and the holdall might weigh more than she did.

He nodded.

"You don't have a sticker," the woman said. "You need a sticker, so we know you're one of us. I have spares." She opened her doctor's bag, rummaged inside, and plucked out an *On Tour* sticker. After peeling the backing off, she reached up and slapped it on Ryan's chest.

He smiled, amused. "Thank you, I'm Ryan." He held out his hand.

"Judith Medwin." The woman grabbed his hand and shook it firmly. "Direct descent of the Hobart Medwin. I'm her Glover fan. I come to every tour. I just can't get enough of him. Are you a fan?"

"Yes, I am," Ryan said with conviction. "Is the whole hour on Glover?"

"We wish." Judith let out a joyous shriek. "Wouldn't that be fun? Perhaps—"

"No, it wouldn't," Louie said, joining them.

Spinning around, Ryan saw Louie standing behind him. A concerned, thoughtful expression on her face. Ryan knew the look—it was her serious work face—and it was one of his favourite expressions. She tried so hard at everything she did, which made him wonder why she hadn't tried harder with their relationship. Why had she let what they had slip away so easily?

He watched as she placed her hand into the pocket of her sundress—also one of his favourites—and held her stone.

His heart flipped.

"Judith, we've talked about this. It's not going to happen," Louie continued. "Nobody wants to talk about Glover for an hour."

"Well, I do. I could talk about him all day."

"You're in the margins."

Louie turned her attention to Ryan. "I'm sorry I haven't answered your calls, but right now I'm at work. If it's closure you're after, then I can't help you. It's overrated anyway."

"I'm here for Glover, like Judith." He held her gaze, unable to turn away. "Closure is the last thing I want."

Louie stared at the floor. Taking a deep breath to steady herself, she said, "Honestly, it's too late. I let you go. I had to. It hurt too much . . ." Her voice trailed.

Ryan sucked in a breath of air.

"How many in today's tour?" Judith asked, scouring the gallery, searching for more sticker-clad Glover fans.

"Twenty. It's booked out." Then it dawned on Louie, Glover was never booked out. She glanced at Ryan. "Did you . . . ?"

"I did. I bought every ticket, except Judith's, which was already sold."

"What a good idea." Judith plucked her phone from her doctor's bag. She started scrolling. Then she began tapping.

"Judith, what are you doing?" Louie asked.

"I'm booking every ticket on the next tour . . . and the one after that." She smiled. "It'll just be the two of us. We can talk about Glover for hours." She dropped her phone back into her bag. "Technology is life-affirming."

Louie narrowed her eyes, glaring at Ryan. This was not one of his favourite expressions, but he'd take anything he could get.

Ryan turned to Judith. "I need some time alone with the tour guide. Perhaps if I buy you lunch, could you give us half an hour?"

"You're not a Glover fan at all, are you?" Judith said.

"No. I'm a Louie fan."

"Okay. But you get the half hour where she talks about the other colonial fellows—that sentimental narrative rubbish and the bushman mythology nonsense."

"That actually sounds quite interesting," Ryan said.

"Trust me, it's not," Judith said.

"Come on," Louie coaxed. "The story about Tom Roberts and the gum leaves was nice."

"It was," Judith conceded. She turned toward Ryan. "That was a very nice story."

Judith and Louie shared a smile.

"Is someone going to tell me about the gum leaves?"

"Let me tell it," Judith burst. "In the late eighteen

hundreds, when Tom Roberts went to London, his artist friend Frederick McCubbin would send him parcels of gum leaves to burn, the scent evoking memories of the Australian bush. I guess it helped with the homesickness."

"That's a great story," Ryan confirmed.

"It's still mythmaking," Judith dismissed. "Instead of lunch, I'd like twenty dollars to spend in the museum shop."

"That much?"

"Trust me, it's not cheap."

Ryan pulled out his wallet. He handed Judith a fifty, claiming he had nothing smaller. "Don't spend it all on Glover. Save some for the mythmaking colonials."

Judith giggled. She plucked the note from his hand and scurried toward the shop.

"You have a super fan." Ryan dug his hands into his pockets. "Let's go outside."

They sat in the shade on the museum steps, close but not touching. Louie crossed her arms tightly over her chest.

"There are things I have to say. It won't take long. I just need you to listen. Can you do that, for me?" Ryan asked.

Louie nodded.

"We both fucked this up. It wasn't just you," he said. "There were things I should have told you. One of the reasons I didn't want to wait." He paused, rubbing his palms together. "Before you, I was in a relationship with someone else . . . and she also asked me to wait. And I did—I waited. A few months turned into a year. It was shit. The worst time of my life, and I swore I would never do it again."

Louie rubbed her forehead. "Oh, my god. You should have told me."

"I know. And you should have answered my calls, and I should have replied to your pictures. I've thought a lot about what happened. Sometimes it's all I think about. There are things in my past—stuff about my father leaving—that I'm working on. But I wanted to tell you how sorry I am. I'm very sorry. Can you forgive me?"

"Yes. Of course." She uncrossed her arms and rested her hands in her lap.

"And for the record, I knew exactly what your photos meant. Light *is* everything."

She smiled. "It really is."

He took her hand and rubbed his thumb back and forth over her skin. "But it wasn't just me. You have a few locked doors. I got some things wrong, but so did you."

She looked at her shoes. "I have so many issues—anxiety, time management, sometimes my self-esteem is so low —it's a lot for anybody to take on."

"We all have stuff." He shrugged. Then he turned and caught her eye. "Louie . . . my feelings for you haven't changed. I love you, more than ever. I thought we could try again. I think what we had was special. It doesn't come along that often and—"

"I can't." She pulled her hand away. "I'm sorry, but I can't."

He dipped his head and smiled at her. "Hey, I understand. A lot has happened, but I had to ask."

A wave of contentment washed over her. She hadn't felt this calm in months. She wanted to crawl underneath his shirt and feel his bare skin. Kiss his chest, his lips, his eyes. She wanted to climb into his pocket and go home with him. But she was not going to do any of those things. It was easier to walk away. She had made it clear—she had let him go and that was the truth. To do otherwise would have been too painful. The past was the past for a reason, and the future had to be shaped to protect the heart.

"I guess we live and learn," she said. "Thank you for coming. Closure is not overrated."

"How's Tara? How's her trip?" Ryan asked.

"She's happier than a person her age has the right to be. She's even painting flowers."

"Good for her."

"And what about Freddie and Henri—they're in love?" Louie said.

"I know. They'll need to keep their fluoride intake up."

Louie smiled. "At least something good came of this."

A short silence.

She turned to him. "Good luck in love and life."

As Louie walked home through the park, the summer light filtered through the canopy of the Morton Bay fig trees, and a warm feeling settled inside her heart. Branches moved gently in the breeze, and the air was filled with bird songs. She passed a banksia, littered with deep red flowers. Then, the flouncing trail of a purple jacaranda tree. After months of rain, the sunshine was restorative. The world seemed cohesive, and she felt safe.

She sighed. Ryan was a lovely man. Very good at apologies . . . and sketching. She felt lucky to have known him. She would miss him; he understood her ideas about light. Finding a person willing to discuss chairs at length was rare.

Her heart stirred. It felt like she had misplaced something important. Searching for clarity, she retraced the events of the afternoon: Ryan had bought every ticket on her tour; he gave Judith fifty dollars to spend at the shop; he apologised, touched her hand, looked into her eyes, told her he loved her . . . and then he left. He got up from the step of her favourite building, and she watched him walk away—but he still had something of hers. A small piece of her heart. He'd taken it on the day they'd met.

Sometimes in life you had to bounce because existence was forged with courage, but it was also forged with love. Louie couldn't linger in the park; she needed one more favour from Uncle Filip.

26
IMPRESSIONS

THE FOLLOWING WEEK, a small cardboard box was delivered to SLD Projects. It was addressed to Ryan McDermott, and Freddie took delivery, placing it with the incoming packages on a side table near reception. *Samples or product catalogues,* Freddie thought. One of the graduates—probably Sophie—would open it later in the day, or maybe tomorrow. The sample library was the graduate's responsibility, and they needed to keep it organised, neat, and tidy; it was part of their job description. But the library shelves, which lined the back wall of the office, looked like they'd been bulldozed. The task was at the bottom of everyone's to-do list, and Freddie could understand that; they currently had thirty-five projects on their to-do lists, and the library was not a priority.

Freddie knew it wouldn't take long to stack the stone samples in order of classification—granite, marble, sandstone, limestone. Gather the mosaic tiles into a basket. Hang the fabric swatches neatly. At the very minimum stand the information folders on end. But he couldn't do it. Once he started, he would not be able to stop, and the library was not his responsibility. So, he did his best to avoid eye contact with the shelves.

When Sophie walked through the door later that morning, Freddie pointed at the boxes of samples on the side table.

"Right, I'm onto it," she said with conviction.

She was not onto it. The boxes stayed on the side table unopened.

Ryan walked past the carton dozens of times—they all did. No one realised what might be inside.

Kat had spent the last few hours at a networking lunch for the Women's Building Council, which was a productive but exhausting way to spend a Friday afternoon. Talking about herself, especially her past, was difficult. But she knew how to condense her childhood into three phrases that explained her love of construction; her dad was a builder; she grew up on a building site; her first words were *floor joist.*

She had also reduced her résumé down to a few key points that piqued the other members' interest: she studied design and history at university; she had a business degree; for the last three years she was acting CEO at Volt Construction; now she worked as a heritage consultant. She kept the conversation centred around her academic and career highlights. No one needed to know about her failed marriages. Business was business.

Kat stepped into the foyer of her house and dropped her keys on a side table. The walls were navy and Ryan had selected the colour. He flew down a week after she'd bought the place and they'd painted the room together. He'd wanted to see the foyer renovated before he returned to Sydney. He liked the idea of Kat coming home at the end of the day—key in the lock, walking through the front door, stepping into a beautiful space. He had also hung a new coat rack, fixed the flickering light, caulked the holes in the walls, and put graphite in the locks so the keys slid smoothly into the keyholes.

She headed for the kitchen and slipped off her jacket—a purple Victoria Beckham blazer, which she found online for half price—and left it over the back of a chair. She half-filled the kettle. From her tote bag, she retrieved her mail—a few letters and a package, which looked like a book. Probably something on construction, or sustainable building, or living with less, or small houses, or efficient carpentry. People sent her all sorts of things now that she was a member of the Women's Building Council. Last week she'd received a book on traditional Japanese joinery, which she'd enjoyed. She hoped this new book also had some grace about it.

She made jasmine tea, sat down at her kitchen table, and glanced at the logos and return addresses on her letters. Then she opened the package.

She was right—it was a book, but not what she expected.

Goose bumps shimmed up her arms.

She reached for her bag, grabbed her phone, and called Ryan. With her other hand, she flicked through the pages of the book.

Early Friday evening, Ryan was still in the SLD Projects office. Sitting at his desk, he was finalising the documentation on a house for a bushfire zone. When his phone rang, he picked it up, leaned back in his chair, and said, "Kat Girl, what's up?"

"Nothing's up with me. What's up with you? Where are you right now?"

"Right now, I'm at work." He yawned. "I'm always at work."

"Have you . . . by any chance, received a package today?"

Ryan glanced at the pile of unopened boxes and packages on the table near reception. "No idea. Why? Did you send me something?"

"You might want to check."

Still on the phone, Ryan eased his way out of the chair, walked to the table that held the post, and scanned the parcels. "What am I looking for?"

"Small, rectangular packet—about the size of a book."

"Isn't that the definition of post, something small and rectangular."

He picked up a few packages, examined the labels, and cast them aside. "I can't see anything out of the ordinary."

"Oh, for god's sake, I can tell from here you've not had a proper look. Have a proper look, and then call me back." She ended the call.

Placing his hands on his hips, he scanned the parcels once more.

His gaze rested on the unopened carton. It was addressed to him and delivered by a private courier company. He tipped the box to the side—it was heavy.

Grabbing a Stanley knife from reception, he sliced open the packing tape. Inside were a dozen books, all the same. Picking one up, he considered the cover image—a photograph of the light shining through the trees. The book was called *Impressions*, and the name *Louie Leon* was written across the bottom.

He exhaled; he had been holding his breath. Slowly, he opened the front cover. The dedication read, *For Tara. Always.*

He smiled and turned the page.

The book was signed, and underneath her name were the words: "I love you."

The book fell from his hand. He plucked another from the carton. Opening the front cover, he read the hand-written inscription. "I love you."

He pulled out another copy, and then another, checking every inscription. They were all the same. "I love you."

She had signed every copy.

"Thank god," he said.

Ryan parked his Defender outside Louie's house. Clutching a copy of her book, he walked to her side gate, then paused. He could no longer punch in the code and let himself inside. Instead, he rang the buzzer.

No answer.

Scanning the cars parked in the street, he spied the Elantra at the end of the block. She must be close.

It was a beautiful summer evening, so he jogged across the road and scoured the line of Norfolk pines that boarded the park. He figured she might be playing Frisbee with Eva. The park was filled with women walking their dogs, but no sign of Louie or Eva.

There was one other place they might be. The duck pond.

As the sun was beginning to set, he headed down the hill

toward the wetlands. He spied the wood duck couple first, towing their ducklings across the golden water of the pond. It wasn't long before he saw Louie and Eva lying on a blanket under a gum tree. Louie was reading a book, and Eva was staring at something in the grass.

Sensing Ryan was close, Eva lifted her head and turned toward him. She shook with joy and excitement, unable to contain herself.

Louie looked up and spied Ryan walking across the grass. Rising on her elbow, she pulled Eva close and whispered, "Go get him."

Eva sprinted.

Ryan dropped onto one knee and the dog jumped into his arms. "Hey, princess, I've missed you."

You've got no idea, Eva thought. She looked him in the eye, then gently pressed her wet nose to his cheek and held it there for several seconds, her tail wagging.

"Thank you." Ryan smiled, stroking her head. He looked deep into her amber-coloured kelpie eyes and quickly kissed the top of her head. Together, they walked over to Louie, who was standing against the tree trunk, her hands behind her back.

Ryan held up her book. "This is amazing."

She crossed her arms over her chest. "Well . . . it's just an ARC—advanced reader copy—"

"I know what an ARC is."

"It doesn't come out for a few months, but I had a box printed—so I could surprise you. They gave me an advance because I'm Filip's niece."

"They gave you an advance because it's great."

She rubbed the back of her neck. "You don't know that, and—"

"Yes, I do." He stepped closer and caught her eye, disarming her.

"Okay, they gave me an advance because I have a pushy agent, and they liked the book—that's the best you're going to get."

"Give me the pitch. What's it about?"

"It's about art—and the effect it has on us. There's also a lot about light. The importance of nature. The power of wonder—that sort of thing. The publishers think it's a relevant topic. People searching for meaning. Turns out it wasn't a very good thesis after all. In fact, it was a terrible thesis, which is why I couldn't finish it. There was too much reflective thought, and god forbid, conjecture and personal opinion."

"Sounds like my kind of book. I can't wait to read it."

"I met with the publishers a year ago—gave them a draft. I thought the thesis would have to be published first, but I signed the contract for the second book a few weeks ago."

"I'm so bloody proud of you—it's a huge achievement."

"Well, it took ten years, and most books only take—"

"I don't want to hear it."

She nodded.

"God, I've missed you," he said. "I love you. I want you back in my life. I can't imagine a future without you."

Pushing herself off the tree, she stepped toward him and smiled. "Me too. That's what I want. I am completely in love with you. I can't believe I let you go and . . ." Her eyes began to well with tears.

"Hey." He grabbed her hand, pulled her into his chest, and hugged her. She dropped her head onto his shoulder and wrapped her arms around him. This was home.

When his lips pressed against hers, she closed her eyes —they both did—and at that moment they fell off the edge of a high cliff and landed together, standing under a gum tree, by a duck pond, with a black and tan kelpie by their side.

"Come back to my place," she said. "We can set the fire; it's still cold inside the house. Then you can take all my clothes off." She sighed. "I'll cook pasta for dinner, and we can have a glass of wine—cheap wine, so be prepared—and we can talk about chairs or cross-laminated timber. I'll even listen to you talk about cantilevered concrete staircases, that's how much I've missed you."

"Sorry, I stopped listening after you said I could take your clothes off."

Later that night, after they'd finished the pasta and shared a bottle of cheap red wine, they lay together on the sofa, Louie's head in Ryan's lap. But conversations about chairs and cross-laminated timber never came up. Instead, Louie told Ryan why she had never let him read her drafts.

"Perfection," she said. "Anxiety's evil twin. I wanted it to be perfect. I didn't want to show you or anyone else something that wasn't flawless. People love perfect things, and I wanted to be loved . . . by you. But after you left, I realised it was a huge mess and it would never be finished. I had to forgive myself for the catastrophe."

"And have you?"

She looked up at him. "I'm a work in progress."

"We all are. For the record, I didn't leave. It turns out I did wait—because here I am." He grinned.

"Semantics . . . and you went on a date."

"A glitch."

After Louie went to bed, Ryan cleaned the kitchen and

restacked the dishwasher. He walked around the house, happy to see that nothing had changed. The flower artworks were still hanging on the walls. On the kitchen table, was a dish filled with pears. The bookcase hadn't changed. The bowl of rocks was still there, next to Louie's desk in the sitting room. Her star chart showed her runs with Lila, her publication date, and Tara's return date. He was pleased that the house faced south and that it would be cool inside throughout the summer months. The house was Louie, and Louie was the house, and he had missed them both.

He climbed into bed next to her, pulled her close, and wrapped his arms around her. This was his home.

Then, he realised he had forgotten something. He climbed out of bed, walked into the sitting room, hovered over Louie's open computer, and selected control-save. Then he went back to bed.

Eva looked up from her mat. *Good man.*

ACKNOWLEDGMENTS

I loved writing this book. It was one of the easiest, most rewarding novels to write, and Louie and Ryan are two of my favourite characters. I hope you fall in love with them as much as I did.

Thank you to my running companion Desmo, my Australian kelpie, for her endless inspiration. Desmo has been remarkably supportive throughout the writing of this book.

Thank you to my early readers, including Tracey Learmont, Annie Aitken, Jenny Watts, and Lulu Howes with special thanks to Lori Learmont for her brilliant early edit and to Jordan Howes for her meticulous proofreading. My professional editors, Claire Ashgrove and Sandra Ogle helped me pull this book into shape. Laura Shellcrass delivered a fabulous image for the cover.

As always, my greatest love and admiration goes to Jordan, Lulu, and Hamish.

Andrew Aitken, thank you for facilitating my Great Escape to a faraway country town—you have my love, as always.

And thank you to my readers.

ABOUT THE AUTHOR

Sarah Lahey writes genre-bending romance, women's fiction, and science fiction that explores love, connection, and what it means to be human. Her romance novel, *Louie the Lynx and Ryan the Lion,* won the IndieReader Discovery Award, and her award-winning Heartless sci-fi series won the Chanticleer Book Awards, the American Fiction Awards, the Independent Publishers Award (IPPY), and the Indie-Reader Discovery Award.

A former interior designer, she now teaches sustainable design, emerging technology, and creative thinking at a university in Sydney. When she's not writing or teaching, you'll find her on her rural property on the south coast of New South Wales with her Australian kelpie (the best dog in the world), cooking, reading, or building architectural LEGO while pondering her next story.

For more information about her life and writing, subscribe to her Substack newsletter, Story Blueprint.

THE SOUTHERN SKIES SERIES

A collection of smart, slow-burn, contemporary love stories. From a prestigious university in the city to a heritage building site, wine-country back roads, and a rugged Tasmanian fishing village, each book in the series is a complete standalone romance that can be read in any order.

Perfect for readers who love mature characters (30+ and 40+), emotional depth, he-falls-first heroes, loyal dogs, and guaranteed happily ever afters. Dive in wherever calls to you first—every story in the Southern Skies Romances series offers emotional depth, laughs, spice and a satisfying happily ever after.

Louie the Lynx and Ryan the Lion

A smart, witty university romance about an anxious PhD student and a pragmatic architect.

Kat Girl

A later-in-life workplace romance between a twice-divorced heritage consultant and the developer who believes in her.

The Side Road

A small-town wine-country romance featuring a former MotoGP champion, a craft-store owner, and a cosy mystery.

The Southern Kind
A coastal Tasmanian romance between a burned-out celebrity chef and a local photographer.

Tropes
Slow Burn 🔥
30+ and 40+ main characters
He falls first (and hard)
Second Chance 🖤
A guaranteed HEA ✅
Spice 🌶️ 🌶️ 🌶️